PENGUIN BOOKS

The Other People

Praise for *C. J. Tudor*

'If you like my stuff, you'll like this' Stephen King

'A labyrinthine tale that kept me guessing right to the end'
Val McDermid

'Utterly hypnotic . . . A dark star is born' A. J. Finn

'Dark, compelling, unsettling' J. P. Delaney

'A tense gripper with a leave-the-lights-on shock ending'
Sunday Times

'Confirms Tudor as Britain's female Stephen King' *Daily Mail*

'A must-read' *Daily Express*

'C. J. Tudor's hybrid of horror and mystery is deeply enjoyable'
Sunday Express

'Deliciously creepy' *Good Housekeeping*

'Plenty of plot twists and a riveting read' *Guardian*

The Other People

C. J. TUDOR

PENGUIN BOOKS

PENGUIN BOOKS

UK | USA | Canada | Ireland | Australia
India | New Zealand | South Africa

Penguin Books is part of the Penguin Random House group of companies
whose addresses can be found at global.penguinrandomhouse.com.

First published by Michael Joseph 2020
Published in Penguin Books 2020

003

Set in 12.29/14.57 pt Garamond MT Std
Typeset by Jouve (UK), Milton Keynes
Printed and bound in Great Britain by Clays Ltd, Elcograf S.p.A.

A CIP catalogue record for this book is available from the British Library

ISBN: 978–1–405–93962–1

www.greenpenguin.co.uk

For Mum and Dad. The best people

'Hell is other people'

– Jean-Paul Sartre

She sleeps. A pale girl in a white room. Machines surround her. Mechanical guardians, they tether the sleeping girl to the land of the living, stopping her from drifting away on an eternal, dark tide.

Their steady beeps and the laboured sound of her breathing are the sleeping girl's only lullabies. Before, she loved music. Loved to sing. Loved to play. She found music in everything — the birds, the trees, the sea.

A small piano has been placed in one corner of the room. The cover is up but the keys are coated in a fine layer of dust. On top of the piano sits an ivory shell. Its silky pink insides look like the delicate curves of an ear.

The machines beep and whirr.

The shell trembles.

A sharp 'C' suddenly fills the room.

Somewhere, another girl falls.

I

He noticed the stickers first, surrounding the car's rear window and lining the bumper:

Honk if you're horny.
Don't follow me, I'm lost.
When you drive like I do, you'd better believe in God.
Horn broken — watch for finger.
Real men love Jesus.

Talk about mixed messages. Although one thing did come through loud and clear: the driver was a dick. Gabe was willing to bet he wore slogan T-shirts and had a picture at work of a monkey with its hands over its head and the caption: *You don't have to be mad to work here but it helps.*

He was surprised the driver could see out of the back at all. On the other hand, at least he was providing reading material for people in traffic jams. Like the one they were currently stuck in. A long line of cars crawling through the M1 roadworks; it felt like they had started sometime in the last century and looked set to continue well into the next millennium.

Gabe sighed and tapped his fingers on the wheel, as

3

though this could somehow hurry along the traffic, or summon a time machine. He was almost late. Not quite. Not yet. It was still within the bounds of possibility that he might make it home in time. But he wasn't hopeful. In fact, hope had left him somewhere around Junction 19, along with all the drivers savvy enough to take their chances with their satnav and a country-lane diversion.

What was even more frustrating was that he had managed to leave on time today. He should easily have made it home by six thirty, so he could be there for dinner and Izzy's bedtime, which he had promised – *promised* – Jenny that he would do tonight.

'Just once a week. That's all I ask. One night when we eat together, you read your daughter a bedtime story and we pretend we're a normal, happy family.'

That had hurt. She had meant it to.

Of course, he could have pointed out that *he* was the one who had got Izzy ready for school that morning, as Jenny had had to rush out to see a client. *He* was the one who had soothed their daughter and applied Savlon to her chin when their temperamental rescue cat (the one *Jenny* had adopted) had scratched her.

But he didn't. Because they both knew it didn't make up for all the missed times, the moments he hadn't been there. Jenny was not an unreasonable woman. But when it came to family, she had a very definite line. If you crossed it, then it was a long time before she let you step back inside.

It was one of the reasons he loved her: her fierce devotion to their daughter. Gabe's own mum had been more devoted to cheap vodka, and he had never known his dad. Gabe had sworn that he would be different; that he would always be there for his little girl.

And yet, here he was, stuck on the motorway, about to be late. Again. Jenny would not forgive him. Not this time. He didn't want to dwell upon what that meant.

He had tried to call her, but it had gone to voicemail. And now his phone had less than 1 per cent battery, which meant it would die any minute and, typically, today of all days, he had left his charger at home. All he could do was sit, fighting the urge to press his foot on the accelerator and barge the rest of the traffic out of the way, tapping his fingers aggressively on the steering wheel, staring at bloody Sticker Man in front.

A lot of the stickers looked old. Faded and wrinkled. But then, the car itself looked ancient. An old Cortina, or something similar. It was sprayed that colour that was so popular in the seventies: a sort of grubby gold. Mouldy banana. Pollution sunset. Dying sun.

Dirty grey fumes puffed intermittently out of the wonky exhaust. The whole bumper was speckled with rust. He couldn't see a manufacturer's badge. It had probably fallen off, along with half of the number plate. Only the letters 'T' and 'N' and what could be part of a 6 or an 8 remained. He frowned. He was sure that wasn't legal. The damn thing probably wasn't even roadworthy, or insured, or driven by a qualified driver. Best not to get too close.

He was just considering changing lanes when the girl's face appeared in the rear window, perfectly framed by the peeling stickers. She looked to be around five or six. Round-faced, pink-cheeked. Fine blonde hair pulled into two high pigtails.

His first thought was that she should be strapped into a car seat.

His second thought was: *Izzy.*

She stared at him. Her eyes widened. She opened her mouth, revealing a tooth missing right in the front. He remembered wrapping it in a tissue and tucking it under her pillow for the tooth fairy.

She mouthed: 'Daddy!'

Then a hand reached back, grabbed her arm and yanked her down. Out of sight. Gone. Vanished.

He stared at the empty window.

Izzy.

Impossible.

His daughter was at home, with her mum. Probably watching the Disney channel while Jenny cooked dinner. She couldn't be in the back of a strange car, going God knows where, not even strapped into a car seat.

The stickers blocked his view of the driver. He could barely see the top of their head above *Honk if you're horny*. Fuck that. He honked anyway. Then he flashed his lights. The car seemed to speed up a little. Ahead of him, the roadworks were ending, the 50mph signs replaced by the national speed limit.

Izzy. He accelerated. It was a new Range Rover. It went like shit off the proverbial shovel. And yet the battered old rust bucket in front was pulling away from him. He pressed the pedal down harder. Watched the speedometer creep up past seventy, seventy-five, eighty-five. He was gaining, and then the car in front suddenly darted into the middle lane and undertook several cars. Gabe followed, swerving in front of an HGV. The horn's blare almost deafened him. His heart felt like it might just burst right out of his chest, like bloody *Alien*.

The car in front was weaving dangerously in and out of the traffic. Gabe was hemmed in by a Ford Focus on one side and a Toyota in front. Shit. He glanced in his mirror, pulled into the slow lane then darted back in front of the Toyota. At the same time a Jeep pulled in from the fast lane, just missing his bonnet. He slammed on his brakes. The Jeep driver flashed his hazards and gave him the finger.

'Screw *you*, too, you fucking wanker!'

The rust bucket was several cars in front now, still weaving, tail lights disappearing into the distance. He couldn't keep up. It was too dangerous.

Besides, he tried to tell himself, he must be mistaken. *Must be*. It couldn't have been Izzy. Impossible. Why on earth would she be in that car? He was tired, stressed. It was dark. It must be some other little girl who looked like Izzy. *A lot like Izzy*. A little girl who had the same blonde hair in pigtails, the same gap between her front teeth. *A little girl who called him 'Daddy'*.

A sign flashed up ahead: Services ½ mile. He could pull in, make a phone call, put his mind at rest. But he was already late; he should keep going. On the other hand, what was a few more minutes? The slip road was sliding past. Keep going? Pull over? Keep going? Pull over? *Izzy*. At the last minute, he yanked the wheel to the left, bumping over the white hazard lines and eliciting more horn beeps. He sped up the slip road and into the services.

Gabe hardly ever stopped at service stations. He found them depressing, full of miserable people who wanted to be somewhere else.

He wasted precious minutes scuttling up and down, past the various food outlets, searching for a payphone, which he eventually found tucked away near the toilets. Just the one. No one used payphones any more. He wasted several more minutes looking for some change before he realized you could use a card. He extracted his debit card from his wallet, stuck it in and called home.

Jenny never answered on the first ring. She was always busy, always doing something with Izzy. Sometimes she said she wished she had eight pairs of hands. He should be there more, he thought. He should help.

'Hello.'

A woman's voice. But not Jenny. Unfamiliar. Had he called the wrong number? He didn't call it very often. Again, it was all mobiles. He checked the number on the payphone. Definitely their landline number.

'Hello?' the voice said again. 'Is that Mr Forman?'

'Yes. This is Mr Forman. Who the hell are you?'

'My name is Detective Inspector Maddock.'

A detective. In his house. Answering his phone.

'Where are you, Mr Forman?'

'The M1. I mean, in the services. On my way back from work.'

He was babbling. Like a guilty person. But then, he *was* guilty, wasn't he? Of a lot of things.

'You need to come home, Mr Forman. Right away.'

'Why? What's going on? *What's happened?*'

A long pause. A swollen, stifling silence. The sort of silence, he thought, that brims with unspoken words. Words that are about to completely fuck up your life.

'It's about your wife . . . and your daughter.'

2

The thin man drank black coffee, plenty of sugar. He rarely ate anything. Once, maybe twice, he had ordered toast and then left it after a couple of bites. He had the look, Katie thought, of someone closer to death than their years should have taken them. Clothes hung off him like they would a scarecrow with the stuffing removed. Emaciation had carved chasms out of his face, beneath his eyes and cheekbones. His fingers, when he grasped the coffee cup, were long and delicate, bones so sharp they looked like they might slice straight through the thin covering of skin.

If Katie didn't know better, she would have said he was terminally ill. Cancer. Her nan had gone that way and they shared the same look. But he had a different kind of illness. A sickness of the heart and soul. The best medicine and doctors in the world couldn't cure what afflicted this man. Nothing could.

When he first started visiting the services, once or twice a month, he used to hand out leaflets. Katie had taken one herself. Pictures of a little girl. HAVE YOU SEEN ME?

9

Katie had, of course. Everyone had. The little girl had been all over the news. Her and her mum.

Back then, the thin man had hope. Of a sort. The insane kind of hope that fuels people like a drug. It's all they have. They draw on it like a crack pipe, even when they know that the hope itself has become an addiction. People say hate and bitterness will destroy you. They're wrong. It's hope. Hope will devour you from the inside like a parasite. It will leave you hanging like bait above a shark. But hope won't kill you. It's not that kind.

The thin man had been eaten up by hope. He had nothing left. Nothing but a lot of road miles and coffee club points.

Katie picked up his empty cup, wiped down the table.

'Can I get you another?'

'Table service?'

'Only for regulars.'

'Thanks, but I have to get going.'

'Okay. See you.'

He nodded again. 'Yeah.'

That was the total sum of their conversations. Every conversation. She wasn't sure if he even realized he was speaking to the same person each time he came in. She got the feeling that most people were just background to him.

Katie had heard that this was not the only coffee shop he visited, nor the only service station. Staff moved around, and they talked. So did the police officers who often came in. The rumour was that he spent every day and night driving up and down the motorway, stopping in different service stations, looking for the car that took his little girl. Searching for his lost daughter.

Katie hoped it wasn't true. She hoped that the thin man

could eventually find some peace. Not just for his sake. Something about him, his quiet desperation, scraped at a raw nerve. Most of all she hoped that one day, she would come into work, he would be gone, and she'd never have to think about him again.

3

Night driving. Gabe never used to like it. The flare of the oncoming headlights. The patches of unlit motorway where the road ahead seemed to melt away into infinite nothingness. Like driving into a black hole. He always found it disorientating. Darkness made everything look different. Distances changed, shapes distorted.

These days (nights), it was the time he felt most comfortable. Cocooned in the driver's seat, playing something low and ambient. Tonight, Laurie Anderson. *Strange Angels*. It was the album he played the most. Something about the otherworldliness, the weirdness, resonated with him. Seemed to fit his journey up and down the black tarmac.

Sometimes, he imagined he was cruising along a deep, dark river. Others, he was drifting through space, into eternal blackness. Strange, the thoughts that sleepwalked through your mind in the small hours, when you should be putting your brain safely to bed. But although he let his mind wander, he always kept his eyes firmly on the road, alert, on the lookout.

Gabe didn't really sleep. Not properly. That was one of the reasons he drove. When he needed a break, more because he felt he *should* than because he felt tired, he pulled into one of the service stations he had come to know so well.

He could list them all, up and down the M1: the facilities, the ratings and the distances between them. They were, he supposed, the closest things he had to any sort of home. Ironic, really, considering how much he used to dislike them. When he wanted more than just a refuel of black coffee, he parked his camper van in one of the HGV bays and lay down in the back for a couple of hours. He often resented the time he was wasting, not doing anything, not searching. But, while his mind never rested, his eyes, wrists and legs needed the respite. Sometimes, when he climbed from the driver's seat, it felt as though he were a stooped Neanderthal attempting to stand vertical for the very first time. So he forced himself to close his eyes, stretch out his six-foot-three frame as much as he could in the camper van for a maximum of 120 minutes every twenty-four hours. And then he got back on the road.

He had everything he needed with him. Toiletries, a few changes of clothes. Sometimes a trip to the launderette necessitated a small detour off the motorway and into a town. He didn't like these trips. They reminded him too much of the normality of most people's everyday lives. Shopping, work, meeting for a coffee, taking the kids to school. All things he no longer did. All the things he had lost, or let go.

On the motorway, in the service stations, normal life was suspended. Everyone was on their way somewhere, at a point in between. In neither one place nor another. A little like Purgatory.

He kept his phone and laptop close, along with two spare chargers and several battery packs (he would never make that mistake again). When he wasn't driving, he spent his time drinking coffee, scanning the news – just in case there *was* any news – and checking the missing-persons websites.

Most of these were little more than noticeboards. They ran appeals for the missing, posted updates on progress, held events to raise awareness. All in the desperate hope that someone out there might see something and get in touch.

He used to trawl them religiously. But after a while it got to him: the hope, the desperation. The same photographs again and again. The faces of people who had been missing for years, decades. Preserved in a camera flash. Their hairstyles becoming more dated, their smiles more frozen with each missed birthday and Christmas.

Then there were the new faces that appeared almost daily. Still with an echo of life. He imagined that a dent remained in their pillows, a toothbrush hardened in a holder, and the clothes in their wardrobe still smelt of fresh laundry and not yet of mould and mothballs.

But it would happen. Just like the others. Time would roll on without them. The rest of the world would continue to its destination. Only their loved ones would remain on the platform. Unable to leave, unable to abandon their vigil.

Missing is different to being dead. In a way, it's worse. Death offers finality. Death gives you permission to grieve. To hold memorials, to light candles and lay flowers. To let go.

Missing is limbo. You're stranded; in a strange, bleak place where hope glimmers faintly at the horizon and misery and despair circle like vultures.

His phone buzzed from the holder on the dashboard. He glanced at the screen. The name on it made the hairs stir on his neck.

The other thing you found, if you spent your time travelling the tributaries of the country in the dead of night long enough, was other night people. Other vampires. Lorry and van drivers on long-haul deliveries. Police, paramedics, service staff. Like the blonde-haired waitress. She had been on again tonight. She seemed nice, but she always looked worn out. He imagined she had had a husband once, but he left. Now she worked nights, so she had time for her kids in the day.

He often did that with people. Invented back stories for them, as if they were characters in a book. Some you could read right away. Others took a little more time. Some you could never fathom, not in a million lifetimes.

Like the Samaritan.

'Where r u?' his text read.

Normally, Gabe couldn't stand people using abbreviations, even in texts – a throwback to his former profession as a copywriter – but he forgave the Samaritan, for a number of reasons.

He tapped the microphone icon on the phone's screen and said: 'Between Newton Green and Watford Gap.' The words flashed up as a message. Gabe tapped send.

The text came back: 'Meet me @ Barton Marsh, off J14. Sndng direcs.'

Barton Marsh. A small village not far from Northampton. Not very pretty. A good fifty minutes away.

'Why?'

The reply was just three words. Words he had been waiting to hear for almost three years. Words he had dreaded hearing.

'I found it.'

4

Tibshelf Services, M1 Junctions 28–9

Fran sipped her coffee. Well, she presumed it was coffee. The menu said it was coffee. It looked like coffee. It smelt vaguely like coffee. But it tasted like crap. She shook out another sachet of sugar. The fourth. Across the sticky plastic table, Alice picked half-heartedly at an anaemic-looking bit of toast that was doing only a slightly better job than the coffee at fitting its purpose under the Trades Description Act.

'You going to eat that?' Fran asked.

'No,' Alice replied absently.

'Don't blame you,' Fran said, smiling sympathetically, even though the effort caused her cheeks to hurt . . . which at least matched her eyes and head.

Her head was throbbing harder than ever in the bright fluorescent light. She hadn't eaten anything since the previous morning. Her belly was past food, but her head was pounding from the lack of nutrition and sleep. That was part of the reason she had decided they should stop for coffee and sustenance. Ha bloody ha. Probably served her right that they weren't getting either. She pushed the coffee away.

'D'you need the loo before we go?'

Alice started to shake her head then reconsidered. 'How far do we have to go?'

Good question. How far? How far would be enough? She had no idea, but she didn't want to say that to Alice. She was supposed to be the one in control, the one with a plan. She couldn't tell Alice that she was just driving, as fast as she dared, trying to put as many miles between them and their last address as possible.

'Well, it's a long way, but there are plenty of other service stations on the way.'

Until they got off the motorway, of course, and then the only option would be a lay-by at the side of the road.

Alice pulled a face. 'I suppose I could go now.'

Said with the same amount of enthusiasm as if she had asked her to step into a cage with man-eating lions.

'You want me to come with you?'

Another hesitation. Alice had, among other things, a phobia about public bathrooms. However, at almost eight, she also had a bigger phobia about acting like a baby.

'No, I'm fine.'

'Sure?'

Alice nodded and then, with a grim-faced determination that made her look oh-so-much older than her years, she rose from her seat. After another momentary hesitation, she reached across the table for her bag: a small pink rucksack decorated with purple flowers. Alice never went anywhere without it, not even to the toilet. As she slung it over her slight shoulder, it rattled and clicked.

Fran tried not to frown, tried not to let the fear show on her face. She lifted her coffee cup and made a pretence of drinking from it as Alice walked away; long, brown hair caught up in a high ponytail, jeans tucked into fake Uggs, a large duffel coat swamping her skinny frame.

A surge of primeval love overpowered her. It got you like that sometimes. Terrifying, the love you had for a child. From the minute you cradled that soft, sticky head in your arms, everything changed. You lived in a state of perpetual wonder and terror: wonder that you could have produced something so incredible, terror that at any moment they might be taken from you. Life had never seemed so fragile or so full of menace before.

The only time you shouldn't worry about them, she thought, was when they slept. That's when they should be safe, tucked up tightly in their beds. The problem was, Alice didn't sleep in her bed. Not always. Alice could fall asleep anywhere, at any moment. On the way to school, in the park, in the ladies' toilets. One minute awake. The next gone. It was scary.

But not as scary as when she woke up.

Fran thought about the rucksack. That restless rattling. Panic fluttered like a dark moth in her chest.

Alice stared at the sign for the Ladies. A woman in a triangle skirt. When she was little, she used to think it meant if she was wearing trousers she couldn't go in. She didn't want to go in now. Fear gripped her belly hard, which of course just made the urge to wee even greater.

It wasn't the toilets she was afraid of. Or even the noisy hand-dryers (although they used to scare her a bit). It was something else. Something it was hard to avoid in any bathroom, but especially in public toilets, with their row upon row of sinks and unexpected corners.

Mirrors. Alice didn't like mirrors. She had been scared

of them ever since she was little. One of her earliest memories was of playing dress-up and sneaking upstairs to look at herself in her mum's big mirror in the bedroom. She had stood in front of it, resplendent in her Elsa dress . . . and she had started to scream.

Not all mirrors were a problem. Some were safe. She didn't know why. She couldn't explain it any more than she could explain why some were dangerous. Unfamiliar mirrors were riskier. Mirrors she didn't know. Those were the ones where she saw things; those were the ones that could make her fall.

It will be all right, she told herself. *Just look down. Keep looking down.*

She took a deep breath and pushed open the door. The cloying smell of air freshener and harsh disinfectant caught in her throat and made her feel a little sick. No one else was in the toilets, which was unusual, but then, it was still early, and the services were quiet.

She hurried to the closest toilet, keeping her eyes to the floor, and shut the door. She lowered herself onto the loo, had a wee then quickly dried, flushed and slipped out again, still trying to keep her eyes down. Now was the hard part. Now she had to get to the sink and wash her hands.

She almost made it. But the soap wouldn't work. She pushed and pushed and then she glanced up. She couldn't help it. Or maybe there was just something about that forbidden gleam that called to her, like a door left slightly ajar. You couldn't help pushing it wider to see what lay on the other side.

She caught sight of her reflection. Except, it wasn't her. It wasn't really a reflection at all. It was a girl, similar looking, although a few years older. But whereas Alice was dark-haired with blue eyes, this girl was pale, almost albino, with white hair and eyes like milky-grey marbles.

'*Alisssss.*'

Even her voice was pale and insubstantial, like it was being carried away on a breeze.

'Not now. Go away.'

'*Sssssh. Sssssh now.*'

'Leave me alone.'

'*I neeeed you.*'

'I can't.'

'*I need you to sleeeeep.*'

'No. I'm not . . .'

But before the word 'tired' could leave her mouth Alice's eyelids snapped shut and she slumped to the floor.

5

I found it.

Was it really possible, after all this time? And, of course, Gabe was very aware of what the Samaritan had *not* said. He'd said, 'I found it.' Not 'I found her.' Unless he was sparing Gabe. But, then, why call him out here? There was something more contained within those words. He felt it. A lie by omission. *I found it.* And?

He squinted at the unfamiliar road signs and guided the camper van along roads that felt too narrow and twisty. Gabe always felt a momentary dislocation when he pulled off the motorway. Like he had cut a safety line. Severed the umbilical cord. Jumped into the abyss without a chute.

Panic scratched with feverish claws at the back of his mind. Panic that he could be missing her. Panic that he was letting her slip away. All over again. Irrational, insane. But he couldn't help it. The motorway. That was his only link. The place he had last seen her. The place he had lost her.

You're supposed to do anything for your child. Anything. And he had just watched his daughter disappear. Just let those tail lights pull away. Gone. Vanished. He had replayed it over and over in his mind. If only he had done things differently. If only he hadn't turned off. If only he had followed that damn shitty old car. If only, if only.

Glorious hindsight. But hindsight isn't glorious. Hindsight is a shabby conman. A gameshow host in a gold lamé suit and bad hairpiece who mockingly shows you what you could have won:

If you had been faster, braver, more committed. If you weren't such a coward. But, ladies and gentlemen, give him a round of applause. He's been a great contestant. Still a loser, though. Still a fucking loser.

He gripped the steering wheel tighter and glanced at the clock: 2.47 a.m. The sky was still a deep swathe of velvety black pierced through with a few tiny pinpoints of light. It would be a while before dawn dragged it aside. In mid-February that wouldn't happen for another three hours, at least.

He was glad. He preferred the darkness. Preferred this time of year. When the days first began to shorten, during October, he both welcomed and hated it. The long hours of summer were bad. Sunny days brought more people to the motorway: cars packed with families heading off on holiday. Smiling, eager, happy faces. Sweaty, screaming, exhausted ones. He saw Izzy in all of them.

Once or twice, at the beginning, he had almost run after a couple of little girls, convinced they were her. Both times he had realized, just before he made a fool of himself (or earned a punch in the face from an angry father), that he was wrong. He had been saved from humiliation. He hadn't been saved from the gut-wrenching disappointment.

By October, the hordes of families had dissipated: back to school and work, the mundane commute. But in their place came other events. Other celebrations. Halloween, Bonfire Night. Throughout the year, it seemed, there were events designed to remind the lonely that they were indeed alone. No children, eyes illuminated by the flare and sparkle of fireworks. No other half to wrap an arm around and draw close against the autumn chill.

Christmas was the worst because it was the most invasive. On the roads, the motorway, in the service stations, you could escape the other occasions, for the most part. But Christmas – *bloody* Christmas – pervaded everywhere, creeping in earlier and earlier each year.

Even the service stations would make meagre attempts at decorations and erect lopsided Christmas trees, badly wrapped empty boxes beneath them. The shops would be full of Christmas 'goodies' for those who had forgotten a present for Auntie Edna and were on the way to a family gathering. And the songs. That was what really drove him past the edge of insanity. The same dozen Christmas songs played again and again, and not even the originals but irritatingly bad copies. After the first year, he had bought himself a very expensive pair of noise-cancelling headphones so he could shut them out and listen to his own, more maudlin, less full-of-good-cheer song selection.

Gabe hated Christmas. Anyone who has ever lost someone hates Christmas. Christmas takes your pain and turns it up to eleven. It taunts your loss with every glistening treetop and 'First Noel'. It reminds you that there is no respite, no let-up. Your grief is unrelenting and even if you manage to put it away, like a box of decorations, it will always come back. Reappearing every year, as familiar as Jacob Marley's rotting ghost.

The further away from Christmas it was, the more settled he felt. Not happy. Gabe never felt happy. He wasn't sure that that particular emotional avenue was open to him any more. But he had found a kind of acceptance. Not acceptance that Izzy was gone. An acceptance that this was now his life. Relentless, joyless, tiring, hard. But that was okay. It was what he deserved. Until he found her. One way or another.

A green sign emerged from the darkness ahead: BARTON MARSH, 2 MILES. Next right. A filter. He signalled and pulled over. Laurie Anderson sang about Hansel and Gretel, all grown up and sick of each other. No such thing as a happy ever after, he thought.

The turn took him on to an even narrower, twistier country lane. No streetlights. Just sporadic cat's eyes, winking at him from the centre of the road. His phone pinged with a text:

'How close?'

'2 miles.'

'Passed a farm?'

'No.'

'After the farm, look out for a lay-by. Pull in. Footpath into woods.'

'Okay.'

Footpath into woods.

His scalp prickled. Momentarily, he wondered what had brought the Samaritan here, to such a secluded spot. Then he decided he really didn't want to know.

He dragged his concentration back to the road. To his left, a sign sprang out of the gloom: OLD MEADOWS FARM. Sure enough, just a few yards down, on his right, he spotted a lay-by, the 'P' sign almost totally obscured by overgrown trees.

He pulled in behind the only other car parked there. A black BMW. A few years old, the number plate partially obscured by dirt. Not enough to attract the attention of the police but just enough to make it difficult to make out, at a glance. The back and rear windows were tinted, although Gabe doubted that was for the comfort of the passengers.

He turned off the camper van's engine, which was probably loud and chugging enough to be heard back at the farmhouse, opened the glovebox and took out a small torch. Then he grabbed his thick parka from the passenger seat and shrugged it on. He climbed out of the van and locked the doors. Probably unnecessary. He was procrastinating. Putting the moment off.

He zipped up the parka, right to his chin. It was cold tonight. His breath puffed out like cigarette smoke. He looked around. To his left, a half-rotted public footpath sign pointed to a narrow gap between overgrown bushes.

Footpath into woods.

Gabe wasn't sure anything good ever came from taking a footpath into the woods, at night, alone.

He flicked on his torch and headed through.

6

Eight minutes. Fran checked her watch. Alice had been gone too long. Even taking into account her bathroom phobia, eight minutes was still too long. Fran grabbed her bag and pushed her chair away from the table.

She hurried down the main thoroughfare, almost empty at this time in the morning. Past a bored-looking cleaner, squeezed into a uniform several sizes too small for his burly frame, sweeping randomly at the floor. Past the W. H. Smith and the gaming section where – even at this hour, and probably even after hell froze over – one sad loner sat tapping at the flashing buttons of a bandit like some kind of fruit-fixated zombie. She rounded the corner and went into the ladies' toilets.

'Alice!!'

She lay on the floor, curled into a foetal ball, halfway along the row of sinks. Her hair had fallen over her face and one hand still loosely clutched her bag. A bit of toilet paper was stuck to the bottom of one boot.

'Shit.' She knelt down and pushed back Alice's dark hair. Her breathing was shallow but steady. When Alice went deep, her breathing was so slow Fran had often feared the worst. But now, as she cradled her head on her lap, she could feel it becoming more regular. *Any second now,* she thought. *Come on . . .*

Alice slowly opened her eyes. Fran waited, watching her blink away the fogginess of sleep. Even though she had been out for only a few minutes, Alice fell hard and fast. Right down to the depths, where the true nightmares swam. *Here be monsters.*

Fran knew a little about those nightmares.

'I'm here, sweetheart. I'm here,' she soothed.

'I'm sorry, I –'

'It's okay. Are *you* okay?'

Alice blinked, sat up. Fran helped ease her into a sitting position. Alice looked around blearily.

'Toilets?'

'Yeah.'

It usually was. Bathrooms, changing rooms. Anywhere with mirrors. Fran used to think that Alice's fear of mirrors was irrational, but no fear is truly irrational. To the person who is afraid, it makes perfect sense. She understood better now. Something about mirrors seemed to trigger Alice's condition. But that wasn't all.

Heels tapped around the corner. Fran turned. A woman in a crumpled sales suit, scuffed stilettos and too much eye make-up walked in. She glanced briefly at Fran and Alice, walked straight past then paused at the mirrors and frowned.

Fran followed her gaze. She had been so focused on Alice that only now did she realize that one of the mirrors above the sinks was shattered. Shards of fine glass littered the floor nearby.

The woman tutted. 'Some people.' She glanced back at Fran and Alice. 'Is your daughter okay?'

Fran forced a smile. 'Oh, yes. She just slipped over. We're fine.'

'Right.' The woman nodded, offered a quick, tired smile and pushed open the door to a cubicle.

She was probably relieved she didn't have to help. Most people were. They pretended they did. But really, no one wanted to put themselves out for someone else. We all live in our own personal fortresses of self-concern.

The woman in the scuffed heels and eye make-up would probably forget them before she washed her hands, sinking back into the folds of her own life, her own routine, her own problems.

But then again, she might not. She might remember the woman and girl on the floor in the toilets. She might mention it to someone; a friend or work colleague, an acquaintance online.

They had to move.

'Come on, sweetheart.' She stood and eased Alice to her feet, holding her arm. 'Can you walk?'

'I'm fine. I just fell.'

Alice picked up her bag – *clickety-click* – and slung it over her shoulder. They walked towards the door. Alice paused.

'Wait.'

She turned back.

'*What?*' Fran hissed.

Alice walked over to the sinks, feet crunching on broken glass. Fran glanced nervously at the closed cubicle door and then followed. Her own fragmented reflection stared back at her from the remains of the shattered mirror. A black hole in the centre of it. Hard to recognize the stranger in those splintered shards. She tore her eyes away and looked down, into the sink.

A pebble lay by the plughole, too large to wash down, although Fran had a childish urge to try and do just that.

Alice picked it up and slipped it into her bag, along with the others. Fran didn't try to stop her. She couldn't interfere in this ritual, whatever it was, wherever the pebble had come from.

The first had appeared almost two years ago. Alice had just suffered one of her episodes, crumpling into a ball on the living-room floor. When she woke, after twenty minutes, Fran saw something in her hand.

'What's that?' she asked, curious.

'A pebble. I brought it back.'

'From where?'

Alice smiled and a frisson of fear skittered down Fran's spine.

'The beach.'

Since then, every time Alice had an episode, she woke clutching a pebble. Fran had tried to think of a rational explanation. Perhaps Alice was picking the pebbles up somewhere else, hiding them and then, by some clever sleight of hand, producing one when she woke. Rational, but still not very convincing.

So where did the damn things come from?

The toilet flushed.

'We'd better go,' Fran said briskly.

They reached the door. Fran glanced back. Something else was bothering her about the mirror. The hole in the middle of it. Glass all over the floor but hardly any in the sink.

Had Alice thrown the pebble at the mirror?

But if you smash a mirror the glass falls straight down. It doesn't explode outwards.

That would only happen if something was thrown *through* the mirror.

From the other side.

She sleeps. A pale girl in a white room. Nurses tend to her on a regular basis. Even though she is not in a hospital, she receives the best twenty-four-hour care. The nurses are well paid and not too much is asked of them except that they turn the girl, wash her, ensure she is kept comfortable. Aside from that, the machines monitor the rest.

Despite this, the turnover of staff is high. Most don't stay more than a few months before moving on. The usual assumption is that the work is not challenging enough. They need more variety, more stimulation.

But that's not true.

Miriam is the longest-serving staff member, here from the beginning. Before the beginning. Long enough to have formed an attachment to the girl. Perhaps that's why she has stayed, despite everything.

It started a couple of years ago. That was the first time. She was downstairs, making a cup of tea, when she heard a single note. Played on a piano. Not repeated. Could she have woken? Impossible. But then, miracles did happen.

She hurried up the stairs and into the girl's room. Everything looked as it always did. The sleeping girl slept. The machines whirred: all readings normal. She walked over to the piano. The keys were coated in dust. Nothing had disturbed them.

She put it down to her imagination. A week later, it happened *again. And again. Every few weeks, that single note would ring out from the girl's room. You never knew when it might happen, day or night.*

Some of the staff began to talk about ghosts, poltergeists, telekinesis. Miriam wouldn't hear of such nonsense. And yet she couldn't summon up a better explanation. So she continued to do her job and tried not to think about it at all.

Tonight, when the note rang out, she walked wearily to the girl's room. She checked the piano, the machines. And then she stood over the sleeping girl and stared at her white face, her mass of flaxen hair. Still just the same. She stroked her thin arm and let her hand drop to the bedsheets. She frowned. They felt gritty. But that wasn't right. They had only just been changed. How could they be dirty?

She ran her hand along the sheets, raised it and rubbed her fingers together.

Not dirt.

Sand.

7

The pathway was narrow and muddy. Heavy woodland crowded in from either side. It didn't strike Gabe as a particularly picturesque or pleasant walk, even on a summer's day, let alone in the pitch black and freezing cold of a February night.

The twisted trunks of the trees pushed over the rickety fencing on either side. In some places, the crooked boughs met overhead, branches entwining with each other like lovers' fingers, crooked as a fighter's knuckles.

He fought down a shudder. A curse, sometimes, being a writer. Or ex-writer, he supposed. But then, did you ever stop being a writer? Like an alcoholic, the urge was always there.

When he was a kid he had dreamed of writing books, like his heroes Stephen King and James Herbert. But growing up in a small, run-down seaside resort with no dad and a mum who spent most of her dole money at the pub, that idea had been quickly knocked out of him.

The people where he lived were suspicious of aspiration. Other people's hard work and success simply reminded them of their own failures and poor choices. Those who tried to claw their way out weren't encouraged, they were mocked: *'Getting a bit lah-di-dah.' 'Get you with your posh degree.'*

He pretended not to care about school in front of his friends while he spent night after night swotting for his exams in his room. He got decent enough grades and, despite almost trashing his dreams before they started in his teens, he was given a second chance. He secured a place at the local polytechnic and then a poorly paid job at a small advertising agency. Just before he started, his mum died. Everyone from their community came to the funeral but no one chipped in a penny to help. Gabe had to pawn what was left of her possessions to help pay for the coffin.

Another three years spent churning out product leaflets for pessaries, and he was offered a job at a big agency in the Midlands. During a pitch, he met a freelance graphic designer called Jenny. They fell in love, got married . . . and Jenny fell pregnant. Happy ever after.

Except there's no such thing.

He often used to joke that he got to lie for a living. *Haha*. No one knew how close it was to the truth.

I lie for a living. I live a lie.

Ahead of him, the path was widening and the last of the trees straggled away. Gabe found himself upon a narrow bank. A starved sliver of moon floated on a still expanse of water. A lake.

Not a large lake. Maybe ten metres across, fifteen wide. On the other side, it was hedged in by more trees. Slightly to the right, a high ridge of hill. Secluded. Hidden. Like the wooded walk, it was not pretty. It smelt dank and fetid. The bank dropped away steeply, littered with cans and ancient plastic bags. The surface of the water was covered in brown algae.

And in the middle, half submerged in the filthy water, was a car.

It must have been fully submerged, once. But the weather had been abnormally dry for the last couple of years. The water levels were at a record low. Bit by bit, the lake must have retreated until the car was revealed. That explained the cans and carrier bags stranded on the bank.

Gabe walked down to the edge of the bank. Water crept over the toes of his trainers. The car was rusted and draped in slimy weeds. In the darkness, it looked almost the same colour as the lake. But he could still see, just visible in the rear window, illuminated by his torch:

Ho k if you e orny.

Horn bro en. W tch or ing r.

He took another step, not caring about the dampness seeping through his socks, and then a voice said:

'Am I right?'

'Fuck!'

He spun around. The Samaritan stood behind him. He must have stepped out of the trees, or simply emerged in a cloud of smoke. Either, Gabe thought, was feasible.

The Samaritan was tall. And thin. As always, he was dressed in black. Black jeans, long black jacket. His skin was almost as dark. His shaved skull glinted in the moon-light. His teeth were a startling white. One was inlaid with a small iridescent stone, like a pearl. When Gabe asked him once what it was, he had frowned.

'I brought it back, from a place I visited. I keep it with me.'

'Like a souvenir?'

'Yeah. To remind me never to go back.'

The subject was closed. Gabe knew better than to reopen it.

He stared at the Samaritan. 'You almost gave me a heart attack.'

'Sorry.'

The Samaritan grinned. He didn't look sorry. Gabe did not pull him up on it. Just like he didn't ask the Samaritan what he was doing here, by a lake, in the dead of night.

'Is it the car?' the Samaritan asked.

Most of the stickers had faded or peeled off. Half of the vehicle was submerged in water and the number plate was completely gone. But Gabe knew.

He nodded. 'It's the car.'

A wave of weakness swept over him. He felt himself sway. For a moment, he thought he was going to throw up. *It's the car.* Saying the words. After all this time. He hadn't imagined it. The car was real. It existed. It was right here in front of him. And if the car was real . . .

'She's not inside,' the Samaritan said.

The nausea subsided. Izzy hadn't died in a stinking swamp, her last breath stolen from her by the stagnant water as she clawed at the windows, unable . . .

Stop it, he told himself. *Fucking stop it.* He dragged his hands through his hair, rubbed viciously at his eyes. Like he could somehow scrub the bad thoughts away with his hands. The Samaritan simply watched and waited for him to gather himself.

'There's something else you need to see.'

He walked past Gabe and waded straight into the water. In a way, Gabe wouldn't have been surprised if he had just glided on top of it. Or maybe that was the wrong brother.

He reached the car and looked back at Gabe.

'I *said* you need to see this.'

Gabe didn't wait to be asked again. He waded into the

water after the Samaritan. The water wasn't as cold as he expected but his skin still shuddered with goosebumps and his breath caught in his throat. He gritted his teeth and pushed through the rotting algae, the murky water lapping at his crotch, the smell slithering up his nostrils and making his stomach roll.

He reached the car. The smell was even worse here.

'What the –?'

The Samaritan replied by stretching out one long arm and popping the boot. It gave with a rusty squeal. He hauled it all the way open.

Gabe looked in the boot.

He looked back at the Samaritan.

He threw up.

8

Fran gripped the steering wheel tightly. Beside her, Alice slumped in her seat, staring out of the window. Her iPad rested in her lap, but she didn't seem inclined to turn it on. She only had limited internet access anyway. Just like she only had a basic pay-as-you-go mobile for emergencies. Fortunately, Alice was still too young to complain about these restrictions. In truth, she was often happier reading than using her tablet or phone. But Fran still felt the familiar ache of guilt.

She was denying Alice so many things, internet access being the least of them. And it was only going to get harder as she edged towards her teens. But Fran had no choice: it was what she had to do, to keep her safe.

After they ran the first time, Fran home-schooled her. It stopped the authorities from knocking on their door, asking too many questions, and it meant that Alice was always within her sight. She was still vulnerable, traumatized. She needed time to adjust. They both did.

But as Alice grew older, Fran knew she needed more normality, to mix with children of her own age, so she had buckled and enrolled her at the local junior school.

That had been a mistake. Alice was smart but she was

also young, and it was so easy to forget a lie. Plus, people talked – at the school gates, in the staff room. A misplaced word repeated to a stranger. A slip of the tongue to a teacher or parent. A friend of a friend who posted a picture on social media.

Really, it was only a matter of time.

They had escaped. But at a price.

This time around, Fran had tried to be even more careful. No more school. A nondescript house in a small town. She found work at a local café and the owner didn't mind if Alice studied quietly in the back. They tried, as far as possible, to live under the radar.

They had lasted a year.

She had known something was wrong as soon as they got home yesterday evening. Fran didn't really believe in a sixth sense. But she did believe in some kind of primeval alarm, wired into our DNA, that warns us about danger; danger even our brain hasn't consciously registered.

She had stood in the kitchen and listened to the house, every sense twitching. Alice had already gone upstairs to her room. Fran heard the clump of her footsteps, the creak of her bed. Then silence. Not even the usual faint chunter of the television from next door. The house rested. Fran's nerves thrummed.

She had walked across to the window. At six o'clock on a February evening the light was getting thin. The street-lights were just starting to stutter on. She looked up and down the street.

Her battered Fiat Punto sat outside, half propped on the kerb. Her neighbour's blue Escort was parked next to it, almost bumper to bumper. She knew every one of the cars on this street, as well as the cars of all the people who visited. That way, she could spot anyone unfamiliar. Out of place.

Yesterday, she had. Parked a few houses down, on the corner, behind the yellow Toyota that belonged to the Patels at number 14. A small white van. Innocuous. The sort of van people hired if they wanted to do their own removals; and it was true that the Patels had sold their house a while ago. But they were a family of six. She was pretty sure one small white van would not carry all of their possessions.

The van should not be there. Of course, there were probably any number of reasons why it *could* be. Rational, simple, normal explanations. But she dismissed them.

The van should not be there.

The van had come for them.

As she watched, the driver-side door opened. A man climbed out. Stocky, wearing a baseball cap, a green sweatshirt and jeans. He carried a parcel. Of course. People were always ordering things online now. A delivery driver wouldn't arouse suspicion. Except Fran didn't order anything online for that exact reason.

She didn't have much time. She ran upstairs and threw open her wardrobe. Everything she needed was packed into a small rucksack at the bottom. The house was rented fully furnished. They had no keepsakes or mementoes.

She knocked on Alice's door and eased it open. Alice lay on her bed, reading, long legs bent up behind her. She was growing fast, Fran thought. There would come a time when there would be questions; when she would no longer acquiesce to this life. Fran pushed that terrifying thought to one side.

'Sweetheart?'

'Yes?' Alice looked up. A few strands of dark hair fell over her face.

'We have to go. Now.'

Fran ran to the wardrobe, grabbed the rucksack and chucked her a hoodie. Alice pulled it over her head and got to her feet, stuffing them into her fake Uggs. Then she hesitated, looking around. Fran fought the urge to grab her, hurry her along.

'Alice. *C'mon,*' she hissed.

Alice spotted what she was missing. The small bag of pebbles, sitting on the bedside table. She snatched it up and slung it over her shoulder.

They crept out onto the landing and padded softly down the stairs. Just before the bottom, Fran paused, Alice's small, warm body pressed closely behind. She peered around the corner of the wall. The front door had opaque glass at the top so she could see people approach. She had attached a sign to the door. Casual, handwritten:

Parcels and deliveries, please use the side door. Thanks (smiley face).

Fran saw a shadow at the frosted glass, waited as the man read the note, then saw the shadow move again, around to the side of the house. *Now.* She grabbed Alice's hand and they ran down the hallway. She quickly unlocked the front door. She heard a knock on the side door. They bolted down the short pathway to the car. Beeped it unlocked. Chucked the rucksacks into the back. Alice climbed in the front; Fran threw herself into the driver's seat. She started the engine.

She was already accelerating away when she saw the

man run down the side path of the house, looking confused and annoyed. Fleetingly, she wondered whether he really *was* making a delivery. Perhaps he had just got the wrong house. Then she saw the flash of metal in his hand. No. She wasn't being paranoid. He had come for them. She knew.

Within ten minutes, they had been on the motorway, their old lives abandoned behind them, again.

Apart from the brief stop at the services, they had been driving ever since. They hadn't made bad time to start with, but then they had hit a massive traffic jam on the M5 and, even at such a late hour, been hindered by an endless procession of lorries blocking both lanes on the M42. They were heading up the M1 towards Yorkshire now.

Making time, Fran thought, a line from an old film popping into her mind. *I'm making time*. What was it? Then she remembered. *Withnail and I*, the perennial student favourite. *We've gone on holiday by mistake*. We appear to be running for our lives by mistake.

'Where are we going?' Alice asked.

'I don't know. Scotland, maybe? Somewhere safe, sweetheart. I promise.'

'You promised before.'

And she shouldn't have. She shouldn't now. But what else could she say? We'll never be safe. We'll never stop running. She couldn't admit that to herself, let alone to a not-quite-eight-year-old.

'We'll have a nice new house.'

'Can I go back to school?'

'Maybe. We'll see.'

Alice didn't reply.

She was getting used to being let down. To being disappointed and feeling distrustful. Shadows shouldn't darken her eyes, Fran thought. They should be fresh and bright with hope and expectation. Not fear. Her mind flashed back to Alice on the toilet floor, waking from her sleep.

'Are you feeling okay?' she asked.

'Yeah.'

'You didn't hurt yourself earlier when you fell?'

'No.'

'You broke the mirror.'

Alice frowned. 'I don't remember.'

'D'you remember anything?'

She risked a quick sideways glance. Alice had stopped frowning. Her face looked calm again, serene. She was thinking about the dream.

'I saw the girl.'

The girl. Alice had mentioned a girl before but, when pressed, she had clammed up.

'D'you know who she is?'

Alice shook her head.

'Did she speak to you?'

A nod.

'What did she say?'

'She said . . . she's afraid.'

Fran swallowed. *Tread carefully. Don't let her slip away from you.*

'Did she say why?'

A pause. A longer one. A car flashed them then darted out and undertook in the inside lane. Fran realized she was dawdling in the middle lane. An annoyance to other motorists and a way to draw attention. She signalled and pulled over.

Alice sat, fingers fiddling with her bag of pebbles. *Clickety-click, clickety-click*. The sound set Fran's teeth on edge. Restless, insistent. *Clickety-click, clickety-click*.

Just when she thought she wasn't going to answer, Alice whispered:

'She said that the Sandman is coming.'

9

Gabe had never seen a dead body before. Not in real life. When his mum finally succumbed to cirrhosis of the liver he had been too much of a coward to view her body in the hospital.

Later, he would wish that he had. It would have made her death more final, more complete. As it was, for weeks afterwards he would wake from vivid dreams convinced that she was still alive, that the hospital had made a mistake. Even visiting her graveside felt unreal. It didn't seem possible that she was gone, for ever. It felt more as if she had simply walked away from him, part way through a conversation that remained unfinished, without ever uttering a final goodbye.

This body was some way past goodbyes. It didn't look much like a body at all. Not any more. It was mostly bone, with a thin covering of rotted flesh. The skin was stippled a hideous marbled green. In places it had split open, revealing more yellow bone and some kind of unidentifiable grey mush. The face, or what had once been a face, was just a skull, the eyeballs yellow and deflated, cracked lips leering over stubs of yellow teeth.

Gabe's mind flashed to a drawing Izzy had done in

pre-school. It was supposed to be her childminder, Joy (no *Mona Lisa*, to be fair), but it came out looking more like a cross between Slimer from *Ghostbusters* and Nosferatu as drawn by someone with psychotic tendencies.

That was what this body looked like. But worse. Definitely worse. *A billion, trillion, squillion, minion times worse*, as Izzy used to say. And that was before you got to the smell. *Jesus Christ, the smell.*

Gabe turned and retched. Nothing in it but bile. Still, he heaved several more times before he managed to regain some control.

The Samaritan stood beside him, seemingly oblivious to the smell, the cold water – upon which now floated the contents of Gabe's stomach – or the rotted corpse.

'Can you close that?' Gabe asked, straightening. 'I think I've seen enough.'

The Samaritan obliged. He pulled the boot down again with a dull clunk. He patted the top.

'I'd say your man here has been dead for around a year.'

'Not longer?'

'Old car. Boot ain't going to be air- or watertight. It might have slowed decomp a bit, but not much.'

'You're sure it's a man?'

He nodded. 'He's naked. Didn't you notice?'

'The whole stinking-decomposition thing kind of distracted me.'

But now the Samaritan had mentioned it, Gabe realized he was right. No clothes. Just a putrefying body, locked in the boot of a car Gabe had last seen driving away with his daughter inside it. He swallowed.

All these years he had been searching, waiting for this.

But *this* was not what he had expected. Shit. What the hell *had* he expected? And what the hell did he do now?

'Is there . . . I mean, anything to identify him?'

The Samaritan shook his head. 'No clothes. No wallet. No ID.'

He looked at Gabe meaningfully. 'But I haven't checked the front of the car.'

Gabe looked at the Samaritan, then back at the car, the front still almost submerged in the lake. He sighed and waded further in. The water crept up to his thighs.

'Deeper than it looks, man.'

The Samaritan was right. Two more tentative steps and it was up to his waist. Gabe's foot slipped on the muddy lakebed. He flailed with his arms, splashing foul water into his face, but just managed to regain his footing.

'Jesus Christ!'

'You okay?'

He glanced back. The Samaritan had glided back to shore and now stood on the bank, watching him with the hint of an amused smile. He took a vape out of his pocket and drew on it. He barely looked damp.

Gabe rubbed at his face with the cuff of his coat.

'Yeah, great.'

He reached the passenger door. Tugged. The weight of the water was keeping it pushed shut. He pulled again. This time it gave a little. Gabe wedged his leg in the gap, fighting against the rancid water. He pulled out his torch and shone it inside. The seats were ancient leather, torn and mouldy with water damage. More water filled the footwells. There was nothing in the driver's or passenger's side except for some slimy-looking weeds and an ancient rusted drinks can. Fanta.

Izzy didn't like fizzy drinks, he thought.

He wedged himself in further, stretched out his arm and yanked at the glove compartment. It fell open. Inside there were a few sodden bits of paper so waterlogged they fell apart the minute his fingers touched them. But there was something else: a clear plastic folder. Gabe took the folder out and trained the torch on the contents inside. A pocket Bible, a folded map and a slim black notebook, like a diary or an address book.

Gabe let the door fall shut. He waded awkwardly back out, clutching the plastic folder. He was cold now, shivering. Well, his top half was shivering. His bottom half could well have been doing a tango beneath the water for all he knew – he had lost all feeling below the waist a while ago.

'I thought you couldn't get any whiter, but right now you look transparent.'

'Thanks.'

'You find anything?'

Gabe held up the folder. 'Maybe the police can still get some fingerprints –'

'Whoah.' The Samaritan held up a hand. 'Who said anything about police?'

Gabe stared at him. 'This is the car. The car they told me didn't exist. I *have* to call the police. It's evidence.'

The Samaritan looked at him with his blacker-than-black eyes.

'The police believe your daughter is dead. This car is not going to change that.'

'But what if they can get Izzy's DNA or identify the body?'

The Samaritan rolled his eyes. 'This ain't like the TV. You know how hard it is to retrieve DNA after all this time, from a car that's been swimming in Lake Murk?'

'Oddly, no.'

'Almost impossible. Any DNA would have degraded in days.'

Gabe wanted to argue but he got the impression, as far as this subject was concerned, the Samaritan knew what he was talking about.

'What about the body?'

'Even if you can identify your man here, what have you got?'

Before Gabe could reply, the Samaritan continued: 'You got a dead dude who has been dumped in the boot of a car *you* have been searching for and only one person with a motive to kill him.'

Gabe blinked. *'Me?'*

'You.'

'So, what should I do?'

The Samaritan nodded at the folder. 'You could start by looking at what you *have* got. Unless you're planning to keep it for a souvenir?'

Gabe debated with himself, then crouched down and carefully opened the folder. A small dribble of water trickled out. The Samaritan trained his torch on him. Gabe took out the Bible first and thumbed through the pages. They were mouldy and stuck together in clumps. No divine inspiration. He put it aside and reached for the notebook. If he had been hoping to find a confession and an address inside, he was out of luck. Most of the pages had been torn out. The remaining few were blank. He felt hope begin to wane. Finally, he reached for the map. One of the old-fashioned Ordnance Survey types that nobody had used since the last century. Gabe opened it up. Something fell out.

He stared at it.

A pink hair bobble. Dirty, damp, frayed.

Daddy.

He looked up at the Samaritan. 'She was in the car.'

The Samaritan regarded him steadily. 'Then I refer you back to my previous point.'

'What?'

'If this is the car, and this is the man who took your daughter – who the hell killed *him*?'

IO

The young woman behind the hotel reception desk looked no more than twenty-five; her accent was Eastern European. She was polite but disinterested, which suited Fran just fine. A motorway hotel was hardly the Ritz, but it would be clean and anonymous. They could rest and Fran could try to plan their next move.

They had a room available, the receptionist informed them. But because they hadn't booked online, they couldn't take advantage of the special rate. Fran expressed an appropriate level of disappointment, tried not to seem impatient and said it would be okay. She paid with a credit card. She had a few, with slightly different names. Surprisingly easy to obtain. She could have paid in cash, but that just made you stand out more. No one paid in cash for anything these days.

'Number 217.' The receptionist gave them their key card. They climbed the stairs and shuffled along the bland, fusty-smelling corridor to their room. Fran buzzed them inside and they threw their rucksacks on the beds. She stared around. It looked, well, like every other budget hotel room in every other city up and down the country. The carpet was worn, the fittings chipped. And it smelt faintly of cigarettes, despite the 'No Smoking' sign on the door. But the beds looked large and comfortable and Fran really *was* exhausted. After almost eight hours on the road, she just couldn't drive any further.

When they first fled, she had taken them north, to Cumbria. When the man had found them, she had driven to the opposite end of the country, the tip of the coast. Where now? Scotland? Abroad? But that meant passports, something she didn't have.

She glanced at Alice, who stood in the centre of the room, shoulders slumped, arms hanging at her sides, too tired even to sit down on the bed. The weariness on her small face cleaved Fran's heart in two. It was like this at the start. Anonymous hotels. Always running, always afraid. No child should live like that. But then, no child should die a bloody, violent death either.

Her throat constricted. Sometimes it hit her like a sledge-hammer. Grief. A desperate, unrelenting sense of guilt. *All your fault.* But she couldn't change things now. She couldn't look back. She'd rather be blinded.

She smiled wanly at Alice. 'C'mon. Let's get some sleep.' She bit her tongue to stop herself saying something else, like, *Things will look better after we get some rest*, because that would be another lie. Instead, she added. 'I'll treat us to a McDonald's for breakfast.'

Alice managed the weakest of smiles in return and pulled out her toiletries bag. They brushed their teeth in the harsh bathroom light, pulled on fresh T-shirts and leggings, placed their packed rucksacks beside their beds.

Fran checked the windows were locked and pulled the heavy blackout curtains. They were on the second floor, which was good. She always refused ground-floor rooms. Finally, she slipped the security chain on the door and tested it a few times.

Satisfied, preparations done, she climbed into bed. Alice lay in the other double, cover pulled up to her chin, eyes already closed. The bag of pebbles sat on the table beside her.

Clickety-click. The Sandman is coming.

Fran shivered, despite the thick duvet and the warmth of the room.

She didn't understand Alice's odd sleeping episodes, although she had done her best to research the condition (narcolepsy, she had found out it was called). Unfortunately, there weren't any easy answers. No simple cause and effect. One of those medical anomalies that prove science doesn't have all the answers.

And *nothing* she had read could explain the pebbles. Fran had exhausted Google and racked her brains but couldn't find anything comparable. Eventually, she had given up trying. What was it Holmes said? 'When you eliminate the impossible, the only answer must be the improbable'? The problem was, dear Holmes, in this case the answer *was* the impossible. Stick that in your crack pipe and smoke it.

Alice stirred a little and snuffled into the pillow. During one of her 'episodes', she would fall straight into a deep, silent sleep. At night, when she should be sleeping peacefully, she was never at rest. Turning, crying out, moaning. Often, she thrashed around, screaming, gripped by terrible nightmares. When Fran went to try to comfort her, she pushed her away.

It hurt. But it was understandable. Despite everything

they had been through, all that Fran had done for her, the bond they shared, it was not Fran she cried out for in the dead of night. It was not Fran she wanted to soothe the nightmares away.

It was her mummy.

11

Routine. You became a creature of it in a job like hers, Katie thought. The same hours, the same tables, the same bright fluorescent lighting bearing down. You had no real sense of time in a service station. No clocks. No windows in the café where she worked. A bit like a casino, or an institution of some kind.

It messed with your mind and your body. Katie would find herself eating cereal at dinner time and craving a steak at dawn. Then there was the scratchiness in her eyes and throat from constantly breathing recycled air. Oh, and the glamour of always smelling like stale food. She could never seem to get it out of her clothes, hair or nostrils.

Sometimes, when she emerged after her shift, blinking into the pre-dawn, she had to take a moment. The daylight, the fresh air, the noise. It felt overwhelming. It took her most of the thirty-minute drive home to adjust, recalibrate. To ease the stiffness in her muscles and mind; to relax into being human again.

Every action became so robotic in this artificial world you functioned like a slightly battered and badly maintained machine yourself, performing your tasks with minimal power input, brain engaged elsewhere. Put into neutral. Humming over but only half alive.

Unless something happened to jar you awake. Something unusual, something out of the routine.

The thin man was back.

This was more than unusual. This was wrong. Very wrong.

The thin man had his own routine. He visited approximately once a week; never more than nine days between visits, never less than six.

He never returned on the same day. Ever.

But here he was.

She had just finished her shift and was heading out, hoodie over her uniform, rucksack slung over her back, when she spotted him.

He sat at his usual table, near the front, behind a pillar, where he could watch people coming and going but remain unobserved himself. Often, he had his laptop open, but this morning he had what looked like a notebook and paper spread out on the table in front of him.

She frowned. Something about him looked different, too. Hair? No – that was the usual dark, unkempt non-style. *Clothes*. He was wearing different clothes. Earlier he had been wearing a grey sweatshirt and black jeans. Now, he wore a checked shirt and blue jeans. He had changed. Why? *And why had she even noticed?*

She shoved the thought to one side. That wasn't the only thing that was different. Normally, like her, the man operated on autopilot. Breathing, moving, performing all the tasks required of life (except, perhaps, eating), but not actually living. That vitality, that energy, had been sapped from him.

This morning, he looked as if he had some of it back. She wouldn't go so far as to say he had colour in his cheeks, but he didn't look as much like a walking corpse as usual.

Something had happened, she thought. Something that had forced him to change his clothes, alter his routine. Despite herself, despite wishing that he would disappear for good, she wondered what.

She walked over to the lanky, bearded youth she was working with on this shift (Ethan? Nathan? Or was it Ned?). That was the only thing that *did* change here on a regular basis. Her co-workers. The pay wasn't bad, but the rotten hours, stifling environment and the need for your own car to get you here made the services a less than desirable workplace.

It certainly wasn't what Katie had imagined herself doing with her life. Sometimes, she could see the pity in her young colleagues' eyes. Most of them were only here to fund their way through university en route to something better. But she was stuck here permanently. This *was* her better life.

'You're a trier, Katie,' she remembered the careers advisor at school telling her, with a smug smile, comb-over slicked fast to his freckled head. 'You work hard. You're a good student. But let's be realistic, you're never going to be Oxford material.'

Patronizing dick. But then, he had been right. Because here she was, a single mum, working in a dead-end job that a robot probably *would* be doing in ten years' time.

'When did the thin man come back?' she asked Ethan/ Nathan/Ned.

He barely grunted, 'Dunno,' intent upon attempting to either break or dismantle the coffee machine. Whatever he was doing, it certainly wasn't making coffee. She knew they received training, but sometimes she wondered. Oxford material, indeed.

'Here,' she sighed, dropping her bag behind the counter. 'I'll do this one.'

Gabe hadn't meant to return to the same services so soon. Normally, he would be miles away by this point. But things were not normal. Not even close. Not even *his* normal, which was, by most people's standards, pretty insane.

He had changed out of his wet clothes in the camper van, thought about trying to sleep, but every time he closed his eyes, all he saw was that damn liquefied body seeping into the car boot. And then he saw Izzy, in the back of the same car.

Who was the man? What had happened to him? What had he done with Izzy?

He needed to stop somewhere. Stop and think. And this place was as good as any. He ordered a black coffee from a harassed-looking young man at the counter and sat down to wait for it at his usual table. The table hadn't been cleared. Same with a lot of them. In fact, the young man looked like the only staff member on. He wondered where the blonde waitress was. Maybe she had finished her shift. He couldn't help feeling a tiny bit disappointed.

He reached into his bag and took out the items he had retrieved from the car, still wrapped in plastic. He laid them on the table, and paused, feeling suddenly furtive. The Samaritan had once told him: *'We're all being watched. The Man has got eyes everywhere. Internet, CCTV, traffic cameras. You've always got to act like somebody is watching.'*

He looked around the coffee shop. In one corner, an older couple in matching Barbour jackets sipped lattes. They probably drove a Volvo and owned a spaniel, he thought. At another table, a young woman in a business suit, and heels that were entirely impractical for driving, tapped furiously at her mobile phone. Finally, there was a mum and dad with a sleeping baby in a car seat. They gulped gratefully at their coffees and threw annoyed glances at anyone who made a noise.

None of them was paying Gabe the slightest bit of attention.

He slipped the items from the plastic bag and stared at them again. He tried to view them objectively. The bobble looked so much like the bobbles Izzy had been wearing that morning. But then, lots of little girls had bobbles exactly the same. There were no stray strands of hair attached and, if the Samaritan was right, it was too late to get any useful DNA anyway.

Of course, he could still call the police, but he already knew what they would say: So, he had found a car. So what? No one denied there might have been a car. But it wasn't Izzy he'd seen in it. Oh, they would be nice. Patient. Understanding. To a point. The point where they treated him like he was crazy. Just like before. He had grown used to them rolling their eyes whenever he came into the station. The polite but firm tone. The suggestions of talking to someone, of counselling. People he could see, numbers he could call.

In a way, he had preferred it when the police thought he was guilty of something. At least they listened to him. At least they treated him like a grown man, rather than some pathetic figure of pity. That was the worst. Becoming invisible, soundless. The assumption that everything he said was nonsense.

There is, Gabe had learned, more than one way to become lost.

For now, he supposed, he was on his own. If he were some hard-boiled detective, he might add, *Just the way I like it*. But he didn't like it. He found himself thinking about the blonde waitress again. He wasn't sure why. Yes, she was attractive, and she seemed kind. But then, that was her job – to be nice to customers, to smile politely. It wasn't as if he really knew her. Besides, she looked like she had plenty going on in her own life as it was. She certainly didn't need his problems. And, aside from a rusty old camper van, that was all he had to offer.

He opened the map and spread it out on the table. A few places had been marked with an X, but they didn't mean anything to him. He folded it back up and picked up the Bible. He had glanced at it only briefly before, the soft, mouldy feel of the pages putting him off handling it for too long. Besides, he remembered the stickers on the back window of the car.

When you drive like I do, you'd better believe in God.

Real men love Jesus.

The Bible seemed appropriate. But now, as he thumbed through the still-damp pages, he noticed something else. Certain passages had been underlined:

But if there is any further injury, then you shall appoint as a penalty life for life, eye for eye, tooth for tooth. (Exodus 21: 23–25)

If a man injures his neighbour, just as he has done, so it shall be done to him. (Leviticus 24: 17–21)

You shall purge the evil from among you. The rest will hear and be afraid and will never again do such an evil thing among you. (Deuteronomy 19: 18–21)

He will avenge the blood of His servants and will render vengeance on His adversaries. (Deuteronomy 32: 43)

Real men may love Jesus, but it seemed that this one was strictly Old Testament. Vengeance, retribution, blood. Gabe felt an icy nail scrape down his spine.

He put it to one side and opened the notebook. Ripped edges. Blank pages. Why rip them out? What was written on them?

'Americano?' a voice asked.

He jumped, looked up. The blonde waitress with the kind eyes stood by his table holding a coffee.

'Oh, yes, thanks.'

He noticed that she wore a hoodie over her uniform.

'On your way home?'

'Just heading off.'

She put the coffee down and nodded at the notebook. 'Looking for a message in invisible ink?'

He glanced at her more sharply. 'What?'

'Sorry. You were just staring really hard at a blank page and . . . just a joke.' She started to turn away.

'Wait!'

Something sparked suddenly in his brain. Pages torn out. There must have been something written on them. Maybe something someone didn't want anyone else to see. 'Have you got a pencil?'

'Err, yeah.' She fumbled in her pocket and produced a stub.

He took it and started tracing it over the paper. He wasn't sure it would work. He had only ever seen people do this on TV. But as he watched, words appeared faintly through the lead, an imprint from the previous page.

Gabe held the notebook up and stared at it. He frowned. 'Don't suppose that means anything to you?'

The waitress shrugged. 'Sorry.'

He nodded, deflated. 'Here's your pencil.'

'You keep it.'

She walked away. Gabe stared back down at the notebook. Several fragments of words and letters had overlapped. But three stood out. A ghostly imprint of a dead man's hand.

THE OTHER PEOPLE.

12

Tentative streaks of silver were just starting to lighten the sky when Katie emerged from the services. Despite feeling tired to the marrow of her bone, every limb aching with exhaustion, she liked this time of day. There was a calmness to the first hours of dawn. The day just waking, nothing to spoil it. A new beginning. A fresh start.

All rubbish, of course. There were no fresh starts. Not really. We're all too entrenched in our own personal ruts, unable to summon up the energy to dig ourselves out. Life, as we know it. Or as she knew it, anyway.

This morning, like most mornings, she would drive to her younger sister Lou's house to pick up her children and make breakfast. Then she would see Sam and Gracie off to school and finally get home to bed for some sleep. At 3.10 p.m. she would pick the children up, make dinner, drop them at her sister's again and, after they were in bed, head back up the motorway to work. Like bloody Groundhog Day. Although, at least, she reminded herself, she had a couple of days off before the routine started again.

She walked across the car park and climbed into her battered Polo. She turned on the engine and selected a CD.

Yep, her car was so old it still had a CD player and she was so old she still had CDs.

Tom Petty seeped out of the speakers as she drove, singing about a good girl who loves her mama. Lucky her. Maybe 'Mama' wasn't a bitter drunk (mental note – better call Mum tomorrow). She turned the song up. *Free fallin'*. Just what she felt like doing sometimes. Forgetting everything, putting her foot to the metal, driving past the turn-off that would take her home: to the dirty dishes, toys scattered across the floor like a Lego and Barbie obstacle course, the bills on the doormat, the sheer drudgery of everyday life. Driving as far as she could, to places she had never been.

Of course, it would never happen. She would tear her own heart out before she ever left her children. And don't get her wrong – life wasn't *bad*. She was luckier than most. She had a job, a house, her health. But she still couldn't help wishing there was something more. Problem was, she didn't know what. Perhaps it didn't even exist. You could spend a lifetime running from one life and chasing another. Gold at the end of the rainbow. Greener grass across the meadow. But, in most cases, the gold would be fake and the green grass would be AstroTurf.

When she got married, she had dreamed of a perfect family. A lovely home with a big garden. Maybe a dog. Holidays in a pretty cottage in Cornwall. She and Craig would watch their children grow up and grow old together.

Hah! Some dream that was. When Sam was five and Gracie barely one, Craig had left her for a sales rep called Amanda. The family home was swapped for a modern apartment (all tiled floors and white bloody sofas) and couple's holidays in Dubai.

'*I just think we rushed into things*,' Craig had told her with his earnest, brown-eyed stare. The same one he had used on her when he told her he wanted to settle down and start a family.

'*I need to have my life back again.*'

Never mind about her life. Or their children's. Never mind that when you committed to bringing new lives into the world, yours went on hold. You didn't get to just pick it back up again, like a discarded coat, slip it on and head off out of the door.

But then, Craig had always been selfish. She should have seen it before but, as always, she had fallen into the role of pacifier, making allowances so as not to let her marriage fall apart. More fool her. It had happened anyway.

Now, Sam was ten and Gracie was five, and the best they got from their dad was an occasional trip to the park and age-inappropriate birthday and Christmas presents. Still, at least he paid maintenance. That was one thing. Without it, her meagre salary wouldn't cover the basics, let alone the extras children needed. Like clothes and shoes.

No such thing as a happy family, she thought. We're all sold a lie. Adverts and sitcoms – even bloody *Peppa Pig*. Families were just strangers, bonded to each other by accidents of birth and misplaced duty.

You couldn't choose your family. You couldn't even choose whether to love them or not. You just sort of had to. Whatever they put you through.

She thought about Mum, eaten up by bitterness and alcohol, Lou with her string of failed relationships, and her older sister, who she hadn't seen for nine years. Ever since the funeral. What had she found at the end of her rainbow?

Her foot pressed down a fraction on the accelerator. The

sign for her junction drew into view: 14. Barton Marsh. She left it a few moments longer than normal, then flicked on the indicator to change lanes and pulled off on to the slip road.

Tom warbled that he was, '*Gonna leave this world for a while.*'

If only, she thought. But then, that could well be her mantra for life. If only she hadn't gone back to the coffee shop today. If only she had gone straight home. If only she hadn't served the thin man. If only she hadn't seen the words emerge in the battered notebook, like a bad dream resurfacing from the depths of her subconscious.

THE OTHER PEOPLE.

You wanted something more, Katie, she thought bitterly. Well, there you go. Be careful what you wish for.

When he had asked if it meant anything to her, she managed to shake her head, even as her stomach twisted itself into a tight knot. Then she walked away, as quickly as she could, without breaking into a run.

He obviously didn't know what the words meant. And hopefully, he wouldn't find out. Besides, it was not her problem. She couldn't help him. She didn't even know him.

But she knew them.

13

Gabe lay on the narrow camper-van bed. His feet hung over the edge. His arms, even folded on his chest, poked off the sides. He closed his eyes, but his mind kept on whirring away. The Bible. The notebook.

The Other People.

He had tried googling it, but the only things his search had thrown up were an old Netflix show and an Indian rock band. He didn't think that was what he was looking for. But then, he didn't really *know* what he was looking for. He didn't even know if the words had anything to do with Izzy or were just something random jotted down, like a scribble on the back of your hand to remind you to pick up milk.

He opened his eyes and stared at the ceiling. There was no point in even pretending to sleep. That ship had sailed. He'd never been a good sleeper anyway. Never found respite in the darkness. Every whisper of wind or slight creak of the house would send his eyes shooting open. He would lie, for hours, tense as a board, staring into the shadows, senses alert. Waiting for the nightmares to begin.

Sometimes, when Izzy couldn't get to sleep, he would curl up next to her and sing lullabies or read her stories until they both dozed off. He never admitted to Jenny that this was as much for his comfort as hers.

After Izzy vanished, the nightmares worsened, shredding his nights into sweat-soaked fragments of terror. Again and again their black claws tore him from the edge of oblivion and he'd be screaming so hard that, come the dawn, his throat would be raw and his eyes speckled with burst blood vessels.

Gabe didn't really believe in karma. But there had been times in the last three years when he had wondered. Was this it? The world's way of keeping balance? Taking away the most precious thing in his life to remind him that he didn't deserve to be happy, not after what he had done. Except, *Izzy wasn't dead.* Despite what everyone believed, he knew there had been a mistake. A terrible, terrible mistake.

The Samaritan was right. He couldn't go to the police. Not yet. First, he needed to speak to someone else. Someone he had avoided challenging, had tiptoed around, unwilling to inflict more pain. But this changed things.

He had to know for sure. He had to speak to Jenny's father.

Gabe lifted his arm, checked his watch. Dawn was creeping around the camper van's thin, pull-down blind. Six thirty a.m.

Still early. But he had a feeling that Harry didn't sleep much either.

He sat up, swung his legs off the narrow bunk and pulled out his phone. After the funeral, Jenny's mother, Evelyn, had changed the home phone number to stop him calling. But Harry had taken pity on him and given Gabe his mobile.

'If you ever need to talk.'

74

Surprisingly, Gabe had found he did. Although, on one occasion, he didn't talk, he just wept.

He typed out a text: 'Harry, it's Gabe. Could we meet today?'

His phone almost instantly pinged with a reply.

'8am? Usual place.'

It wasn't a question. With a heavy heart, Gabe typed, 'Okay.'

Farnfield Cemetery was an hour's drive away, not far from the home he had once shared with Jenny and Izzy in Nottinghamshire. It was as pleasant a space as somewhere like this could be. The Garden of Remembrance had plenty of green, neatly mown grass. Smart wooden benches. Trees to provide shade and lots of flowering bushes and evergreens.

Gabe appreciated the sentiment, but he wasn't sure if it was here that people really remembered their loved ones. Memories were entwined with the everyday minutiae of life. The scent of a certain perfume. Writing a shopping list and still including Marmite because your wife loved it. Finding a mug with 'Best Mum in the World' on it in the cupboard. A song on the radio. The smell of food drifting from a restaurant where you once shared a ridiculously expensive bottle of wine that neither of you really liked. Those were the memories that seized you out of nowhere, grabbed you by the heart and squeezed until your chest felt like it would explode. Raw, visceral, uncensored.

Here, memories were filtered through rose-tinted glasses. You selected the things you wanted to remember and put aside those you would rather forget. You left bright bunches of flowers to disguise the fact that all around you was death, your loved ones just a small pile of milky ashes in an ugly pot that Gabe was pretty sure Jenny would have stuffed at the back of a cupboard or 'accidentally' dropped if she had received it as a present.

He smiled. A real memory. Jenny was a woman of taste and limited tact. She knew what she liked and what she didn't and wasn't afraid to say so.

He sat down on a bench and stared at her small headstone, beneath which the offensive pot was buried:

> Jennifer Mary Forman
> 13 August 1981–11 April 2016
> Wife. Beloved daughter. Devoted Mummy.
> In our hearts, minds and memories always.

'Wife'. That was all they had given him. The tiniest of gestures. He hadn't been involved in choosing the headstone. Just like he had been excluded from most of the funeral arrangements. At the time, he was relieved. And, of course, at the time, he was still under suspicion of murder.

'Gabriel?'

He started, looked around. Harry stood beside the bench. Always a well-preserved, fit-looking man (a respected doctor and surgeon in his day), today he looked every one of his seventy-nine years. The thick white hair was still perfectly styled, combed back from a face bronzed by regular winter sun. But there was a slight sagginess around his jaw and eyes. The lines on his forehead carved deeper. One hand leaned heavily on a stick. In the other, he held flowers. Two bouquets.

As Gabe watched, he bent and placed one in the vase beside Jenny's headstone. Then he turned. To the other headstone. The one Gabe had carefully avoided looking at since he arrived. Because, despite what he believed, despite what he had discovered, the sight of it still filled him with a grief that was almost too much to bear. A black, swollen tide that threatened to drag him down and engulf him.

> Isabella Jane Forman
> 5 April 2011–11 April 2016
> Cherished daughter and granddaughter.
> Borrowed from Heaven, returned to the arms
>   of angels.

Jenny. Izzy.

'It's about your wife . . . and your daughter.'

Harry sat down heavily next to him. 'So what do you want to talk about?'

14

The estate where Lou lived was a cramped quadrangle of pebbledashed houses on the outskirts of Barton Marsh village. Sustainable, affordable housing. Translate as: cheap, small, ugly.

Katie squeezed into a space a few doors down from her sister's mid-terrace. The small square of grass outside was uncut. A trike lay on its side, weeds poking through the spokes. The rubbish bin by the front door overflowed with bulging black sacks. She tried not to tut.

She loved Lou. God knows what she would do if she couldn't have Sam and Gracie overnight. But she hated that she had to leave her children with her. She hated how she couldn't be sure that Lou would put them back to bed if they woke up in the night, rather than letting them stay up and watch TV. She hated that Lou's own little girl, Mia, always looked a bit dirty and hastily dressed, often wandering around in just a T-shirt and a nappy.

She knew it wasn't up to her to tell her sister how to live her life. She knew that, as the youngest, she had been hit hard by what had happened. But then they all had. You couldn't use that as an excuse for the rest of your life. Eventually, you had to grow up, take responsibility. Lou didn't seem to want to try. She was only twenty-seven and it felt like she had already given up on life.

Katie walked up the short front path, stepping over an empty McDonald's wrapper and a packet of half-used wet wipes. She let herself into the hall with the key Lou had given her. It smelt of stale food and dirty nappies.

'Hello?' she called quietly.

No sounds from upstairs. She wondered what time they went to bed. Waking up grumpy, tired children when she was feeling grumpy and tired herself was the last thing she needed.

'Sam? Gracie?'

She traipsed upstairs, shoved open the door to their bedroom. Sam and Gracie were already sitting up sleepily in the bed they shared. Mia rolled over and blinked at her from her cot bed, a dummy hanging out of her mouth.

Sam yawned. 'Did we sleep late?'

'No, no, It's okay. I just wanted to come in and surprise you!'

From next door, she heard her sister's sleepy grumble: 'For God's sake.'

She smiled grimly.

'Okay, well, up you get. I'll start breakfast.'

Lou emerged downstairs just as Katie was dishing up toast and cereal. She managed to clear a space at the cluttered table for Sam, Gracie and Mia. She had stuck the television on to keep them happy, although there had been a brief dispute over whether they should watch *Clone Wars* or *PJ Masks*.

'Christ – can you turn that down a bit?' Lou yawned.

Her blonde hair was a tangled haystack, make-up

smudged beneath her eyes. She wore a grubby dressing gown knotted loosely at the waist.

Katie picked up the remote and deliberately nudged the volume up. Then she gathered up the pile of rubbish she had picked up from the floor and went to stick it in the bin. She flipped open the lid and paused. The bin was crammed with Guinness cans.

'Has Steve been round?'

'Oh yeah. Just for a bit, last night.'

Steve. The latest in a long line of useless boyfriends that Lou seemed to pick up like other people pick up chewing gum on the soles of their shoes. The only difference being that Lou's boyfriends didn't stick around as long.

It was probably giving Steve too much credit to even call him a boyfriend, really. The relationship seemed more off than on. He wouldn't call for weeks on end, then he'd turn up, out of the blue, whenever he felt like it. And it was pretty obvious *what* he felt like. Katie knew that he was just using her sister. But Lou refused to see it, trotting out all the usual excuses: he worked shifts, he was busy, he had a demanding job.

Katie supposed that at least he *had* a job, which was more than could be said for some of the walking disasters Lou had dated, like Mia's dad, who had disappeared faster than you could say 'unpaid child support' once he knew she was pregnant. But ultimately, none of that really mattered. Steve could have been a millionaire entrepreneur or a saint. The point was that Katie had one firm ground rule in the babysitting arrangement with her sister: no boyfriends stopping over when her children were here.

'When did he leave?' she asked now.

'Last night. He had to be up early for work.'

'Right. So, how did he get home?'

She saw Lou hesitate.

'He drove, didn't he?'

'He doesn't live that far.'

'Of all people –'

'Oh, here we go.'

'Here we go what?'

'You – being all judgemental. You never like any of my boyfriends.'

'That's because they're all idiots.'

'Yeah, well, at least I *have* boyfriends.'

'Yeah, well, at least I have my self-respect.'

'You're such a –'

'Mum, Auntie Lou, can you stop *arguing*?'

Gracie stood behind them in her My Little Pony pyjamas, hair full of morning static, hands on her tiny hips. 'You always tell Sam and me not to argue.'

Katie forced a smile. 'We're not arguing. We're just . . .'

'Discussing,' Sam said, spooning cornflakes into his mouth. 'That's what you always say. Sounds just like arguing, though.'

Katie glanced at Lou. Her sister offered a small shrug.

'Little ears hear big mouths,' she muttered.

It was what Dad used to say to Mum when they were kids and overheard something they shouldn't. *Told you to be quiet – little ears hear big mouths.* Her mum would mock-scowl and whip at Dad with a tea towel. *Who you calling Big Mouth?*

Right on cue, Gracie giggled and pointed at Katie: 'Ha – Big Mouth.'

Katie poked her tongue out and tried not to feel irritated that her kids always took Auntie Lou's side in an argument.

Still, the moment was deflected. Mia banged her spoon on the table and started to wail. Sam screwed up his face: 'Eurgh. Mia stinks. She's done a shi— . . . a poo in her nappy.' Then, in the same breath, 'I've finished breakfast. Can I play *Super Mario*?'

'No,' Katie and Lou said, for once in unison, and then smiled tentatively at each other.

'I'd better deal,' Lou said, bending to pick up Mia.

Katie nodded and sipped at her cup of tea. Even though she rarely drank, right now she wished it were something stronger.

Fifteen minutes later, she was loading Sam and Gracie back into her car. She waved at her sister, who stood in the door, still in her dressing gown, a cigarette in one hand and Mia clinging to her leg.

Katie sighed. What was the point? she thought. You do your best. You try. But you can't force people to change. Maybe they never will. Not unless something drastic happens to shake them out of their apathy.

Or maybe that was the problem. Something drastic *had* happened. Something terrible. Something that had splintered their already fragile family into pieces.

Someone had murdered their dad.

15

There are many things you don't consider about death. Especially bloody, violent death. For a start, you don't consider that it will ever happen. Not to you. Not to someone you know. Not to someone you love.

We live our lives in a state of denial. A blinkered belief that we are different, special. Protected by a mystical force field that deflects all the bad stuff.

Terrible things happen, of course, but they happen to other people; the ones you read about in newspapers. The haggard, tear-ravaged faces you see on the television.

We sympathize. We shed tears. Maybe we even light candles, leave flowers, create hashtags. And then we get on with our lives. Our special, safe, protected lives.

Until one day, one phone call, one sentence.

It's about your wife . . . and your daughter.

And you realize it's all an illusion. You're not special. You're just like everyone else, skipping across a minefield, trying to pretend that your whole world can't, at any moment, be blown apart.

You never consider how that will feel. Not really. Because you have spent a lifetime *not* imagining it, as if to do so might tempt Fate to turn his ravaged face your way and see something he likes.

You never consider that you will have to drive for miles, the resonating aftershock of those words ringing in your ears, desperate denials still raging around your head. You never consider that you will arrive home not to a home but to a crime scene. Your personal mementoes now evidence. Men and women in uniforms and white suits shuffling around silently while you are shut outside. You never consider that you will have to explain your actions to strangers; lay your secrets bare before people you do not know, in a situation you still cannot understand. You never consider that you will need an alibi or a lawyer.

And you never consider that, amidst your grief and terror and confusion, you will be asked to identify the bodies.

The bodies. No longer people, full of warmth and hope and fears and dreams. No longer living, breathing souls. No longer Izzy or Jenny or Bubs or Mummy. Those wonderful, frustrating masses of human contradictions were gone. For ever.

Except he had seen her. He had seen Izzy.

Gabe had stared at the detective, DI Maddock, through eyes that felt lined with grit and swollen with grief.

'Identify them?'

'It's standard procedure, Mr Forman. Based upon photographs obtained, we've no reason to doubt the bodies are those of your wife and daughter –'

Photographs, he thought. They hadn't taken any new ones in a while. There just hadn't been that many happy family moments recently, he thought bitterly. The ones up on the walls were old. Izzy when she was two or three.

They had talked about putting some new ones up. So many things we talk about doing, he thought. Always thinking we'll have another day, another week, another year. As if our future were a certainty. Not just a fragile promise.

Gabe shook his head. 'I told you. There's been a mistake. I *saw* my daughter. In a car. Someone has taken her, maybe my wife, too. You need to be out there, looking for them.'

'I understand – and we have your statement, Mr Forman. That's why I think it's even more important for you to provide a formal identification.'

Gabe let the words sink in. 'Formal' identification. Gentlemen must wear a tie. If you're wearing trainers, you're not coming in. He choked down a hysterical giggle.

The police didn't believe him. Fine. He would show them. It wasn't Izzy lying cold and still in some damn morgue. She was alive. She had only just turned five. And he had seen her. In that rusty wreck of a car. *Honk if you're horny.* Two blonde pigtails. *Real men love Jesus.* One tooth missing in the front.

'Fine. But you're wrong. I saw my daughter being taken. She's alive.'

DI Maddock had nodded, something Gabe couldn't quite decipher flitting across her face. 'Once you've seen the bodies, I'm sure we'll have more questions for you.'

The identification was scheduled for the following afternoon. Gabe felt frustrated by the lack of urgency. But he also felt too shell-shocked and exhausted to argue.

The house, which a couple of days ago had hosted Izzy's fifth birthday party, was now a crime scene. Gabe couldn't stay there. In the absence of any friends who could put him up, he booked a room at a nearby Premier Inn. A stout woman in a white shirt and black trouser suit arrived and introduced herself as: 'Anne Gleaves, your family liaison officer.' She drove him to the hotel and, uninvited, accompanied him to his room. She sat with him for a while and talked. Lumpen words that had no meaning. He stared at her kind, sensible face and wished she would jump out of the window. When she asked if there was anyone he would like her to contact, he thought of Jenny's parents and, reluctantly, refused. He should do it. After she had gone, he called Harry and Evelyn, destroyed their world with a single sentence, and then sat up, staring at old photos of Izzy and Jenny on his phone, crying himself hoarse.

When dawn edged around the thin curtains, he showered, shaved and pulled on the same clothes from the day before – a black shirt and jeans. He took a crumpled tie from his pocket and knotted it around his neck, pulling it a little tighter than necessary. He regarded himself in the mirror. Aside from the pallid colour of his skin and blood-streaked eyes, he looked almost presentable. *Formal identification*, he thought again, grimly.

Then he sat back down and waited.

All a mistake. A terrible mistake.

Harry and Evelyn called him back just before midday. Evelyn sounded surprisingly calm. No trace of the hysterical woman from the night before. They wanted to come with him, she said. For support. Gabe didn't want them to. He told them it was unnecessary. But Evelyn insisted: *'You can't do this on your own. Harry will drive. In case it's too much for you.'*

Back then, before the accusations and suspicions had broken down their tenuous relationship completely, he supposed they were still playing the role of supportive in-laws, the three of them united briefly in their loss.

'*Have you eaten?*' Evelyn asked when they arrived. '*You need to eat. You need strength.*' As though food would somehow fill the aching hole in his heart.

They took him to the pub next to the hotel. The lights felt too harsh, the decor too bright. Gabe had no idea what they were doing there. The scrape of cutlery on plates set his teeth on edge. Evelyn chattered resolutely about nothing, her voice a little too brittle and high. He could see her eyes were sore and red-looking. Once or twice she took out some eye-drops and squeezed them in. Harry made intermittent grunts and funnelled a cheese sandwich into his mouth. Gabe managed one bite of stale bread and ham and two cups of black coffee. It was cold and bitter. An apt metaphor. Life had lost its taste.

It was a twenty-minute journey to the hospital, which was on the outskirts of town, near the ring road. The same hospital where Jenny gave birth to Izzy. He thought his heart had wrung itself dry with grief, but now he felt it twist again. Bitter drops that burned his soul and made his gut convulse with nausea. He clutched his stomach.

'Are you all right?' Evelyn clasped his hand.

He nodded. 'Fine, I'm fine.'

She reached into her purse, took out a small vial of pills and shook two out into her hand. She offered them to him.

'What are they?'

'To help, with your nerves.'

That explained some of the odd, manic chatter. He looked at the small pink tablets and started to shake his head. Then he felt his stomach clench again. He changed his mind. He took the tablets and swallowed them dry. *Bitter*, he thought again.

They parked in the visitors' car park, adding to Gabe's

sense of unreality, but then they were hardly going to have spaces marked 'Morgue Only', perhaps with a white outline of a coffin, were they? Wouldn't want to remind people that hospital isn't always a place where their loved ones get better.

Anne Gleaves met them in the reception. She held out a hand. He took it, but it felt like shaking Plasticine. Maybe the tablets were kicking in. Every part of him felt numb.

'If you'll just come this way.'

A cliché to say the rest was a blur. But there it was. He felt like he was walking through a world made of fuzzy felt, all the sharp edges rubbed off. They padded down soft-blue corridors. Muffled voices settled like sludge in his ears. The only thing that felt sharp and clear to him was the smell. Chemical. Medicinal. Embalming fluid, he thought. To stop the bodies rotting. His stomach rolled again.

They reached a small waiting room. He supposed it was meant to look homely. More pastel hues. Grey sofas. White flowers in a vase. Fake – their fabric petals faded and dusty. Leaflets were spread out on the table. Dealing with Bereavement. Counselling Services. Explaining Sudden Death to a Child. A picture of a wide-eyed toddler stared up at him. He looked away.

Anne Gleaves sat down. Explained about 'the process'. It was nothing like you saw on TV. There would be no hideous, dramatic pulling back of a sheet. Jenny and Izzy would by lying on tables, just their faces visible. Gabe could spend as long with them as he wished, but he mustn't touch the bodies. When he was ready to leave, he would be required to sign a form confirming that the deceased were his wife and daughter. Did he need a drink of water before he went in? Did he want someone to accompany him?

He shook his head. He stood. He made it to the door.

Everything swam. His vision was distorted by wavy lines. He tried to breathe deeply, but all he could smell was that damn chemical stench.

'Mr Forman? Do you need a moment?'

He opened his mouth to reply. His stomach knotted and vomit spewed from his throat. He couldn't stop. He threw up again and again, all over the soft-blue carpet tiles.

'Oh God.' He heard Evelyn's voice. 'We should never have let him come.'

He wanted to tell her he *had* to come. He had to do this. But his head was a grey, fuzzy cloud. His ears buzzed. His knees buckled. He collapsed to the floor.

Distantly, he heard Anne Gleaves say: 'I'll get a nurse. We can do this another day.'

And then Harry's voice. Surprisingly firm. 'No. It's all right. I'll do the identification. It's for the best.'

For the best. For the best. The words thrummed around Gabe's head.

Later, he had asked if he could go back and see them. But by this point, after he had been released from hospital, where they put him on a drip and asked repeatedly if he had 'taken anything', the police had arrived. His world tilted on its axis again. He was no longer a grieving husband and father. He was a murder suspect. He found himself in another bland, featureless blue room. But there were no flowers or comforting leaflets here. Just a tape recorder, DI Maddock and another grim-faced detective, and a young solicitor, hastily found and seemingly more nervous and unprepared than Gabe.

He sat by, looking helpless, as the detectives asked Gabe

about his relationship with his wife, his job, his background . . . and oh, what exactly had he been doing between the time he left home at 8 a.m. and the time he made the phone call from the Leicester Forest East Services at around 6.15 p.m., seeing as he hadn't been at work?

He didn't want to answer. Didn't want to confirm their suspicions about him – that he was the type of man who could hurt or kill somebody. But it was futile. They knew about his record. They had tracked his phone. It had all come out anyway. Most of it, at any rate.

Things between him and Jenny's parents had disintegrated fast after that. Even when he was eventually released without charge, Evelyn refused to take his calls, changed their number. Shut him out completely. He found out the date of the funeral through his solicitor. He had to take a taxi to the crematorium because his car was still impounded for 'evidence' and Evelyn wouldn't allow him to travel in the funeral car.

As it was, he didn't even make it through the service. He couldn't sit there, listening to the minister's meaningless words, staring at the coffins. Jenny's was a gleaming oak that was, no doubt, the most expensive Harry's money could buy. Izzy's was a miniature version, painted pink and decorated with brightly coloured flowers. As if that could make the awfulness, the horror of that tiny coffin, more palatable. Instead, it just made it worse. No coffin should ever be so small. No child should ever lie so cold and still. Children were light and warmth and laughter. Not darkness and silence. It was all wrong, and he couldn't – *wouldn't* – accept it.

He had risen with a strangled cry and run from the chapel, collapsing onto the damp grass outside. He lay there and screamed into the earth, until his throat was raw and his suit and shirt were sodden and stained with grass. No one came to help him. Even as the other mourners filed out, not a single person paused or offered their hand. No one wanted anything to do with a man tainted by murder.

At some point, lying there on the wet, muddy grass, he came to a decision. He could never get up again, he could kill himself, or he could find the car – find an answer, one way or another. Only then would he allow himself to grieve. Only then would he accept that Izzy was gone for ever, carried away in a tiny pink coffin painted with bright, scentless flowers.

As the sun started to falter in the sky, he staggered to his feet and walked away: from the chapel, from the ashes of his family and from his life.

A week later, as he was loading his final few possessions into the boot of his recently purchased second-hand camper van, he had received the text from Harry. He had been surprised. Then angry. He had thought about deleting it. But something stopped him.

Gabe didn't have any parents, no close friends. He had become accustomed to keeping people at a distance, scared that if he let them too close they might see through his façade. Or worse, that one day someone from his past might emerge, strip away his emperor's new clothes and expose him for who and what he really was.

He had work associates, but it's funny how a murder accusation can cause those colleagues to fall away. He was aware that, had he not resigned, it would only have been a matter of time before the agency found a reason to let him go.

He didn't even have a home any more. Despite the clean-up team eliminating any trace of what had happened, he could still see the blood spatter on the walls. He could still hear the screams. Every morning when he walked into the kitchen he saw Jenny standing there, body bloody with bullet holes, eyes cold and accusing.

'Why did you let this happen? Why weren't you here to protect us?'

A week after he was cleared to return home he called an estate agent and put the house on the market. Then, he packed a small suitcase and checked back into the Premier Inn, returning only to collect post and feed the cat. He didn't care about the house.

The only things Gabe had ever truly cared about in this world were Jenny and Izzy. Now they were gone, and that world had ended. The only remaining link to it was Harry.

He had stared at the text and pressed reply.

They had met a few times since then. Not enough to call it regular. Not always at Gabe's behest. But always here, in the Garden of Remembrance.

They sat, sometimes in silence, which, strangely, had never felt awkward. Mostly, they talked. About Jenny and Izzy. About happier times. Embellished on both sides, Gabe felt sure. But there was no denying that the talking, letting their memories breathe, out here in the open air, amidst the greenery and flowers, eased the hollow ache inside him. Just a little. Just for a short while. Sometimes, that had to be enough.

They discussed other things, too. Banal day-to-day things. Occasionally, one of them mentioned the police investigation. Or lack thereof. How no one had been brought to justice for the crime. How hopes of catching the person responsible grew fainter each day.

Harry knew all about his motorway travels. But he never

mentioned it. Just like Gabe never brought up the identification. A mutual consent of silence. A grenade that could blow apart their fragile bridges.

Despite their past differences, Gabe had always believed that Jenny's father was a good man, a principled man, a decent man.

Today, for the first time, he wondered if he was also a fucking liar.

16

Clickety-click. Alice opened her eyes and blinked blearily. Where was she? It took a moment. The hotel room. Across from her, Fran slept. But something had woken her. *Clickety-click*.

She glanced at the bag on her bedside table. The pebbles. She could sense them, shifting softly inside.

They were restless, she thought.

I'm dreaming, she thought.

Clickety-click, the pebbles whispered.

She sat up. The artificial darkness disorientated her. She had no idea what time it was. She realized she needed to wee. Maybe this wasn't a dream. She slipped out of bed, softly and carefully. She didn't want to wake Fran. She must be tired. All that driving. How far? *Are we there yet?* Would they ever be there?

She didn't remember much before they started running. Or perhaps she had tried to forget. Sometimes it came back to her in dreams. Not the dreams she had when she fell. She wasn't even sure they were dreams at all. But the other ones. The ones that seized her the moment she closed her eyes at night. Dreams that were full of blood and screams and a pretty lady with blonde hair. *Mummy?* Something had happened to her. Someone had hurt her. And they had wanted to hurt Alice, too. But Fran had saved her. Fran had kept her safe. Fran would always keep her safe. Fran loved her. And Alice loved Fran.

Except, sometimes, just sometimes, Fran scared her a little, too.

Her bladder demanded her attention again. She padded to the bathroom, flicked on the light switch and pushed the door open.

The bathroom was small and bright. She shut the door again so as not to wake Fran and sat herself on the loo. She weed, wiped and flushed. Instead of facing the mirror over the sink, she ducked and washed her hands under the bath taps.

Clickety-click. The pebbles sounded louder, which was stupid because they were in the other room. *Clickety-click.* And now she was sure she could hear something else, like the soft washing of waves on sand. Like the sound was inside the room. No, inside her *head*.

She tried to shake it out, but it wouldn't go. *Clickety-click. Clickety-click.* It was hard to resist the pull. And it was getting stronger. Slowly, she raised her eyes. The girl in the mirror smiled.

'*Alissss.*'

'I can't.'

'*Pleeeeease.*'

Alice shook her head. But the movement was slow and sluggish. Her eyelids started to droop. The bath tap gushed, water swirling down the plughole.

Alice stepped into the bath and lay down.

17

'I want to ask you something.'

Harry sighed. 'I may not want to answer –'

'Do you think I'm crazy?'

Harry paused. Obviously not quite what he was expecting. He took a while to reply.

'I think, when something terrible happens, we all deal with it in different ways. We find something that helps us cope.' He coughed, cleared his throat. 'Evelyn volunteers now, at a shelter for abused women.'

'Really?'

Gabe couldn't keep the surprise out of his voice. He found it hard to imagine the perfectly coiffed, starchy, conservative – with a small and big 'C' – Evelyn lowering herself to mix with the desperate and disadvantaged. But then, maybe she'd changed.

'Things had got quite bad,' Harry said. 'She . . . she took some pills.'

That *didn't* surprise him. He remembered the pills Evelyn had given him before the identification. Throughout everything, for as long as he'd known her, Evelyn had always been in control. Even at the funeral, she didn't cry. Not really. Oh, she dabbed at her eyes, she sniffed, she popped eye-drops. But proper snot-dribbling-down-your-chin wailing – no. She kept it all in. Kept up her composed façade. But you can only button yourself inside that chemical straitjacket for so long before you realize that your gaoler is you and there is only one way of release.

'Anyway,' Harry continued, 'it seems to have helped her. Knowing she is doing something positive for other women and children.'

'I'm glad she's found a vocation.'

A thin smile. 'It takes her out of the house. I sometimes wonder if that's her real motivation. If being with me, together, reminds her more.'

His voice cracked a little. He coughed again. Harsh, guttural. Gabe wondered again about his sudden agedness, the limp. If he still had the expensive-cigar habit.

'What about you?' Gabe asked. 'What do you do?'

'I keep myself busy. Golf, gardening. I'm learning archery.'

Gabe raised an eyebrow. 'Right.'

'I'm not sure if it's coping or distraction. But we do what's necessary to get by.'

'I suppose.'

'What I'm saying is, I understand that this obsession of yours is your way of coping. I don't think you're crazy. But I do think it's desperately unhealthy.'

'Thanks.'

'Until you accept that they're dead – both of them – you'll never move on with your life.'

'Maybe I don't want to.'

'Your choice. But you're still young. It pains me to say it, but you could meet someone else, have more children. It's too late for Evelyn and me. But you could rebuild your life. A fresh start.'

Fresh start. Like life was a carton of milk. When one went sour you threw it out and opened another.

'I want to help you, Gabe,' Harry said in a softer voice. The one Gabe imagined he used to use with his patients when he told them that their test results were back and the news wasn't good.

'I know. That's why I called you.'

Harry nodded. 'Well, if I can do –'

'I found the car.'

Gabe took his phone out of his pocket. He had taken several photos the other night. They were a bit grainy, the flash whiting out a lot of detail, but they showed most of what he needed. The car, from several different angles, boot closed. The stickers. Harry peered at them and frowned.

'D'you see?' Gabe said, unable to contain the slight desperation in his voice. He needed Harry to believe him, he realized. Needed vindication.

'I see a rusted old car in a lake.'

Gabe zoomed in on the screen.

'See the stickers?'

Harry peered more closely and gave a small shrug. 'Maybe. I couldn't be sure.'

'It's the *same* car, Harry. The one I saw that night.'

Harry sighed. 'Gabe, maybe you did see a car with a little girl in it. Maybe this is the same car. But it wasn't Izzy. You made a mistake. It was dark, at a distance. Little girls that age can look alike. It was another little girl who looked like Izzy. You must see that?'

'No.' Gabe shook his head. He took the folder out of his pocket and shook out the hair bobble, holding it up for Harry to see.

'I found this. It's Izzy's.'

Harry stared at the bobble and his lips thinned.

'Okay.' Gabe took out the notebook, pulling out the map with it and then somehow managing to drop them both on the ground. He bent and snatched them back up, frantically brushing off the dirt.

'What about this?' He opened the notebook. 'Does this mean anything to you? The Other People?'

'Gabe, this has gone far enough –'

'*No!* Everyone is always telling me I must be mistaken. But what about you? What about Evelyn? You said yourself that little girls that age look alike. What if it wasn't Izzy you identified? What if *you* were mistaken?'

'You really believe that I wouldn't recognize my own granddaughter?'

'You believe *I* wouldn't recognize my own daughter.'

They glared at each other. Stalemate. Harry's face was calm, but Gabe could tell that, behind his eyes, there was a lot going on. Harry was not a stupid man. He never spoke or acted without considering all outcomes.

'Just think for a minute about what you're suggesting,' he said. 'For me to have wrongly identified Izzy's body, there would have to have been another body. Another dead little girl. Who is she? Why has no one reported her missing? What you're saying makes no sense, even if I *was* mistaken, which I was not.'

Gabe could feel his conviction wavering. Harry was good at that – being convincing. His calm, measured tones. His logic, his reasoning. *Trust me, I'm a doctor.*

'This hair bobble, Gabe. It could belong to *any* little girl.'

'It's Izzy's.'

'Okay, then maybe it is Izzy's. Maybe you kept it. Maybe you have convinced yourself you found it in the car.'

'*What?*'

'Not consciously.'

'You think I'm making this up?'

'No, I think *you* believe it. And that's the problem. That's why you need help.'

Gabe snorted out a laugh. 'Help. Right.'

'I have a friend who you could talk to.'

'I bet you do. Let me guess – nice, plush office and a ready prescription of happy pills.'

'Gabe –'

'I don't need a psychiatrist. I need you to tell me the truth about that day.'

This time, Harry's face did change. The bushy eyebrows furrowed, the blue eyes darkened.

'You're accusing me of lying about the identification.'

Gabe didn't reply. He had tried to think of other explanations: Harry and Evelyn didn't see their granddaughter that often – another bone of contention between them and Jenny ('*They live two hours away, not on the bloody moon*'). It must have been at least three months since their last visit. They hadn't even seen her on her birthday. Kids grew fast at that age. Izzy had had her hair cut. Lost a tooth.

Was it possible, in Harry's grief, in the messy confusion of that day, that he had got it wrong? Terribly, hideously wrong? And now, he was too scared to admit it? Or was there another reason?

He still couldn't say it. Still could not accuse Harry of something so awful, so unthinkable. Because to do so raised so many other questions, not least: Why? Why? Why?

'If I was a younger man, I'd punch you in the face for that,' Harry muttered.

He'd like to, Gabe thought, but there was the rub. Harry was not the man he used to be. He had aged in a way that had nothing to do with the march of time. Grief did that to you. Added decades in a day. He recognized the ache in his own weary bones. Sometimes, he felt like a ghost already, draped in the skin of a man who had once lived.

'I'm sorry,' he said.

Harry shook his head, the fight that Gabe had seen fleetingly rise in him subsiding again. 'No, I'm sorry. I always hoped you'd eventually snap out of it, see sense. I even hoped that you *would* find the damn car and realize you were wrong. But it seems that's not going to happen.'

He reached into his inside jacket pocket and took out an A4 envelope folded in half.

'Hope is a powerful drug. Believe me, I've seen it work miracles in my patients. But there's a difference between hope and delusion. That's why I'm giving you this. Evelyn wanted you to see it before. I didn't want to hurt you. But it's time, Gabe.'

'What is it?'

'The post-mortem report.'

Gabe felt a hollowness opening in his stomach. 'I read the post-mortem report. There's nothing in it that says the body is definitely Izzy.'

Harry sighed. 'Age, weight, hair colour, even the missing front tooth.'

We'll leave it under the pillow, for the tooth fairy.

'It all matches. But you don't want the truth. You want to cling to a fairy tale.' He placed the envelope down on the bench between them and slowly stood. 'I think it's best if we don't meet again for a while.'

Gabe didn't reply. He was barely aware of Harry leaving.

He stared at the envelope as if it were an unexploded grenade. Of course, he could leave it. Not look. Burn it, throw it in a bin. But he knew he wouldn't.

He picked up the envelope and opened the flap. There were two sheets of paper inside. He slid them out. Lines of black type blurred before his eyes. Impenetrable medical terms, but some words stood out. *Gunshot wounds. Artery. Perforation. Organ damage.* He laid the papers to one side. There was something else inside the envelope. He tipped it up. Two Polaroids fell out.

Jenny and Izzy. Just their faces, green sheets pulled up to their necks.

Morgue photos.

He heard a noise. Like a moan. One of the undead. He realized it was him.

How the hell had Harry got hold of these? But then, Gabe supposed, he *was* a doctor. He had contacts.

Gabe reached for the picture of Jenny. Her face was pale, waxen, unfamiliar in death. And yet he knew it was still the face he had once stroked, kissed, loved, dreamed of. He put the photo to one side and forced himself to pick up the second one.

Izzy's face was perfect, unblemished. She looked like she was sleeping. A cold, forever sleep.

He stared so hard his eyeballs burned. No mistaking. Izzy. His Izzy.

He started to cry. He cried until he thought his eyes must surely be squeezed from their sockets; he cried until his chest hurt and his throat felt like he had been gargling ground glass. He bawled like a child, letting snot flow freely, scrubbing at his face and nose with his sleeve.

Evelyn wanted you to see it . . . it's time.

'Are you all right, love?'

Gabe glanced up. An elderly woman stood in front of him. Dirty white hair, skin crinkled into flaccid folds. Her body was bowed by osteoporosis and she wore a stained beige raincoat. Gabe caught a whiff of musty, stale urine.

She pushed an old Silver Cross pram. More rust than silver now. Instead of a baby, a cat was curled up inside it. A large tabby with surly green eyes. It reminded Gabe of their grumpy old cat, Schrödinger. Not that he was ever called that. Izzy couldn't pronounce it, so his name became Soda.

After Gabe moved out permanently, their neighbours had taken him in. Gabe was glad. He had never really liked the mean old tom. One minute he would be purring, the next his claws would rake down the nearest bit of exposed flesh.

'Here you go, love.'

The old woman held out a crumpled pack of Kleenex. Her nails were embedded with black dirt. His first instinct was to tell her to go away, but then his resolve withered in the face of her small act of kindness.

'Thank you,' he croaked, taking one and handing the packet back.

'You keep it.' She shuffled away.

He rubbed at his eyes and blew his nose. Then he picked up the photographs and slipped them carefully into his wallet.

He had been so sure. And they had found the car. But what did it really prove? And the body? Maybe best not to think about that. Could he even trust the Samaritan?

Perhaps Harry was right. He needed help. If not, maybe he was destined to end up like Kleenex Lady, shuffling around a cemetery, smelling of stale piss and wheeling his very own cat in a pram.

And then something poked him in the back of his mind. Hard.

The cat.

Not the cat in the pram.

Their cat. Schrödinger.

'Daddy, Soda scratched me.'

Izzy's tear-stained face. An ugly red line on her chin.

Gabe had applied Savlon. *'There you go. All better.'* But the scratch had still looked sore when he dropped her off at school.

That morning. Before the phone call. Before his life fell off the edge of a cliff.

Gabe fumbled the photographs back out of his wallet. He peered at the one of Izzy more closely. He squinted, held it up this way and that. He could see her eyelashes, the faint freckles on her nose. Every detail laid bare in the unforgiving light.

There was no scratch on her chin.

Of course, when you're young, scratches heal quickly. But not in a few hours. Gabe was no doctor, but he knew that. And he knew something else.

They didn't heal when you were dead.

18

Rain pattered on umbrellas. A bobbing sea of black. Mourners massed outside the Chapel of Rest. Black clothes, grey sky. A picture in monochrome.

Fran watched her family, staggering slowly along the uneven gravel path, her sister supporting their mother, not just through her grief but through her drunken stupor. Fran stood apart, watching from a distance. Why wasn't she there?

Because this is a dream. Of course.

But then, in reality, she always had been on the periphery. She loved her family, but she had never felt close to her mum or her sisters. Maybe that was the way with the eldest. You grew up and away first. It was only her dad she had been really close to. And now he was gone.

The funeral party filed in and sat down. 'Funeral party'. It always seemed an odd name for a mass of mourners. 'A sadness' or 'a weep'. That seemed more appropriate.

The coffin was perched upon a plinth at the end of the chapel. Flowers had been arranged around it. They looked too bright against the dark oak. Out of place. Dad had loved his garden, but he hated cut flowers. Preferred to see them alive and blooming. *'Cut flowers are already dead flowers,'* he always used to say. He didn't want bouquets at his funeral. They'd ordered potted flowers from the florist that could be replanted. And Dad had not been cremated. He was buried.

This was wrong, she thought suddenly. All wrong. This wasn't his funeral. It couldn't be her family.

She walked slowly down the centre of the chapel, between the row of mourners, who had now put their umbrellas back up. Rain poured down and when she looked up the roof of the chapel had disappeared, and tumultuous charcoal clouds rolled by overhead.

She walked up to the open casket and stared at the pale, still body of the little girl inside. Blonde hair fanned out around her small, heart-shaped face. She was dressed in a pretty pink dress that Fran didn't remember buying. But then, she didn't buy the dress, did she? Not for her funeral.

Tears started to roll down her cheeks. The rain darkened the little girl's hair and soaked the pretty pink dress. Fran raised her head and screamed . . . and her mouth filled with water, pouring down her throat, choking her . . .

Water. Running water. Fran blinked her eyes open. Shit. Where was she? The hotel room. So why could she still hear water? She sat up, glanced across automatically at Alice's bed. Empty. *Water. Running water.* She looked back at the closed bathroom door, a dark stain just starting to spread below the chipped edge.

'No.'

She leapt out of her bed and ran over, yanking the door open. The bath was overflowing, a small sea of water flooding the linoleum and seeping out on to the carpet.

Alice lay in the bath, head just starting to slip below the surface of the water. Asleep.

'*Fuck!*'

Fran grabbed her beneath the arms. *Jesus Christ, the water was freezing.*

'Alice. Alice. Wake up!'

Her skin was almost blue, her lips a cracked line of purple.

No, no, no. How had she let this happen?

She grabbed towels, wrapped them around Alice and carried her, dripping, out of the bathroom. She laid her on the bed, rubbing her gently dry, whispering into her wet hair.

'Alice, Alice, wake up.'

'M— . . . Mummy.'

For once she didn't correct her. 'I'm here, sweetheart. I'm here.'

Alice's limp arms encircled her. She felt her body start to shiver. A good thing, Fran thought.

'We need to get you warm.'

She wrapped the duvet tightly around her. She needed more towels. She walked back to the bathroom. The water was still running. Crap. She squelched over to the bath and turned off the tap. She reached for the plug and then paused. *What the?* The plug was still wrapped around the tap. So why wasn't the water draining away?

She stuck her hand into the freezing water and felt around. Something was blocking the plughole, wedged tight. She fumbled around and managed to dislodge it. The water began to gurgle down the drain. Fran pulled her arm back out, peppered with goosebumps, and stared at the object in her hand.

A small, pinky-white conch shell.

She sleeps. A pale girl in a white room.

The nurses look after her well every day. But this morning there is more activity than usual. Today is a special day. Today is visiting day.

Miriam helps the juniors as they hoist the girl and change her bedding. She supervises the cleaners and ensures that every speck of dust has been removed from every room; from the machines, the piano keys and the shell.

She arranges fresh flowers in vases, washes and dries the girl's hair and then brushes it until it shines. Later, she will make tea and cakes and sit with the girl to wait.

This is Miriam's domain. Yes, there are nurses, and a doctor visits occasionally, but she is the one who spends the most time here and has done for over thirty years, since before that awful day. Since before the girl's mother became a virtual recluse and the girl ended up like this.

Perhaps if it had never happened, Miriam wouldn't have stayed. She would have moved on, made a life of her own. But they both depended on her so much. Mother and daughter. She couldn't desert them. She always feared what might happen if she did. So, she had stayed and, in many ways, this was her family now, her life. She doesn't begrudge it. In fact, often Miriam feels that she is here for a reason.

She reaches into her pocket and takes out a piece of paper. Soft and much folded. A child's face stares out. HAVE YOU SEEN ME? *Miriam sighs and looks back at the girl. Then she leans forward and gently pats her still hand.*

'Soon,' *she whispers.* 'Soon.'

19

Gabe drove. It was all he could do. Maybe if he was a detective or a private investigator, someone with 'a team' and experts to summon, he would be doing something more productive.

But Gabe was neither of those. He didn't know *what* he was any more. No job, no home, no longer a father or a husband. A driver with no destination and empty passenger seats.

But now he had something. The photo. The scratch. As he drove, he went over and over it in his mind. Prodding and pulling at his memory, trying to pick holes in his recollection. Was it really *that* morning he had applied the plaster? Could he be getting confused with another morning? *No.* You did not forget something like that. You did not forget the last time you saw your wife and daughter alive.

And that Monday morning had *not* been like any other morning. It wasn't normal for him to take Izzy to school. In fact, he remembered arguing with Jenny about it.

'It's a bit short notice. Can't you change your meeting?'

'No. It's a big client.'

'But I'll be late.'

'So? It's just one morning. Maybe you could actually leave on time, too – push the boat out.'

'Jesus, Jenny.'

'I am serious, Gabe. You missed Izzy's birthday party at the weekend.'

'One party. I had to catch up on work.'

'You almost missed her bloody birth.'

'Oh, here we go.'

'Here we go. Always work, isn't it? Yet whenever I call you, you're never there. You're always at a client's, on the road, or your mobile is turned off. Where were you last Monday, Gabe? Work didn't know.'

'Christ. I thought we'd been through this. All the accusations.'

'I'm not accusing you of anything.'

'Then what are you saying?'

A long pause. A look on her face that almost tore the truth from him. Almost.

'I'm saying – I want you home on time tonight. Just once a week. That's all I ask. One night when we eat together, you read your daughter a bedtime story and we pretend we're a normal, happy family.'

Leaving that barb buried deep, she had shrugged her coat on, flung her bag over her shoulder and gone to say goodbye to Izzy.

Gabe had started after her then almost fell over Schrödinger, who was winding around his feet and mewling for breakfast. Gabe had cursed, shoved the cat roughly aside with his foot and picked up his phone.

That was when Izzy had emerged into the kitchen, sleep-tousled and red-cheeked.

'Hi, Daddy!'

She'd yawned and bent down to pick up the cat . . .

'*Owww!*'

It had *definitely* happened that morning. He remembered the bright red blood welling in the shallow wound. Soothing her a little impatiently. Fumbling for the small Disney plaster to stick on the scratch. He remembered it all.

So where was the scratch on the photo?

He turned the question over and over, wrestled and wrangled with it, but he still kept coming to the same conclusion: if there was no scratch, the photo must have been taken later. *After* the scratch had healed. *After* the day that Izzy had supposedly been killed.

Which meant . . . the picture wasn't real. It couldn't be.

So, what was he saying – someone had set it up? Faked the photograph – to convince him Izzy was dead?

But why? And if Izzy's picture was fake, what about Jenny's?

His throat tightened. He felt an ache somewhere in the region of his heart, or where it used to be. Gabe had thought about this before. Many times. In his long treks up and down the motorway he had had very little else to occupy his mind. So he would run through all the possible scenarios in which Izzy could still be alive. The ways in which a mistake could have been made.

It always came back to one answer. One painful, brutal truth.

The only way Izzy could be alive was if Jenny was dead.

There had to be no doubt, not one iota, that the female body in the house was Jenny. Only then would the police have assumed that the little girl was Izzy. Of course, she would have to be the same age, build, colouring. But it wasn't actually that difficult to confuse one child with another, if you didn't know them.

He remembered Izzy's first school nativity (or, should he say, Jenny never let him forget) when Izzy had told him she was playing Mary. He had arrived late, so had to sit at the back, several rows behind Jenny. But he had spent the performance dutifully snapping away with his iPhone and applauding every mumbled line. Afterwards, he told Izzy what a brilliant Mary she had been.

She had burst into tears.

'What?' he had asked.

I wasn't Mary. I was a shepherd!

Jenny had hugged Izzy and hissed at him. *'She was Mary last night. I told you. They take it in turns.'*

The memory still burned. But the point was, if he could mix up his own daughter with another child, then so could strangers. So could the police. They would have no reason to believe that the little girl in the house wasn't Izzy.

It's about your wife . . . and your daughter.

And, of course, the real rub: Izzy had been positively identified by her grandfather. Harry. A respected retired surgeon. But also, the more Gabe thought about it, a man who was hiding something; something that was eating away at him.

He gripped the steering wheel tighter. Harry. Fucking Harry. All this time. Lying. Pretending to everyone that Izzy was dead.

But why?

Gabe was under no illusion that his relationship with Jenny's parents had never been anything but 'strained'. Or, to put it bluntly, Evelyn had regarded Gabe as something she might scrape off her expensive Louboutins, and Harry had tolerated him, like a vaguely unpleasant smell. He could just about accept that Harry had used him, deceived him. Evelyn would probably have got a perverse kick out of it.

But to lie to the police, to risk his precious reputation, perhaps even prosecution? To go through the charade of a funeral, to lay flowers every month on another girl's buried ashes?

Jesus Christ. There had to be a damn good reason.

And who was the other little girl? It was the point he kept stumbling at. For Izzy to be alive, then there *had* to have been another little girl in the house. Another body to identify. To cremate. But if another child had been killed, why the hell had no one reported her missing?

The police had spoken to the parents from Izzy's school. They had to, because of Izzy's birthday party at the weekend. With so many people coming in and out of the house, it had pretty much blighted any chance of the police recovering anything useful from DNA traces. But no one had said: 'Oh, by the way, Officer, I seem to be missing my daughter.'

His head throbbed. He rubbed at his eyes. A horn blasted, loud enough to jolt him out of his stupor. He had let the van drift. He yanked it back, out of the path of a truck thundering down the inside lane. *Shit. Breathe, Gabe, concentrate. Think.*

Two little girls. Alike enough to be confused. Almost interchangeable.

'I wasn't Mary. I was a shepherd.'

Why had no one reported the other girl missing?

And suddenly he had it. He felt the neurons fire in his brain, making the connection. He had been looking at it all wrong. Arriving late to the scene, sat at the back, snapping away blindly but not really paying attention.

If another girl could be mistaken for Izzy, then Izzy could be mistaken for her.

'*She was Mary last night. They take it in turns.*'

What if the other girl wasn't missing?

What if Izzy was playing her part?

20

'That good?'

Alice nodded, stuffing an Egg McMuffin into her mouth. She was ravenous this morning, Fran thought, guiltily. *Bad mother*, her internal voice – which sounded a lot like her own mother's – scolded. *You're neglecting the basics: food, fluid, rest – oh, and not letting her drown in the bath.*

So far she had trodden carefully around the incident in the hotel room. Her first priority had been making sure that Alice was back up to body temperature, that her breathing and heart rate were normal. She couldn't have been in the icy water for long (and, thank God, she had run the cold, not the hot tap), but this was a new and worrying development.

She took a sip of coffee. 'Alice, can we talk about what happened in the bathroom?'

Alice glanced up at her from beneath her drapes of dark hair. Fran frowned as she stared at the roots. They needed retouching. Small things they couldn't let slip.

'I don't remember,' she said.

'Not anything?' Fran waited.

Alice sighed, looked down at her half-eaten McMuffin. 'I saw the girl again.'

The girl. Fran felt her agitation increase. Who was she? Some kind of imaginary friend? A product of Alice's mind, of the trauma? Or something else?

'Did the girl make you run the bath, get in the water?' Fran asked.

'No. She just wanted to show me something.'

Fran gritted her teeth, pushed her hair behind her ears. *Try to stay calm.*

'What did she want to show you?'

Alice fiddled with the rucksack on her lap. *Clickety-click. Clickety-click.* The sound made Fran's fillings hum. She fought the urge to yell at her to *Stop fucking doing that.*

'Alice, you could have drowned, died of hypothermia. Do you think the girl wants to hurt you?'

Alice looked at her with wide eyes. 'No. You don't understand. It's not like that.'

Fran put her cup down and grabbed Alice's arm. The rucksack fell to the floor with a thud.

'Then tell me. Who is the girl? What's her name?'

Alice wriggled. Fran held on tighter. *Too tight*, the internal voice tutted.

'I don't know.'

'Try – think.'

Something vibrated on the table near her elbow. Alice yanked her arm away and rubbed at the red fingermarks.

'Your phone.'

Fran stared at it. Only one person had this number. And he knew never to use it unless it was important – an emergency. She snatched the phone up, stared at the text.

'He knows.'

21

Sleeping in the day was difficult, no matter how many years you'd been working nights. Katie had blackout blinds and ear plugs, comfy pyjamas and memory-foam pillows, but it didn't matter. You couldn't fool your body clock. Your brain knew that it was daytime and it resisted sleep like an argumentative toddler.

Normally, a good book, some hot milk and cereal – and occasionally a couple of Nytol – helped to ease her off. Today, not even that was working. Her mind was too busy, too distracted.

Despite what she had told herself, she couldn't stop thinking about the thin man. *The Other People*.

Why were those words written in the notebook?

She tossed and turned, thumped her pillow, kicked off the duvet, pulled it back on again and then, eventually, admitted defeat. She heaved herself out of bed and padded downstairs to her tiny kitchen.

She set the kettle to boil, plucked a couple of digestives out of the biscuit tin and pulled open a kitchen drawer. She fumbled among the detritus of takeaway menus, spare keys, paperclips and Sellotape and took out a postcard.

A view from a cliff overlooking a beach. The sun was

shining, the sky was a deep azure, the waves tipped with white. Beneath the picture, swirly writing read: *Greetings from Galmouth Bay.*

They had gone there for a family holiday, their last one all together, staying in a whitewashed B&B run by an eccentric lady in her sixties with an alarming red wig and a snappy white terrier. They had eaten ploughmans at country pubs, built lopsided sandcastles on the beach and even had a photo taken on this very same cliff.

No such thing as a happy family, she reminded herself. She remembered standing there, clutching Lou's pudgy hand as Mum wobbled on her heels, smile already blurred around the edges from one too many G&Ts at lunch, and how her elder sister had sulked and moaned about how she hated her picture being taken.

Only Dad had been genuinely happy and relaxed, wisps of his thinning hair caught by the breeze as he focused his old Kodak camera and tried to goad them all into saying, 'Smelly cheesy feet'. The only solid, stable thing in their lives. The glue that kept them all together.

At least he was. And then, one day, he was taken away. Suddenly, brutally, violently.

And Katie was the one who found him.

Nine years ago. One of those bright spring mornings that fools you into thinking you don't need a jacket and then whips up goosebumps on your arms with a bitter breeze.

Katie had arrived at her parents' for Sunday lunch. It wasn't something they did regularly – Mum was hardly the best cook, even when she was sober – but Katie appreciated that at least her parents *tried* to get them all together as a family every few months.

Out of her sisters, Katie was the one who had remained closest, the one who called when she said she would and visited regularly. She supposed they had all fallen into stereo-typical sibling roles. Youngest – a little spoilt, always caught up in some drama or other. Oldest – the rebel, the one who endured the most difficult relationship with their mother and moved away as soon as she could. And middle. The dependable, dull one. Only Katie could be relied upon to turn up early to help with the cooking, clutching a bottle of wine and a plant for Dad's garden.

This morning Katie had forgotten both, and even the smile was hard work. Sam had chicken pox and he'd kept her up most of the night, applying calamine and kisses. Craig, who never nursed Sam when he was ill, had opted to stay at home with him today rather than endure dinner with her family. She was actually relieved. Things weren't great between them and she didn't need the extra stress of his sniping.

She had felt on edge as she climbed out of her car and walked up to the front door. Her parents lived in a modern, detached house on an estate that had been bright and new when it was built thirty years ago. The houses were square and bland with identikit beige brick, UPVC windows and built-in garages. The suburban dream, or nightmare, depending on your point of view. It suited her parents, though. And every Sunday morning – as per the hidden clause in suburbia – Dad could be found out on the drive-way, washing and polishing his car till it gleamed.

But not this Sunday. The garage door was half open. She could see the bonnet of his car just inside but no Dad waving his chamois. She glanced at her watch. Ten forty-five. She supposed Dad might have cleaned it already, but the driveway was dry. No remnants of foamy suds seeping down to the kerb.

Something felt wrong. She walked up to the front door and rang the bell. She heard it chime faintly inside. She waited. Normally, her mum would be at the door straight away. She rang the bell again. Still no sign of movement, no shadow emerging behind the frosted glass. Concern started to nibble gently at the edges of her stomach.

She fumbled in her bag for her keys, unlocked the door and pushed it open.

'Mu—um. Da—ad? It's Katie!'

The house felt heavy with silence. And there was something else. She sniffed. There was a smell. Not the usual scent of cloying air freshener her mum sprayed everywhere before visitors arrived. It smelt of sweat, she thought, and smoke, stale cigarette smoke. Her parents had never smoked.

She walked quickly into the living room. Her heart constricted. It was wrecked. Drawers had been pulled out of the sideboard. Books tossed from the shelves. Ornaments smashed. The patio doors gaped open.

Her mother lay beside the sofa, still in her dressing gown. Her always perfectly styled blonde hair was matted with dark blood. More blood caked her face, which was bruised and swollen.

'Mum.'

Katie ran forward and fell to her knees. She could hear her mother breathing, but it was faint and raspy.

And what about Dad?

'It's okay. I'm going to call an ambulance, okay?'

She pulled out her mobile and ran back out into the hall. A cool draught brushed her bare arms. She turned. The door between the kitchen and the garage was ajar. Dad? She walked towards it, mobile clutched in her hand, heart thudding, and stepped into the cool, dark space.

The car was backed in as normal, but the driver's door hung open, the keys still in the ignition.

The thief, or thieves, had been trying to steal the car. But something had stopped them. Something had made them panic and run instead . . .

'Dad!'

He was slumped over the boot, almost like he was caressing it. Blood ran down the sides of the car, leaving streaks on the silver paintwork. *He'd be so cross about that*, a small voice inside her chided. *Making his car all dirty.*

She couldn't see the rest of his body. Because it was crushed between the car and the garage wall. With such force the boot had buckled and the rear windscreen splintered.

His face was turned towards her, bright blue eyes, crinkled around the edges with lines drawn by the sun, now as empty as marbles. A look of surprise caught there. That it could have come to this. That his life would end here, in this cold, dark garage, in his pyjamas, as he attempted to stop some low-life driving away with his car. That he would not rise to greet another Sunday morning. That all Sundays, chamois and waxes were over, for ever. She stared back into her dad's empty eyes and she started to scream . . .

Her phone vibrated by her elbow, making her jump and splash hot tea all over the worktop. *Shit.* She picked it up. Marco, her manager at the coffee shop.

'Fancy an extra shift this afternoon?'

One of the Ethans or Nathans obviously hadn't turned up again. She didn't really fancy an extra afternoon's work on top of a night shift. She was supposed to have a couple of days off. And she would have to ask Lou to pick up the children from school. On the other hand, Sam's uniform was getting a little tight and she was never going to get back to sleep now anyway. In fact, it was probably better if she had something else to occupy her mind.

She typed back: 'Okay.'

'Fine. See you later.'

Katie sighed. She looked back at the postcard. It had arrived on the anniversary of his death. She flipped it over. On the back, written in her elder sister's familiar spidery writing:

Remember. I did it for Dad.

xx

But did you really? Katie thought. Or did you do it for you, Fran?

22

Gabe first met the Samaritan on a motorway bridge at two in the morning. He remembered the time because he had just checked his watch. He wasn't sure why. He was about to kill himself and you could hardly be late for your own suicide.

He had thought about killing himself before. Quite regularly over the last six months. Usually at around this time in the morning. That was when the bad thoughts came. The dark hinterland between midnight and dawn. The time when the demons would emerge, slithering and sliding out of the shadows, trailing mucous membranes of bitter bile and stinging misery and regret.

The thought of Izzy had always stopped him. The thought of finding the car. Hope, or perhaps persistent, dogged denial, had managed to ward the demons off. But they were persistent. They didn't tire. They didn't let go. Their claws just dug in deeper and deeper.

At some point along the drive tonight, the despair had overwhelmed him. He hadn't slept in almost forty-eight hours. The nightmares wouldn't let him. He couldn't face sleep. He couldn't face being awake either. He had pulled off the motorway, circled the roundabout off the slip and on to the bridge that crossed to the south side.

Halfway across, he stopped and pulled the car up on to the kerb. He climbed out and walked to the railing. He stood there in the bitter cold, staring down at the speeding traffic below through eyes blurred with tears. White lights, red lights, white lights, red lights. After a while, it became hypnotic.

He swung one leg over the railing.

Somewhere, deep inside, he knew that this was a shit thing to do. That it might not just be himself he killed. But truthfully, that voice was a long way down. All he was really thinking was that he just wanted it over. The pain, the sheer exhaustion of trying to stay alive. It was too hard. Life itself had become an instrument of torture, every minute of every day bearing down on him like the spikes of an iron maiden.

He slung his other leg over the railing. Now he was perched on the narrow metal, gripping tightly with his hands. All he had to do was let go. Let gravity do its job. He took a deep breath, closed his eyes.

'Waiting for something?'

He jumped. Or rather, he didn't. He started, wobbled and grabbed at the railing to steady himself.

'Fuck!'

'Didn't mean to make you jump.' The man chuckled. 'Unless that's what you want.'

Gabe turned his head. The wind grabbed and snagged at his hair with icy fingers. He felt his eyes water and blur. Slowly, his vision drew into focus.

A tall, thin figure stood behind him. All black. Jacket, jeans, hat. Skin. Just the thinnest rim of white around his eyes. Gabe had no idea where he had come from. He hadn't heard another car approach. Insanely, Gabe wondered if the man was an angel, come to visit him at the moment of his death, or maybe it was the other way round and he was a demon, come to drag him down to hell.

He giggled, a mad, shivering thing that dribbled from the corner of his mouth.

The man continued to stand and look at him, placidly, hands stuck in his pockets. He looked like he might just stand there all night.

'Something funny, man?'

'No,' Gabe shook his head. 'No. This is pretty fucking serious.'

'Killing yourself is a pretty fucking serious business.'

'Tell me about it.'

'Why don't you tell me?'

'I don't think so.'

'I'm a good listener.'

'I'm a man of few words.'

A chuckle. Deep, throaty. 'Got a way with them, though.'

'I used to be a writer.'

'Yeah? What did you write?'

'Lies, mostly.'

'Honesty is overrated.'

'Especially in advertising.'

'You worked in advertising? Sounds interesting.'

Gabe smiled. 'This won't work.'

'What?'

'Trying to get me to talk about myself. Distract me. Stop me from jumping.'

'Can't blame a brother for trying.'

'No. No, I can't.'

'So you gonna do it?'

'Yeah.'

'Nothing I can say to stop you?'

'No.'

'Any final words?'

'Always look on the bright side of life?'

'Life's a piece of shit, right?'

'Wouldn't have had you down as a Python fan.'

'Oh, I'm full of surprises.'

The man pulled his hands out of his pockets. One held a gun. He pointed it at Gabe.

'Do it.'

'What the fuck?!'

'You want to die, go on. Jump.'

He moved closer. Gabe gripped the railing tighter.

'Wait –'

'For what?'

'I –'

So close now Gabe could smell him. Expensive aftershave, mints and metal. Gun metal, he thought wildly. The man pressed the gun into his side.

'Jump. Or I will kill you.'

'*No!*'

'No?'

'Don't kill me.'

The man stared at him. No light in those eyes. Gabe's heart pounded. Sweat was gathering on his palms. The wind was buffeting him back and forth. He wouldn't be able to hold on much longer.

The man held out his other hand. 'Get down.'

Gabe hesitated for a moment. Then he grabbed the proffered hand and swung himself back over the railing. His legs gave almost immediately, all strength evaporating. He slid down, until he was sitting on the ground with his back against the railing. He couldn't stop shivering. He wrapped his arms around his body and started to cry.

The man sat down beside him. He waited until the tears had dried. Then he said: 'Talk.'

Gabe talked – about Izzy, the night he saw her taken. About his grief, his torment, losing Jenny. About spending his days and nights driving up and down the motorway, searching. About his desperation. About how he couldn't see any end to the torment. And then he told him more. Stuff he had never told anyone else before, not even Jenny. He told the stranger with the gun everything.

When he had finished, the man said: 'Give me your phone.'

Gabe pulled out his phone and handed it over. The man tapped in a number.

'Any time you need help, you call me. I will look out for you. I'll look out for your little girl, too.'

'You believe me?'

'I've seen a lot of strange things. The strangest things are often true.'

He stood and held out his hand again. Gabe took it and allowed himself to be hauled to his feet.

'You're not done yet,' the man told him. 'When you are, you'll know.'

He turned and walked away, to a car parked further down the bridge. An angel, Gabe thought. Yeah, right. And then something occurred to him.

'Wait!'

The man paused, looked back.

'You never told me your name?'

The man smiled, flashing very white teeth, one inlaid with a small stone. 'I got a lot of names – but some people call me the Samaritan.'

'Right. Cool.'

'Yeah. It is.'

'So that's what you do? Hang around motorway bridges saving people's lives?'

The smile snapped off. Gabe felt a sudden chill enter his bones.

'I don't save them all.'

The café was a small, shed-like building set back from the road on what looked like an abandoned building site. Gabe had passed it a few times. The road led to an out-of-town trading estate he occasionally visited for supplies.

He had always thought the place was closed, perhaps about to be demolished. It didn't even have a name, simply the word 'Café' daubed clumsily on the wood in red paint, which had run a bit, like blood. Two cars sat outside, one of which was missing its wheels.

Even the sign hanging inside the door read 'Closed'. However, when Gabe pushed it, skirting the debris and broken bricks which formed a pathway, it gave with a painful groan.

Inside, the light was so dim it took his eyes a moment to adjust. Tables were arranged in rows either side of a small, square room. A serving hatch and kitchen lurked at the back. Lights glowed dimly. Only one other patron sat at a far table in the corner, almost blending in with the shadows.

Gabe had spent a while driving before he made the call, turning thoughts over and over in his head, kneading them like dough. Could he go to the police with the photo, or would they simply dismiss him, make the right noises then file his statement in the shredder? He could already hear their calm, patronizing tones.

You're suggesting that your father-in-law faked a morgue photograph?

Isn't it more likely you're mistaken? The cat must have scratched your daughter another morning.

And then the Samaritan's voice: *It ain't proof.*

No, he thought. Proof lay with the decomposing sludge of the man in the car. He held all the answers, but the only thing he was giving away was noxious gas. That just left the Bible and the notebook. *The Other People.* What the hell did it mean, if anything? Were the underlined passages and the words he found in the notebook connected or was he trying to link needles in a self-made haystack?

Who could he ask? Not the police. And then a thought prodded him in the gut.

There was one person who probably knew *more* than the police about criminal activity, the darker side of life. If anyone knew what those three words meant, he would.

Gabe walked over to him. 'You invite me to all the best places.'

The Samaritan glanced up. In the dim lighting, his eyes looked like empty holes. 'Don't knock it. This is my place.'

'You own it?'

'Call it my retirement fund.'

The Samaritan must have caught Gabe's dubious look. 'It's a work in progress.'

Gabe couldn't help wondering if it was more about a work in money-laundering, but he knew better than to say anything. He never asked questions about the Samaritan's business or his life. He had a feeling he wouldn't like the answers. And it didn't take much of a leap to assume that a man who worked at night, carried a gun, lurked around deserted woods and refused to divulge his real name wasn't exactly Santa Claus.

Besides, the Samaritan was a friend, of sorts. Perhaps the only friend Gabe had. And who was he to judge? We're all capable of good and bad. Very few of us show our real faces to the world. For fear that the world might stare back and scream.

'So, can I get a coffee?'

'If you make it. Kettle on the side. Instant in the cupboard to your left. There ain't any milk.'

Gabe walked behind the counter, flicked on the kettle, located two grimy mugs in the sink and added the coffee and hot water. He stirred with a stained spoon from the drainer and brought the coffees back to the table.

'I can see you're going high end.'

The Samaritan didn't break a smile.

'You wanted to talk about the Other People.'

So it was straight down to business. Sometimes, Gabe wondered if his perception of their friendship was more one-sided than he cared to admit.

'You've heard the name?'

'How did *you* hear it?'

Gabe fumbled in his bag and took out the notebook. He showed the Samaritan the page with the traced words.

'I found it written here. I wasn't sure if it meant anything, but . . .'

'Burn it.'

'What?'

'Take the notebook, burn it and forget you ever saw those words.'

Gabe stared at the Samaritan. It was the first time he had ever seen him anything less than composed. He was almost – and the idea seemed scarcely believable – rattled. The thought disturbed him.

'Why would I do that?'

'Because you do not want to go anywhere near that shit, trust me.'

'I do if it will help me find Izzy.'

'Are you sure?'

'I'm sure.'

'You were sure you wanted to jump, too.'

'This is different.'

'It really ain't.'

'I told you, I always thought Harry must have been mistaken about the identification. Now I'm sure he deliberately lied. He's still lying. He may even know who took Izzy. But I don't have any proof. If this is somehow connected, if it can help me make sense of anything, I need to know.'

Another long pause. The Samaritan picked up his coffee and took a sip. He sighed.

'You heard of the Dark Web?'

Gabe felt his skin bristle. Of course he had. Every parent or relative who has lost someone would, at some point, hear about the Dark Web. The vast sub-surface of the internet, encompassing everything that's not crawled by conventional search engines. The hidden place beneath the sheen of the official Web.

It was often used by people who simply didn't trust the normal Web. But it was also used by those who wished to operate outside of the law. Like any deep, dark place, it was where the filth and sediment settled. Child porn. Paedophilia websites. Even snuff movies.

It was the place that every parent who has lost a child feared they might end up. Contrary to popular belief, it wasn't that difficult to access. You just needed something called a Tor bundle (a way of hiding your ISP). But once in, you needed to know what you were looking for. Specific links that might just be a cluster of random letters and numbers. It was a bit like searching for a house without a number, street name or key in a neighbourhood full of dead-end streets and locked, steel-reinforced doors behind which who knew what horrors lurked.

'Yes,' he said eventually. 'I've heard of it.'

'It's where you'll find the Other People.'

'It's a website?'

'More a community where you can connect with like-minded people.'

'What sort of like-minded people?'

'People who have lost loved ones.'

Gabe frowned. That wasn't what he had expected.

'So why is it on the Dark Web?'

'Imagine the police found the person who killed your wife, kidnapped your daughter. Imagine that he gets off, on a technicality. He's walking around out there, guilty as hell. What are you going to do?'

'I'd probably want to kill him.'

The Samaritan nodded. 'But you wouldn't. Because you're not a killer. So, you feel angry, powerless, helpless. Lots of people feel like that. Maybe a guy raped your daughter but the police say it was consensual. Maybe a driver mowed down your mum but all that happens is he loses his licence. Maybe a doctor is negligent and your child dies but he just gets a slap on the wrist. Life ain't fair. Ordinary people don't always get justice.

'Now imagine someone offers you a chance to put that right. A way to make those people pay, make them hurt like you do. You never get your hands dirty. You'll never be connected.'

Gabe's throat felt dry. He took a sip of coffee. 'So it's a place where you can hire vigilantes, hitmen?'

'In a way. Some of the people involved are professionals. But money rarely changes hands. It's more like payment in kind. Quid pro quo. You ask for a favour, you owe a favour in return.'

Gabe thought about this, let the concept settle.

'Like *Strangers on a Train*?'

'What?'

'It's a film where two strangers meet by chance and agree to commit a murder for each other. They'll both have an alibi. No one will connect a random stranger to the crime.'

'Kind of the deal. Except we're talking about *hundreds* of random strangers. Everyone has a use, and everyone has a price. That's how the Other People work. You ask for their help, you'll be asked to do something in return. It might be something small. They might not even call in the favour right away. But they will. They always do. And you'd better be damn sure you're up to returning it.'

Gabe thought about the underlined Bible passages again:

'You shall appoint as a penalty life for life, eye for eye, tooth for tooth.'

'What happens if you don't?'

The Samaritan's gaze punctured him like a bullet. 'You run. As far and as fast as you can.'

23

Fran didn't believe in going back. But she had no choice. She had tried so hard. So very, very hard to keep it all together. For both of them. But she could feel her edges fraying, the seams starting to give.

She had had the dream again, the one she thought she had managed to submerge, deep in the murky depths of her psyche, weighted down with heavy chains of denial. But the chains were never strong or heavy enough. Those black, bloated thoughts – guilt, recrimination, regret – kept on floating back up to the surface.

The funeral, the girl in the coffin. Wearing the wrong dress. In some versions of the dream, when Fran drew closer, the little girl sat up and opened her eyes.

'Why did you leave me, Mummy? Why didn't you come back? It's dark and I'm scared. Mummmy!'

Then the little girl reached out her hands and Fran turned and ran, through the congregation, who were no longer mourners dressed in black but huge black crows who flapped and cawed at her as she passed through.

'Cruel, cruel. Cruel, cruel.'

But I'm not, she wanted to cry. She had saved her. If she hadn't run, they would both be dead. She had sacrificed everything to save her. And she would never let her be taken away.

That was why, despite every single nerve ending screaming that this was a bad decision, that she was heading the wrong way, she had to do this. She didn't have a choice.

'I thought we were going to Scotland?' Alice asked when they had bundled back into the car and headed south, on the M1.

'We were. But this is important, Alice. It's something I need to do – to keep us safe, okay?'

Alice had nodded. 'Okay.'

What Fran hadn't added was that this was something she had to do alone. But again, she had no choice. And maybe, just maybe, this was a good diversion. The last thing they would expect from her. The last person they would expect her to visit and certainly the last person she *wanted* to visit.

They were now over an hour from the services. Almost back to where they had started. Their destination was just half an hour away. But it felt like she was driving back in time. Nine years since she had left. Since one terrible night had smashed their family into smithereens. Perhaps it had always been fragile. Most families are. Blood may be thicker than water but it's a pretty useless substance for sticking anything together.

Her dad had been the only constant and, once he was gone, the rest of them had been cast adrift. No anchor, nothing to stop them floating further and further away from each other. Or, in their mother's case, further down into the bottom of a bottle.

Fran's grief had festered and grown. A constant darkness at the edge of her vision. Sometimes the feeling was so intense she imagined she could reach out and touch the dark cloud around her pulsating with pain, anger and resentment. Even when they caught the person responsible, it hadn't been enough. It hadn't eased the constant ache inside.

And then, someone had offered her a solution.

Soon afterwards, when she found out she was pregnant – a stupid, drunken misadventure – she decided to move away. She had never really considered herself maternal, but once she knew she had a tiny human growing inside her she yearned to love and protect it.

She didn't tell her family about her plans. She just found another job, in another town, and left. On the day of Dad's funeral. A fresh start, putting what she had done behind her. At least, that's what she had told herself. She had moved several times since then; made several fresh starts. Unfortunately, Fran's baggage wasn't the kind you can leave at the station. More like a shadow, and you can never escape your shadow.

'Don't we need to turn off here? You said it was this junction?'

'*Shit!*'

Alice shot her a reproving look.

'Sorry. Language. I know.'

She indicated and swerved through the traffic to the slip road. Damn. She was getting stressed, getting sloppy, and they weren't even there yet. Already she could feel the familiar anxiety bearing down on her. She hadn't even thought exactly what she would do when they *did* get there. What she would say. How she would deal with things. None of this was to plan.

But then, you couldn't plan for everything. You couldn't plan for an exceptionally wet year followed by three years of dry winters, lowering water levels. Or for a new housing estate being built and the surrounding land being drained. And you certainly couldn't plan for *him* finding the car. Of all people. *How?* How had he even known where to look?

She glanced at Alice. She was staring out of the window, a familiar lost look in her eyes as she fumbled with the bag on her lap. *Clickety-click. Clickety-click.* The shell from the bath had disappeared, added to Alice's collection. Where did they come from? she thought again. Who was the girl on the beach, and what did she want? *'The Sandman is coming.'* Why did that phrase seem so damn ominous?

Just another thing to worry about. Because, while she could protect Alice here, in the waking world, how was she supposed to protect her from her dreams, her subconscious? She couldn't keep her safe there. And that scared her more than anything.

She tried to shake off the feelings of agitation. Focus on the road. The task at hand. They were nearing the outskirts of the village now. The area where she had grown up. A place she used to know well. But it had changed. She noticed a new speed-camera sign. The last thing she needed now was to be caught on film.

This was a bad idea, she thought again. A bad, bad idea. But she didn't have a better one. Certainly not a good one.

They passed the sign for Barton Marsh, twinned with who gave a fuck. It was a small sleeper estate of once-desirable detached houses. When desirable meant uniform and bland. The sheen had worn off long before she moved away. Now, it was a dozy ditchwater of pensioners unwilling to downsize who spent their days tending their impossibly neat gardens, bitching about parking and every Sunday polishing their cars. Just like Dad, she thought with a pang.

It was easy to spot the house. The lawn was mown but the flowerbeds were empty and bare, the basket optimistically hung outside the front door not just dead but virtually mummified. The UPVC windows and doors were dirty, the net curtains yellowed. A small Toyota with a dented bumper was parked in the driveway.

Fran observed all of this then pulled past the house and parked around the corner, a short way up. She got the feeling that, just like her, the neighbours here were the sort who noticed strange cars visiting.

'Okay,' she said, in what she hoped was a bright voice. 'Let's go.'

She climbed out of the car. Alice gave her a curious look but grabbed her bag of pebbles and followed. Fran looked around, automatically checking for anything odd, out of place. All the other houses seemed quiet. She could hear a small dog barking somewhere. Distantly, the hum of a lawnmower. Normal sounds of suburbia. It didn't quite reduce the hard knot in her stomach.

They rounded the corner and walked up the driveway of number 41. The closer they got, the more her gut was urging her to turn around and drive away again. But she had a job to do. Something to take care of . . . and she couldn't take Alice with her for this. Alice didn't know about the car, or the man. Or what she had been forced to do.

Fran rang the bell. They waited, Alice looking around with mild curiosity. Fran rang the bell again. *C'mon. I know you're here. The car's here. C'mon.*

Finally, she heard movement. A slow pad of footsteps, a mumbled curse. Chains on the door rattled and then it inched open.

Fran stared at the old woman in the doorway. The

immaculate honey-blonde bob, the careful make-up, the smart blouses and slacks. The keeping-up-appearances. All gone.

This woman was scrawny and hunched. Her hair was a dirty yellow with grey showing at the roots. She wore no make-up and was dressed in an old gown over crumpled leggings. Fran could smell stale wine.

Jesus. Things were far worse than she had expected.

The woman squinted at Fran. 'Yes?'

Fran swallowed. 'Hi, Mum.'

Slowly, the woman's eyes widened with recognition. 'Francesca?'

And then her gaze shifted to the small, dark-haired girl beside Fran. She raised a trembling, vein-stippled hand to her throat. 'And who is this?'

Fran felt her own throat constrict. 'This is Alice.' She grasped Alice's hand and squeezed it. A silent signal. 'Your granddaughter.'

She sleeps. A pale girl in a white room. Miriam sits in the arm-chair beside her. The tea in the pot has stewed and the cakes have gone hard.

After a moment, she takes the girl's hand. Physiotherapists visit regularly to ensure her limbs and hands remain mobile, that her fingers don't curl permanently into her palms. But Miriam can still feel the stiffness in her joints. Beneath the crisp sheets, her body is as frail and tiny as that of a child.

The girl's face is calm and smooth, like alabaster. No worry lines mar her forehead and no laughter lines trace happiness beside her eyes. She has not laughed or frowned or cried for years now. Possibly, she never will. While some patients in a permanent vegetative state may make facial expressions, noises, open and close their eyes, the girl does not. She remains frozen. Trapped in a body that has barely aged.

Miriam thinks it would be kinder to let her go. But that is not her decision to make. Not while there is even the faintest possibility that she is still in there, somewhere. The girl who used to love to sing, who loved the sounds of the ocean. The girl who no one remembers, except her. The girl who no one visits, except him.

He has never shirked his responsibility to the girl and her mother. Every week, he sits with the girl. He talks to her, reads. And often, he and Miriam talk, too. Despite everything, she's grown to enjoy these conversations. Neither of them has any family or close friends. They are both tied to the girl, unable to leave her, unable to let her go. And he has never missed a visit. Never even been late.

Until today.

Miriam glances at the clock. He's not coming, she thinks. For the first time.

A shiver of premonition runs through her. Something has happened.

She debates with herself, unsure if she is overstepping her boundaries . . . and then she takes out her phone.

24

Jenny had once told Gabe that his most annoying habit (of which he had plenty, apparently) was his inability to take advice. To listen to reason. His path could be peppered with warning signs and strung with barbed wire, but he would still only believe that the pool was toxic and infested with sharks by jumping in himself. Head first.

She was right, as she was about most things. If she were here now, Gabe might have told her that her most annoying habit (of which there were a few) was always being right about him.

He missed that. He missed a lot of things about Jenny. Not in the same way that he missed Izzy. The pain was different. It wasn't an all-encompassing black hole that obliterated the light from his life. It was more of a dull throb.

That sounded harsh. But it was true. The brutal fact was that losing a wife or partner and losing a child were different. He would have sacrificed himself for Izzy, and he knew Jenny would have done the same. The less palatable truth, the one that nobody liked to admit was, if it came to it, they would have sacrificed each other for their daughter. Jenny would have pushed him in front of a bus without a second thought if it meant saving Izzy's life. And that was fine. That was good. That was how it should be.

It wasn't that they didn't love each other. Once, they had loved each other furiously, relentlessly. But passionate love always dims. It has to. Like anything else, love must evolve. To survive, it needs to smoulder, not rage. But you still need to tend it, to keep it throwing out warmth. Be too neglectful, for too long, and the fire goes out completely, leaving you raking through the ashes, searching for that spark you once had.

They had both been neglectful. The last remaining bit of warmth had almost faded and he knew that they were both fruitlessly throwing on sticks in the vain hope it might reignite. That catch-all cliché – he loved Jenny, but he was no longer in love with her.

It wasn't Jenny's face he saw when he woke screaming in the middle of the night. It was Izzy's. Sometimes – often – he felt guilty about that. And yet, he was pretty sure if Jenny were here right now, she would say, *I should bloody well hope so.*

She would also have told him not to consider what he was considering.

Don't go near this shit. Forget you ever heard about it.

But then, warning signs, barbed wire, sharks . . .

After he had left the Samaritan, he had driven straight back to Newton Green Services, sat down in the coffee shop and pulled out his laptop. This time, there was no sign of the kind-faced waitress. Probably just as well. He didn't really want her appearing at his shoulder and seeing what he was doing. He had deliberately positioned himself in a different seat, tucked right into a far corner. Fortunately, the coffee shop was pretty empty. Just one middle-aged couple and a stocky young man with a shaven head in a fluorescent police jacket. Traffic cop, thought Gabe, although usually, like socks, they came in pairs. Perhaps the other one had got lost in the wash.

He turned his attention to his laptop. He had considered downloading a Tor browser before but never had the nerve. It felt a bit too much like opening Pandora's box. Plus, he wasn't exactly tech savvy. The instructions he had downloaded made it *seem* simple. (If this were a film, he would probably have whacked a few keys and had instant access to the White House security files.) As it was, it took him a good half an hour of disabling and enabling functions on his laptop before he eventually had the browser set up.

He stared at the screen. *Welcome to Tor Browser.*

Now what? He tried typing in 'the Other People' but, predictably, it yielded no results. You didn't just browse the Dark Web, he reminded himself. You needed to know what you were looking for. He didn't know what he was looking for. He didn't even know if he was looking in the right place or just wasting his time.

He could almost hear Jenny muttering smugly, *Told you so.*

Feeling frustrated, he took out the notebook and the Bible. The fusty, damp smell rising from the pages clogged his throat and the underlined passages seem to mock him. He wondered again why Sticker Man had underlined those particular ones.

And then the thought struck him, barrelling into his brain with the force of a small juggernaut.

You didn't just browse the Dark Web. Often the Web addresses were just *random letters and numbers.*

And how did you remember random letters and numbers? You needed a system. One that someone else wouldn't understand, should they stumble on it. He unfolded his napkin. He walked back up to the counter and asked the barista if he could borrow his ballpoint. The barista gave him an odd look but obliged.

Gabe sat back down. He jotted down the four Bible references on his napkin.

Exodus 21: 23–25
Leviticus 24: 17–21
Deuteronomy 19: 18–21
Deuteronomy 32: 43

Okay. Most obvious. The first letters of each of the testaments. He typed into his laptop: *http://ELDD.onion*
No joy.

He tried again but, this time, added the first numbers: *http://ELDD21241932.onion*
Nothing.

He felt his optimism begin to drain away. There could be any number of combinations, and he didn't even know if his theory was right. Maybe Sticker Man just really liked those quotes. Maybe it had nothing to do with the website.

Still, one more go: *http://E21L24D19D32.onion*

He hit return. A blue line appeared at the top of his screen. It trundled along and, when it reached the end, a page popped up.

THE OTHER PEOPLE

'*Shit.*'

Or maybe 'Holy shit.' He hadn't actually believed it would work. He stared at the innocuous home page. Plain white letters on a black background. A little like a chalkboard.

Below the website name, in smaller writing, was a box that read 'Enter Password.'

He looked at the line references. Worth a try.

2325172118213243

He hit enter. Another page flashed up.

WELCOME TO THE OTHER PEOPLE

We know about pain. We know about loss. We know about injustice.

We share the pain . . . with those who deserve it.

Beneath this little mission statement were three links:

Chat. Request. FAQ

He stared at the words, an unpleasant feeling slithering around his stomach.

FAQ.

It seemed a good place to start.

Q: Why are you called the Other People?

A: We all think that tragedy happens only to other people. Until it happens to us. We are people just like you. People to whom terrible things have happened. We've found solace not in forgiveness or forgetting. But in helping each other find justice.

Q: What sort of justice?

A: That depends on the individual. But our ethos is a punishment that fits the crime.

Q: What if I'm not looking for justice?

A: You are free to use our message board to talk to others just like you. However, most people come to our site through invitation. If you've found us, you already need us.

Q: Is this a website for vigilantes?

A: Not at all. We are all ordinary people. However, we have found that by connecting with each other we are able to utilize our unique talents, knowledge and connections.

The Other People pool these resources in order to fulfil each other's Requests.

Q: Do I have to pay?

A: No money changes hands. That way our services are accessible by anybody. Not just those with the financial means. We use a system of quid pro quo. Requests and Favours.

Q: How does it work?

A: If you wish to make a Request, visit the Requests page. You will be asked to submit a form explaining your situation and what you require. TOP will take 24 hours to consider your Request. During this time, you may still amend or cancel your Request.

After 24 hours, if we consider your Request acceptable, you will receive a confirmation that it has been activated. Once a Request is activated it cannot be amended or cancelled. No further correspondence will be necessary. Rest assured, unless there are exceptional circumstances, we fulfil all Requests.

Once your Request has been completed, you will be notified. You now owe a Favour. This can be called in at any time. Once your Favour is repaid, you are under no further obligation to the Other People.

Q: What if I don't repay the Favour?

A: We always try to ensure that the Favour is one you are able to complete, happily and willingly. Failure to complete your Favour threatens the very integrity of our site. That is why we have measures in place to ensure it doesn't happen.

Q: Can I request to have someone killed?

A: If your Request is acceptable, and unless there are exceptional circumstances, we fulfil all Requests.

Gabe stared at the screen.

We fulfil all Requests.

Jesus.

He reached for his coffee and took a sip. His head swam. Maybe the Samaritan had been right. He didn't want to go near this. He didn't want any part of it.

On the other hand, Sticker Man had been part of it. And he had taken Izzy. There had to be a connection. The police believed that his wife and daughter had been killed in a robbery gone wrong. But there were inconsistencies. Nothing had been stolen, not even cash. The caller who had alerted the police to an intruder at his house had never been traced. What if there was more to this? What if his family had been targeted on purpose?

But why? And what did Harry have to do with it? Why was it so important that he convinced Gabe that Izzy was dead? And who was the other little girl? There were still so many things that didn't make any sense.

He sighed and rubbed his eyes. His mobile pinged with a text. He picked it up, half expecting it to be the Samaritan, checking up on him.

It wasn't. It was worse.

He stared at the message and his stomach somersaulted off a steep cliff.

'Isabella missed you today.'

25

Fran hovered at the door of the kitchen while her mother made tea. Alice perched upon the sofa in the living room. A glass of orange squash and a plate of biscuits had been set on the coffee table. The orange cordial had settled at the bottom of the glass. Fran bet that if you bit into one of the biscuits, it would be damp and stale. Small details. Like the dirt around the edges of the carpet. The cobwebs lurking in the corners of the room. The tremor in her mother's hands.

'You should have called,' her mother said. 'I haven't had a chance to tidy up, get myself sorted.'

A lie, Fran thought. She hadn't had a chance to start drinking today and now their visit would delay it.

'Sorry. We were in the area, so we thought we'd drop by.'

'*Drop by?*' Her mother turned, eyes suddenly sharp. 'You've not *dropped by* in over nine years. I didn't even know I had a granddaughter.'

Despite herself, despite everything, Fran felt a leaden punch of guilt.

'I'm sorry.'

'Sorry?' Her mother spat in disgust. 'You disappear without a word, you never call or send a message in all this time. You cut us from your life. And now you turn up, out of the blue. What's really going on, Fran?'

'It's complicated.'

Her mother's lips pursed. The crockery rattled as she stuck cups on saucers. 'If you want money, I don't have any.'

No, Fran thought. You've probably spent it all on booze. She bit back the words. Instead she said: 'I have something I need to do. I need someone to watch Alice, just for an hour or two.'

'And you had no one else you could ask?'

Fran didn't reply. What was the point in lying?

Her mother shook her head, moisture welling in her bloodshot eyes.

'I know what you think of me. But don't you think I deserved the chance to know my eldest granddaughter?'

Fran wanted to reply that she had never made the effort to know her eldest daughter. And what about her other grandchildren? Occasionally, when Alice was in bed, Fran had looked up her sisters on social media. She knew that Katie had two children now and Lou had a little girl. Fran bet her mother never saw them either. But now was not the time to start an argument.

She just said again, 'I'm sorry.'

Her mother turned and walked across the kitchen. She peered through the open door into the living room where Alice still sat, clutching the bag of pebbles on her lap. Fran held her breath. She knew it was a long shot. If they had to leave, she would have to sort something else out . . .

Then her mother turned, smiling sadly.

'I suppose we have to make the best of things, don't we?'

She shuffled into the living room and sat down beside Alice, who started a little.

'Do you like jigsaw puzzles, Alice? I think I still have some somewhere.'

Alice glanced quickly at Fran. Fran gave a small nod. Alice looked back at her grandmother and smiled. 'Yes, that would be lovely.'

Fran felt her heart soften. She reached for her car keys. 'I won't be long.'

The sky outside was heavy with bloated black clouds, the breeze needle sharp. Fran turned the heater in the car up to full.

There was a garage about two miles down the main road. She drove past it and pulled into a turning about fifty yards down. Then she walked back to the garage, where she purchased a petrol can and petrol, made suitably 'I'm such a stupid woman' noises to the disinterested youth behind the counter and carried it back to the car. She hoped it would be enough. Next, she drove to the out-of-town Sainsbury's. She picked up matches and some cheap T-shirts, which she planned to rip into rags. Then she headed off again. She glanced at her watch. Almost forty minutes so far. She felt her stomach tighten.

The thought of Alice, out of sight, was grating on her. She needed to get this done. Quickly. It should take only about fifteen minutes to get to her destination. Hopefully, no more than ten minutes to do what she needed to do, and then back again. Hopefully.

She indicated left and trundled along the narrow lane. After about ten minutes she spotted the farmhouse and then the small lay-by on the right. She pulled in, opened the boot and took out what she needed. In the distance, she heard a car. She stepped back into the embrace of the woods. A blue Fiesta sped past. The driver obviously didn't realize there were cameras further down the road. Serve him right. With a final glance around, she turned and trudged into the undergrowth.

The overhanging branches were wet and dripped fat blobs of icy water on her head as she walked along. Occasionally, a drooping branch whipped her in the face. The petrol can felt heavier with each step.

The woods were far more overgrown than she remembered. When she was a kid, she and her friends used to ride here on their bikes. Far more than her parents ever knew. Back then, before the new housing estate, you could reach the lake from the other side. They would cycle through the fields along an old bridle path. A rough, overgrown track just wide enough for horses, or a car, at a push.

Mum and Dad had told her not to play here, obviously. Mum moaned that she would get all dirty. Dad told her that a child had drowned in the lake, years ago. She wasn't sure she believed him, but the lake was certainly deep. Deep enough to submerge shopping trolleys . . . or something bigger.

But not any more.

As she emerged into the small clearing she caught her breath. Jesus. The lake had shrunk to a puddle. You could plan and plan, but there were always things you couldn't predict. Although, to be honest, dumping the car here had never been a plan. It had been an act of desperation.

She'd like to say she hadn't meant to kill him. But that wasn't true. As soon as she had held the kitchen knife in her hand, she knew what she had to do. Survival. Once, she would never have thought herself capable of such violence. But she had done a lot of things over the last three years that she had never thought herself capable of. None of us know, until pushed, what our limits truly are. How far we would go for those we love. The greatest acts of cruelty are born of the greatest love. Wasn't that some famous quote? Or maybe she was making it up. These days, she was no longer sure.

She was sure of one thing. The man who had broken into their house that night had come to kill *them*, and he probably had his reasons, too. Good reasons. Reasons which he could use to justify his actions. But he had been careless, and Fran had been ready, waiting. The weird thing was, when she drove the knife into his flesh, it hadn't felt wrong, or strange, or even that terrible. It had felt necessary. And then she had stabbed him again, and again. To be sure.

Once he was dead, practicality took over. She had loaded him into the boot of the old car, roused Alice from her bed (thank God she hadn't woken in the middle of it all) and told her they had to leave. They had driven south, avoiding main roads where possible, and checked into a hotel nearby. She had been forced to leave Alice alone for a couple of hours while she took care of things. A *huge*, *huge* risk. One she couldn't bring herself to repeat. But she saw the chance to kill two birds with one stone. Dispose of the body *and* the damn car. She knew the perfect spot. One where neither would ever be found. Or so she thought.

She stared at the car, the boot sticking up out of the murky water. At first, she had been amazed that he could have found it. Now she was here, it made more sense. Someone was bound to find it eventually. Still, the chances of him just *stumbling* over it were still remote. Not many people visited this place, or even knew about it. Someone must have told him it was here. But who?

A worry for later. For now, she had to make sure no one

else found the car or, more importantly, what was inside it. She swallowed. There probably wasn't that much left. She remembered stripping off the man's clothes and burning them. A sudden, sickening reality check. She had struggled to force his stiffening limbs from the grubby sweatshirt and jeans. His underwear was slightly stained and she had felt absurdly embarrassed, as if taking off his clothing were a greater desecration than taking his life. The sight of his flesh, pale and hairless, sticky with drying blood, had almost made her throw up. She had managed to hold her stomach and checked his pockets. No wallet or ID. Some car keys (despite no car parked near their house), which she had chucked into the lake. But she had been hasty and had panicked. Desperate to get away from the body, the dank lake, the consequence of her actions.

She hadn't cleared out the car. She had just shoved stuff in the glovebox without checking if there was anything incriminating that could lead them to her and Alice.

That had to be rectified.

She ripped up the T-shirts. Then she quickly wriggled out of her jeans and trainers, grabbed the petrol and rags and waded into the stagnant water.

The cold made her gasp. Sticky mud squelched beneath her toes. She grimaced and gritted her teeth. She needed to do this fast. She reached the car. She pulled at the back door. The water pushed against her. She managed to yank it open and chucked some of the rags onto the back seat, which was virtually dry. It should catch. She doused the rags and seat in petrol. Was it enough? No. She needed to make sure that the contents of the boot burned, too. She stepped away from the car and waded around to the back. She steeled herself and then cracked the boot open.

That was when she heard the splash behind her. She turned, a moment too late, and something heavy crashed into her skull. Her head exploded and her knees buckled, the petrol can slipping from her hand. She sank, dazed, into the water, suddenly up to her chest. She gasped and floundered, arms splashing weakly.

A figure loomed over her. And then his hands were on her throat and he was pushing her head down, into the freezing water. She tried to fight it. She grabbed at his hands, but they were so strong. She twisted and writhed. She kicked out with her feet and felt her heel connect soundly with his crotch. The grip around her throat loosened. She dragged her head up, out of the water, seizing a precious breath.

He punched her in the face. She sank again, his grip even tighter. She scrabbled and scratched at his fingers, but her strength was fading. She needed air. Her lungs were about to explode. She felt her lips part slightly, her brain desperate and conflicted. *Don't open your mouth. But I need to breathe. Just hold on.* She would not die in this stinking, filthy pool. She couldn't. Alice was waiting and Fran had to get back because . . .

Something gave. A sharp pain in her neck. A sudden lightness in her head. Her lungs were no longer burning because she could no longer feel her body. Her limbs floated uselessly. She couldn't fight. She couldn't stop this. Her mouth lolled open. And her last thought as the water rushed in was . . . *Alice hates jigsaws . . .*

26

Gabe had tried to talk Jenny out of it. He'd practically learned the *Big Book of Girls' Names* off by heart. But she had been adamant: *'I want to call her Isabella.'*

And they had had a deal. If it was a girl, she would choose. A boy, and the choice would be Gabe's. Gabe had thought it was a little sexist, but he also knew not to argue with a pregnant woman.

The more he tried to persuade her, the more Jenny dug in her heels. He had always loved that about her. Her stubbornness. Her unwillingness to buckle just to please or pacify someone else. But on this issue, he wished she could be just a little more compliant.

'Most wives wouldn't want to choose a name their husband didn't like,' he had pointed out.

'Most wives don't have such arseholes for a husband. What is your bloody problem with Isabella anyway?'

He couldn't answer her. Couldn't explain. He certainly couldn't persuade Jenny to change her mind, so he tried to persuade himself that it was just a name. A pretty name. And this was *their* Isabella. Their baby. A completely new person.

It was true that when she was born he very quickly forgot everything except how beautiful she was, how noisy she was, how incredible and exhausting it was now that one tiny little person had completely taken over their lives.

But he still chose to call her Izzy instead.

And the nightmares came back.

He told himself it was just the stress of fatherhood. He told himself it was only natural; his head was all over the place. He would adjust. Things would settle down.

He tried not to listen to the insistent little voice that told him that calling their precious little girl Isabella was a portent of doom. A jinx.

He stood, so quickly the coffee cup wobbled and slopped cold dregs over his saucer. How could he have forgotten what day it was? *Visiting day*. How could he not have heard his phone ping with the reminder? *Shit, shit, shit*. He gathered his things and stuffed them back in his bag. He had to go, now.

He hurried across to the camper van and pulled out his keys. He frowned. The side door was open, just a fraction. Had he forgotten to lock it, or had someone broken in? He pulled the door open and climbed inside.

There was a man in the van. Sitting calmly on the small bunk seat. Even more oddly, Gabe recognized him. It was the young police officer he'd seen in the coffee shop. The traffic cop flying solo.

The disparity, the sheer strangeness, threw him for a moment.

'I'm sorry, but wha——?'

The man rose and struck him in the face. It was so sudden, so unexpected, that Gabe didn't even have a chance to raise an arm to defend himself. His head rocked back against the side of the van. His legs wavered. Before he could straighten, the man punched him again, in the throat. Gabe gasped, choking, trying to draw breath, his throat burning like someone had rammed hot coals down it.

The man picked up Gabe's messenger bag.

No! he tried to yell, but it came out: 'Nnurrrggghhh!'

Gabe grabbed for the bag. Managed to snag the strap. The man threw another punch. Gabe ducked his head to one side. He held tight as the man pulled at the bag. They tugged back and forth, Gabe somehow finding strength in desperation.

The man drew back his arm and punched him sharply in the side. Hot, burning pain. Gabe grabbed instinctively at his stomach, letting go of the bag. The man snatched it, shoved the door open and jumped outside. Gabe lurched after him, but the pain reeled him back. He fell to the floor. Through the open door, he could see the man sauntering casually away.

He tried to reach for the door to pull himself up, missed and fell out of the van, onto the rough tarmac. He screamed, clutching at his side, which seemed to be leaking something hot and wet. The man was just a silhouette now. *He couldn't let him go.* The bag held everything. His laptop, the Bible, the notebook, the hair bobble. It was all he had.

He tried to drag himself along the ground, but his energy was seeping out of him. He rolled onto his back, gasping for air. It was too thick with petrol and fumes. The sky was too bright. He closed his eyes. Faintly, he could hear shouting. Then, closer, a voice:

'Oh my God. Christ – what's happened?'

He couldn't answer. The darkness was soothing. Like a balm. There would be no more pain there.

But the voice was insistent.

'Open your eyes. Look at me. I'm calling an ambulance, but you have to wake up.'

He opened his eyes. A face loomed over him. Familiar. Nice, but tired. The kind waitress.

'I . . .' He drew his hand away from his side and stared, bemused, at the red dripping from his fingers. 'I think I've been stabbed.'

27

Alice waited. She tried not to look as if she was waiting. Or worried. Or afraid. But actually, she was all of them and more.

Fran should have been back by now. She had said it wouldn't take more than an hour. One and a half tops. That was over two hours ago. They had exhausted the old woman's old (and frankly pretty rubbish) jigsaw puzzles and had struggled through some stilted conversation. Fran had told her what to say, but it was still difficult, remembering stuff, trying not to say the wrong thing, just like sometimes she forgot to call Fran Mum. She got pretty annoyed about that.

Something about the old lady scared Alice a bit, too. She smiled too much. Alice didn't like that, not just because her teeth were all yellow. And she was so jittery. Her hands shook when she was trying to put the jigsaw pieces down. There was this odd, sour smell about her, too.

Her twitchiness was making Alice more on edge. She kept asking if Alice wanted another drink or something else to eat, even though Alice's glass was still half full and she had already forced down three of the stale biscuits. Eventually, just to keep her quiet, Alice said yes, some more squash would be nice. This seemed to make the old lady happy, so Alice took her opportunity:

'Can I use the toilet, please?'

'Oh, of course. It's just upstairs, first on the left.'

'Thank you.'

Alice grabbed her bag, walked up the stairs and onto a narrow landing. The bathroom door was open, but she didn't really need the loo; she just needed to get away from the old lady for a bit. It looked old-fashioned anyway, a hideous shade of green, shaggy mats on the floor all flattened and manky.

There were three more doors. The nearest one was ajar. Alice peered inside. It was obviously the old lady's room. There was a lot of dark furniture, a double bed covered in a quilted bed cover. On the bedside table were two pictures in fancy silver frames. Alice hesitated. She wasn't normally a child who sneaked around. But being here, in this house, had made her curious.

She padded across the carpet and picked up the first photo. Four people stood on a clifftop in the sunshine. She recognized the old lady, younger and happier, and Fran, looking very young. Not that much older than Alice. There were two little girls in the photo, too. Fran's sisters. Alice had never thought of her as having a family. It had always been just the two of them. The second photo was of the old lady and a man. He had thinning hair, a wide smile and crinkly blue eyes. He looked nice, she thought. Kind.

She put the photo back down. From the kitchen she could hear the sound of glasses clinking. The bedside table had two small drawers. She yanked one of them open. Neatly folded hankies, a pot of Vicks and, just poking out from underneath the hankies, what looked like newspaper cuttings. Alice took them out. She was a good reader, but the small print of newspapers was a little difficult. Still, she could make out the headlines.

HOME-OWNER KILLED IN BUNGLED BURGLARY

HORROR IN SUBURBIA

She recognized the house in the pictures. And the man who was in the photo on the bedside table. Nice, she thought. But dead.

She stared at the pages. Then she stuffed them back in the drawer and shut it. She crept from the room and started to make her way downstairs. Halfway, she paused. She could hear the old lady talking in the kitchen. Momentarily, her heart lifted. Fran. She had come back. She peered over the banister. But the old lady was alone, clutching a glass of something red in one hand and a phone in the other.

'Yes. She's here now. No, I don't think her mother is coming back. I think she's in some kind of trouble.'

A pause.

'About eight years old. Can you come quickly? Thank you, Officer.'

The police. The stupid old lady had called the police. Alice had to get out. Now. She ran down the stairs and darted to the front door. Locked. Crap.

From behind her, she heard a shout: 'Alice!'

The old lady stood in the kitchen doorway. Alice looked around desperately and then spotted the keys on the hall table. She snatched them up and stuck them in the lock.

'Stop right there!'

'No. You called the police.'

The old lady moved faster than Alice had expected. She grabbed her arm.

'Listen to me –'

'Get off!'

Alice yanked her arm away.

'Come back here!'

Alice pulled the door open and stumbled outside. The old lady screamed after her: 'Your mother isn't coming back. She's left you. Wait and see.'

Alice didn't wait. Tears blinded her eyes. She had no idea where she was going. But she did what she had been told to do, trained to do.

Alice ran.

28

'Seven stitches. No major organs. You're lucky it was just a graze.'

Gabe stared at the young doctor. Thin, with bright red hair and a dour northern accent. It was hard to tell whether she was joking or not.

'Err, thank you,' he murmured.

'Of course, if your friend hadn't found you, you could be dead.'

'From a graze?'

'Shock and blood loss at your age can often lead to heart failure.'

'Well, thanks – again.'

She nodded briskly, satisfied he appreciated the magnitude of his near-death experience.

'Do I need to stay in hospital?' he asked.

She regarded his chart, obviously debating whether 'near-death' really required taking up a bed for the night.

'I'll get you some antibiotics to take home,' she said, and hurried away.

He lay back on the hard hospital pillows. Compassion, he thought, like everything else in the NHS, had been cut back to the bone.

His side throbbed and felt tight with the stitches. Lucky. He had been lucky, he reminded himself. And actually, the doctor was right: if the blonde waitress hadn't been getting out of her car when he had stumbled out of the van, he could have lain there for vital minutes, the blood seeping out of him. But she had seen him and staunched the wound with her scarf, called 999. Then she had talked to him, trying to keep him conscious, until the ambulance arrived. Her name was Katie, she had told him. A pretty name.

He owed her his life. In fact, he was rapidly beginning to think of her as some kind of guardian angel, appearing at his hours of need. Or perhaps that was the painkillers talking.

He closed his eyes and, this time, he saw the man again, plunging the knife into his stomach, calmly walking away with his bag. The policeman from the coffee shop. It couldn't be a coincidence. Either there was a blip in the Matrix, or he had been following Gabe, waiting for his chance. But why? The Samaritan's voice echoed in his head:

'Forget you ever saw those words . . . don't go anywhere near that shit.'

Could it be connected with the Other People? Had Gabe stumbled over something important? Something worth attacking him for? His ancient laptop could hardly be the motive, but what about the website? Or was it what was contained in the notebook or the Bible. The codes?

It seemed far-fetched, but then the last forty-eight hours had been a vertical plunge down the rabbit hole. The car, Harry, the photos. Not exactly his normal daily routine. And the worst part – aside from almost being killed – was he no longer had any of the things he had retrieved. The map, the notebook, the hair bobble, the Bible. They were all gone.

'Mr Forman?'

He opened his eyes at the doctor's clipped tones. She wasn't alone. Another woman stood behind her, at the side of his bed. Late forties, petite, with cropped blonde hair and a weariness to her face. A face that said: *Really? You expect me to believe that?*

Gabe knew that look only too well. He had felt it levelled at him a number of times during the investigation into the murder of his family.

If it weren't for the stitches and the drugs, he was pretty sure he'd have felt his stomach sink.

'Gabriel.' DI Maddock smiled thinly. 'What have you got yourself into now?'

29

Katie wiped tables, collected empty mugs, filled clean ones, smiled, took money and gave change. At least, that's what her body did. Her mind was elsewhere. It wandered around in circles but kept coming back to one thing: the sight of the thin man on the ground, leaking dark blood from his side. His panicked eyes. Déjà vu. It reminded her a bit too much of Dad. Except the thin man was alive. So far.

When people talk about dying, they often talk about peace and acceptance. That wasn't what she had seen in her dad's eyes. It was terror, shock and disbelief that life, this thing that we take for granted, that we kid ourselves is constant and fixed, could be snatched away, just like that.

We try not to think about death. And if we do, we view it as something distant and abstract. We never expect it to ambush us in our own garage one late-spring night. Just like we convince ourselves tragedy will never befall us because we are somehow special and immune. The worst that can happen only ever happens to other people.

She swiped viciously at a sticky mark on a table then gave up and stuck a menu on top of it. She kept wondering how the thin man was. *Gabe.* He had told her his name while they waited for the ambulance. She supposed she could call the hospital. Just check he was okay. She glanced at the clock. Only another hour left on her shift. The afternoon rush had subsided. Ethan (she was *pretty* sure this one was Ethan) was occupied at the counter, talking to a pretty female customer.

She stuffed her cleaning cloth in her pocket and hurried out to the staff room. She let herself in and grabbed her mobile from her locker. Hospitals, she thought. She supposed the nearest would be Newton General. She googled the number and hit call.

'Hello, Newton General Hospital.'

'Oh, hello. I'm just calling to check on a patient who was brought in this afternoon. He was stabbed.'

'Name?'

'Gabe.'

'Surname?'

'Oh.' She didn't know his last name. 'Sorry, I don't know.'

'I'm afraid we're not able to give out patient details without more information.'

'I just wanted to check he was okay.'

A pause. 'I don't believe we've received any fatalities.'

'Right. Good. Thanks.'

She ended the call and chewed her lip. She didn't have any other way of contacting him. No surname. No phone number. No – wait. She *did* have his number. On the 'missing' flyer he had handed her ages ago. The one with the picture of his daughter on. HAVE YOU SEEN ME? She was sure she still had it at home somewhere; she had felt bad about throwing it away. She just had to find it again. Well, she didn't *have* to. She could just leave it. He wasn't dead. That was all she needed to know, really.

But she couldn't dispel a nagging feeling of disquiet.

Worry gnawed away at the lining of her stomach. She didn't believe in premonition, or any of that nonsense. The morning she had arrived at her parents' house to find her dad crushed to death she hadn't experienced one iota of foresight, not a shiver, not a cloud skimming the blue sky. Nothing. And yet, right now, she couldn't shake the feeling that something bad was about to happen or was already happening. A seed of unease had been planted and she could feel it growing, stretching out its roots.

She called her sister.

'Hello.'

'Hi, Lou. Just wanted to check everything was okay?'

'Why?'

'Just. I don't know.'

A heavy sigh. 'The kids are fine. They're watching *Scooby Doo*. I'm making fish fingers and chips for tea, like you instructed.'

'Right. Good. Thanks. I'll see you later.'

She ended the call and then gave in to the paranoia and called her mum. It rang for so long she thought it would go to answerphone. Maybe she was still in bed, or already drunk. Then there was a click and she heard her mum's voice snap: 'Where are you? I called hours ago.'

She frowned. 'Mum? It's Katie.'

'Katie?'

'Who did you think it would be?'

A pause. 'Is she there? Is that why you're calling?'

'Is who here? I'm at work. Are you all right?'

'No, of course I'm not. She thinks she can just turn up here after all these years –' Her mum broke off. 'Wait. The police are here. About time.'

'The police? Why?'

'I called them when she didn't come back.'

'*Who*, Mum?'

'Your *sister*. Fran. I have to go.'

An abrupt click as her mum ended the call. Katie stared at the phone.

Fran? Fran had come back? No. Not possible. And surely, the last person she would go to would be their mum. The pair had always had a spiky relationship, even before Dad died. Afterwards, neither felt the need to keep up the appearance of civility. It was no wonder, really, that Fran had wanted to get away, to cut ties completely. She had left for good on the day of Dad's funeral.

But not before she had told Katie. About what she had done.

Katie tried to be rational. You couldn't always trust what her mum said when she was drunk. She became paranoid, abusive. She had called the police before, convinced that her neighbours were spying on her, or someone was trying to break into the house, or there was a man watching her. It always amounted to nothing. But she hadn't sounded *that* drunk today. She had sounded nervous, on edge. And why would she make up a story about Fran?

Katie slipped her phone in her bag. She couldn't wait until the end of her shift. She had to know what was going on. *Now*. She shrugged on her hoodie, grabbed her bag and hurried out of the staff room.

The queue was growing. The pretty girl had been joined by a good-looking young man.

'Where've you been?' Ethan scowled at her.

'Sorry. I have to go. Family emergency.'

'*Now?* You're leaving me on my own?'

'It's only an hour. You'll cope.'

'I should get extra pay.'

'Oh, I think all the change you steal out of the tip pot when you think no one's looking is bonus enough.'

Katie smiled sweetly then scuttled out of the coffee shop, trying to ignore the feeling that, somehow, she was already too late.

30

'*Tell me about the last time you saw your daughter, Mr Forman.*'

'*I told you — it was in a beaten-up old car being driven north on the M1 between junctions 19 and 21.*'

'*We both know that's not possible, Mr Forman.*'

'*Do we?*'

'*You called your house at 6.13 p.m. You claim to have seen your daughter about ten minutes before this and yet we know that your wife and daughter were already dead by this point.*'

'*No.*' He had shaken his head. The effort made it throb. A constant headache that had been festering for days. Pressure. All the pressure building up. Why wouldn't they listen to him? They had got it wrong. All wrong.

'*Mr Forman. We appreciate how difficult this is.*'

'*No, you don't. You keep telling me my wife and daughter are dead, but I saw her. My little girl is out there. There's been a mistake.*'

'*There is no mistake, Mr Forman. Now, can you tell us your whereabouts between 4 p.m. and 6 p.m. on 11 April?*'

Silence.

'*You didn't go into work that day. So, where were you? We can track your mobile, so you might as well tell us. Where were you when your wife and daughter were murdered?*'

*

DI Maddock regarded him now with her pale, appraising gaze. Not an unattractive woman, but something about the insipid colour of her eyes, platinum hair and pale skin give her a chill appearance. Like a stone angel, he thought. No soft edges or warmth. He could throw out the cliché about it being her job, but he suspected that her coolness had more to do with her personality than with her profession. He bet she even greeted her mother with a curt handshake.

'So,' she said. 'I was hoping you might have taken that camper van of yours, hopped onto a ferry and gone somewhere hot and sunny.'

'Given up, you mean?'

'Moved on.'

'I do move on, every day.'

She looked him up and down. 'And how's that working out for you, Gabriel?'

He shifted. 'I would have thought a knifing was a bit small-time for you. Or have they downgraded you from Homicide?'

'Nope. But some people I like to keep tabs on. When your name cropped up on PNC, it was brought to my attention and I thought I'd make a personal visit.'

'Gee. Thanks.'

'You're welcome.' She took out a notebook. 'So what exactly happened?'

He reached for the glass of water beside the bed and took a sip. His throat felt suddenly dry.

'I was attacked.'

'In your camper van?'

'Yes.'

'And your assailant ran off with your bag, containing your laptop, is that right?'

'That's right.'

'Can you describe your assailant?'

'Mid-twenties. Short, stocky. Wearing a police uniform.'

'You're saying a *police officer* stabbed you?'

'No. I'm saying he was *wearing* a police *uniform*.'

'Doesn't sound like your typical opportunist thief.'

'I'm not sure he was.'

'How d'you mean?'

'I saw him in the café, before the attack.'

More note-taking. 'Okay, I can ask some of the staff. They might remember him.'

'What about CCTV?'

'We're looking into that, but if this was planned, your assailant probably knows how to avoid being caught on camera.' A keener look. 'You think he targeted you? Why?'

Gabe stared back at her. Because of what he had found. Because he had got too close to the truth. To Izzy. And he was pretty sure if he said that, then DI Maddock would snap her notebook shut and walk out of here. On the other hand, what did he have to lose?

'I found something. Evidence that Izzy is alive.'

The notebook remained open. For now. But he sensed the effort it was taking for her not to roll her eyes.

'What evidence?'

'The car.'

'You found the car? Where?'

'It had been dumped, in a lake.'

'So why didn't you call the police?'

'You never believed me before.'

'Not true. We believed there was a car. We even had witnesses who saw a vehicle matching the description you gave driving erratically on the M1 that evening.'

'So why didn't the driver come forward?'

'Maybe they were drunk. Maybe they didn't have tax, insurance. Could be any number of reasons. But the point is, it can't have been Izzy you saw in it. Just another little girl who looked like her.'

'Why dump it, then?'

'Who knows? Maybe it was stolen.'

He felt the frustration rise, just like before. A feeling of helplessness, like a child trying to tell an adult that fairies really did exist.

'There were things in the car. A hair bobble just like Izzy's. A Bible with these strange passages underlined. And a notebook. It had something written in it. "The Other People".'

Her gaze became keener. 'The Other People?'

'You've heard the name?'

She continued to stare at him, evaluating. 'These items,' she said slowly. 'I take it they were in the bag that was stolen?'

'Yes.'

'I see.'

'No, you don't. That's why I was attacked. They wanted to destroy the evidence.'

A deep sigh, conveying a faint whiff of mints and a stronger whiff of scepticism.

'What?' Gabe challenged. 'You think I'm making all of this up? That I attacked myself?'

She didn't reply and, suddenly, he was sure that that was *exactly* what she was thinking.

He sank back into the pillows. 'For fuck's sake.'

'Okay,' she said. 'Tell me where the car is and I can at least get someone to tow it out of the lake.'

He hesitated. If he told her where the car was, they would

find the body and then they would ask why he hadn't mentioned the small matter of the decomposing corpse before.

'I can't remember.'

'You can't remember?'

'No. Not exactly.'

'You miraculously find the car you have been searching for, for three years, and you can't remember where, exactly?'

He didn't reply. This time the notebook did snap shut. She shook her head. 'Get some rest, Mr Forman. We've finished here.'

No. He was close. So close to getting her to believe him. But he had nothing else, except . . . the photos. They were in his wallet, not his laptop bag. He still had the photos.

'*Wait!*'

His coat was slung over one of the plastic chairs. He swung his legs out of bed and reached for it, grimacing at the sudden hot burst of pain in his side.

'There's something else. I have these.'

He fumbled in his wallet, pulled out the photos and thrust them at her. She recoiled slightly.

'Where did you get these?'

He hesitated. Even though he was pretty sure that Harry was a lying son of a bitch, he didn't want to hand him to the police. Not yet.

'I can't tell you.'

Her lips thinned. 'Seems like there's a lot of stuff you can't tell me.'

'Look – someone sent me the photos. I think they were trying to convince me Jenny and Izzy were dead, but they got it wrong. Because of the scratch.'

She squinted at the photos. 'I don't see a scratch.'

'Exactly. That morning, our cat scratched Izzy. But there's no scratch in this photo.'

'The cat must have scratched her another morning. You're confused.'

'No. I'm not. I'm just sick of being called a liar.'

'No one is calling you a liar. Despite what you think, I am not your enemy.'

'You thought I was a murderer.'

'Actually, I never really thought that. It didn't work. To drive home, murder your wife and child, get yourself cleaned up, drive back along the motorway and call from the service station, miraculously avoiding all the traffic cameras? Not feasible. And then there was the anonymous caller.'

Gabe had thought about that, too. The call reporting a break-in at Gabe's house, just before the murders. It wasn't a neighbour. The police had decided it must have been a concerned passer-by. But why not come forward?

'There was me thinking it was my honest face,' he said now.

'Never trust an honest face.' A pause. 'Of course, if you'd just told us where you really were from the start, it would have made our jobs a lot easier.'

'And have you judge me for that, too?'

'You were judged by the court and sentenced.'

'Please,' he said. 'Can't you just ask about the photographs, check with the coroner or something? I mean, only Harry identified the bodies. It's just his word.'

'And you think he lied?'

'Maybe. Maybe he was . . . mistaken.'

'You're suggesting that your father-in-law misidentified your wife and daughter's bodies.'

'No, just Izzy's.'

'Do you understand how insane that sounds?'

'Yes. Absolutely.'

Maddock picked up the photos again. She peered more closely at the one of Izzy. He waited, heart thumping. Finally, she turned to him.

'Okay. I'll get someone to look at the photos. But first – where's the car?'

'I –'

'Don't bullshit me.'

He debated. He could lie. Claim he just stumbled over it. Say he never looked in the boot.

'Barton Marsh, off Junction 14. There's a lay-by just past a farm. Follow the footpath till you get there.'

She jotted it down.

'Don't suppose you care to tell me how you found it?'

'No.'

'Fine.' She put the notebook back in her pocket and started to do the same with the photos.

'Wait.'

'What?'

He hesitated. 'The photos. They're all I've got. The only proof.'

'And you think I'm the sort of police officer who would misplace evidence?'

'No, but –'

The 'but' hung in the air, reverberating with accusation.

'You have to trust someone, at some point.'

He debated with himself then nodded. 'Fine.'

She tucked the photographs into her pocket.

'Thank you. Now, if I do this for you, can you do something for me?'

'What?'

'Think about what I said before. Siestas. Sipping margaritas at sundown.'

'I'll think about it.'

'Good. Everyone deserves a second chance.'

'Even me.'

'Especially you.'

31

A police car was parked outside her mum's house.

Katie pulled up behind it, yanked on the handbrake and climbed out. Her heart felt like it was fighting her lungs for space. She couldn't help it. The sight of a police car, outside their house. Too many memories.

However difficult her mum was, however awkward their relationship, she still worried about her, still cared for her. It wasn't until you lost a parent that you understood the magnitude of their presence in your life. So many times, after Dad, she would pick up the phone to call him and pause, mid-dial, remembering that he would no longer greet her from the other end with a cheery 'Hello, sweetheart.' It wasn't a temporary absence. He was gone. For ever. The realization sideswiped her again and again.

This is not the same, she tried to tell herself as she walked up the driveway. Not the same. Still, the feeling of unease that had started back in the café had increased tenfold. She rang the bell. A few seconds later it swung open.

Her mum stood in front of her. She looked thin, haggard and older than ever. She eyed Katie suspiciously.

'Why are you here? Has she called you? Have you seen her?'

'Mum. Calm down. I was worried about you, so I left work and drove straight over.'

Her mum glared at her and then turned abruptly. 'You'd better come in,' she said, and walked back down the hallway.

Trying to fight the irritation nipping at her already frayed edges, Kate followed her into the small, beige kitchen. A young police officer with a ruddy face and sandy-coloured hair sat awkwardly at the table, a mug of tea in front of him. A bottle of red and a full glass sat in front of the other chair.

Just something to steady my nerves, her mum had probably told him. Katie had heard that excuse before. She had heard all of them.

'This is Katie, one of my other daughters,' her mum said as she slumped into the chair and took a sip of wine. The police officer stood and offered a hand.

'PC Manford.'

Katie shook it. 'Could you tell me what's going on?'

'That's what we're just trying to get to the bottom of.'

Katie felt like saying the only thing her mum was trying to get to the bottom of was that bloody bottle of wine, but she bit her tongue.

'My mum called you?'

'Yes, Mrs Wilson wants to report a missing person.'

Katie frowned. 'Who's missing?'

'Your sister, Francesca –'

'My sister moved away years ago.'

'She was here,' her mum said. 'Today.'

Katie stared at her. 'You're sure?'

'Of course I'm sure. Just turned up, out of the blue, then took off again.'

Katie tried to digest this. Fran. Back. After all this time.

'You're positive it was Fran?'

'I know my own daughter.'

'But now she's gone?'

'Yes.'

'Well, I still don't think you can report her missing if she left of her own volition . . .'

'I don't want to report *her* missing. I couldn't care less if she never comes back. She was always trouble. You don't remember, you were too young –'

'*Mum,*' Katie broke in. 'If you don't want to report Fran missing, then why did you call the police?'

'Because of the little girl.'

'What little girl?'

'Alice. She just left her here.'

'Who's Alice?'

'Fran's daughter. My eldest granddaughter.'

Granddaughter? Katie opened her mouth, closed it again. She was about to say that Fran didn't have a daughter, but what did she know? She hadn't seen her sister in almost a decade. She could have a whole brood. Nephews and nieces Katie had never met.

'Well, where's the little girl now?'

'*Missing.* That's what I've been trying to tell you. She ran away. She's out there somewhere all alone –' Her mum's face softened and, for a fleeting moment, Katie could almost see the parent she used to be.

'We have to find her. Before something terrible happens.'

32

It was growing dark, the sky blotted out by heavy clouds, by the time Gabe walked – tentatively, feeling sore and light-headed – from the hospital. His pocket rustled with painkillers and a 'Self-care' leaflet that explained what he should do if the wound started to bleed, became inflamed or wept yellow pus. Surprisingly, this was not 'Carry on and ignore it.'

He had booked a cab to take him back to the services, where he had left his van. A text had just informed him it was on its way. He stood, shivering, outside the hospital entrance, peering at every car that passed by.

A few smokers huddled in dressing gowns and slippers, one clutching an IV stand. Some people might sneer at how ill patients would stand outside in the cold just to get their nicotine fix. But Gabe understood.

We all have our addictions. Things we value even more than life itself. Things we know will probably kill us. In a way, they make life simpler. You know what's going to get you. You're not blindsided. As Bill Hicks said: 'It's you people dying of nothing that are the problem.'

A car horn beeped. He glanced up. A white Toyota with 'Ace Cabs' stuck wonkily on the side had pulled up in the pick-up area. He shuffled over. The taxi driver was a bald Asian man with a small goatee.

'For Gabriel?' Gabe asked.

'Yeah.'

He climbed inside, wincing a little as he did so.

'Newton Green Services, yeah?'

'Yes. Thanks.'

He eased himself into the seat and fumbled for the seatbelt.

'Been in an accident?'

'Sorry?'

'A lot of people we pick up from here have been in accidents on the motorway. Nearest one, innit?'

'I suppose.'

'What happened?'

'Just a shunt.'

'Yeah? We had one the other day where this old dear had a heart attack at the wheel . . .'

Gabe leaned back and tuned him out. He was tired and cold; brittle bones draped in a sprinkling of skin. It felt like going over a bump might cause him to dissolve into dust. He kept wondering if he had done the right thing, telling Maddock about the car, sharing the photos. He worried that the Samaritan would not be happy. But then, this wasn't about him. He yawned. It hurt. The motorway passed in a blur of darkness and light.

'Whereabouts d'you want dropping, mate?'

The taxi pulled into the services car park. Gabe must have dozed off for a few minutes. The driver didn't appear to notice or care. Gabe blinked.

'Erm, could you just go down to the bottom and pull up next to the VW camper van?'

'Okay.'

The taxi trundled down to where the van was still parked. Gabe had a momentary panic. Where were his keys? He patted his pockets and found them in the top-right one, where he never put them.

'Thanks. How much is that?'

'Eighteen forty.'

He had the same fleeting panic about his wallet, and then found it in his other pocket, where he usually put his keys.

He fumbled out a crumpled twenty and handed it to the cab driver. 'Call it twenty.'

He probably couldn't afford to be so generous, but he was too exhausted to care.

'Cheers, mate.'

Gabe climbed out of the cab, clutching at his side. He looked around, feeling nervous. As the cab pulled away, part of him wanted to shout for the driver to come back. Not to leave him here, on his own. Stupid, he knew. The car park was busy. Vehicles came and went. People trudged in and out of the brightly lit services. A thin woman with a large brown Labrador traipsed around a narrow strip of grass, chanting: 'Wees and poos. C'mon, Bourbon. Wees and poos.'

Normal service-station stuff. Except nothing felt normal any more. Everything felt darker, sharper, more suspicious. He had never thought about the danger of sleeping in his van before. He had heard about people being attacked and robbed, but he had always thought that, as a six-foot-three male, he was safe. Now, the tug of the stitches in his stomach reminded him that he was also vulnerable.

'Good girl, Bourbon!'

The dog was taking a crap. The woman sounded delighted beyond measure, and she was hardly going to attack him with a loaded poo bag. He just needed to get some sleep. He was tired and jittery. And this was not a random attack, he reminded himself. The man had what he wanted. Gabe didn't think he was going to come back.

He unlocked the camper-van door, climbed inside and almost imitated the dog as a voice said: 'You gotta do something about those locks, man.'

The Samaritan sipped the bitter coffee that Gabe had heated on the small stove.

'How did you get in here?'

'Told you – you need better locks.'

'You scared the shit out of me.'

The Samaritan shrugged.

Something else occurred to Gabe. 'How did you even know where to find me?'

'I got my ways.'

Wasn't that the truth, Gabe thought.

'I heard some idiot had got himself stabbed at Newton Green Services. White male, early forties.'

'And you just presumed it was me?'

'Someone was always gonna try to kill you some day. So? What happened?'

Gabe told him.

'I think he wanted the stuff we found in the car.'

The Samaritan listened, long legs crossed, face impassive. When Gabe had finished, he didn't speak for a long while.

'Okay,' he said eventually. 'This is what we're going to do.'

'We?'

'You want my help or not?'

Gabe often felt that by accepting help from the Samaritan

he was making a lot of very small deals with the devil. But what choice did he have?

He sighed. 'Okay.'

'You need to leave your van here and then go check yourself in at a hotel.'

'Why?'

'Because, in this van, you're a sitting duck.'

'But the man got what he wanted.'

'And you got a good look at him.'

'You think he'll come back?'

The Samaritan stared at him with his fathomless eyes.

'I would.'

'All right.'

'You can take my car.'

'You're sure?'

'It's just temporary. You keep your head down and wait to hear from me.'

'What about you?'

'I'll stay in your van. If your man comes back, I'll be waiting for him and we'll have a little chat. Understand?'

Gabe nodded slowly.

'All right.'

'Don't worry. He won't bother you again.'

The Samaritan sat back and grinned. The strange, shiny stone in his tooth gleamed. Gabe tried to contain a shiver.

Gabe had found it best not to think about what lay behind that smile. Just like he tried not to wonder who this man really was, why he wanted to help him or what he might want one day in return.

'Some people call me the Samaritan.'

But sometimes, Gabe wondered what the others called him.

33

Alice sat on a swing in the run-down playground, pushing herself slowly back and forth. It was getting dark. Younger children and their parents had gone, heading home for dinner, baths and bed. One group of teenagers remained, pushing each other too fast on the small roundabout.

Alice kept her head down, swinging quietly. No one took much notice of a child in a playground, and she looked old enough to walk home on her own. That was what Fran had always told her. Hide in plain sight. Hang out in a playground, or park, near a school. Near other families and parents. Somewhere that people expect to see children, among other children. If anyone asks where your mum is, point at someone in the distance or say they're just coming. Hang tight and wait for me to call.

'*Wait for me to call.*'

That was the other thing Fran had always told her. If something goes wrong, if I don't reply to your text, wait for me to call you. Don't call me. It's too risky.

She had tried. She had waited and waited. The mobile on her lap remained dark and silent. And then she had broken the rule. She just needed to hear Fran's voice. But the voice she got was automated, telling her the number was unavailable.

She pushed herself back and forth restlessly. The swing squeaked like an animal in pain. There was still time, she told herself. Still time. Even as a weak drizzle began to spit from the sky and her fingers numbed with cold. Still time. Just wait.

Because she didn't want to think about the end of waiting. About what happened if she stopped. About what that meant. About the final thing Fran had told her.

'If I don't call, it means something bad has happened. I might be hurt. Or dead. So, you don't call me. You call this number. And you do what we planned. Yes?'

She remembered nodding, thinking that she was agreeing to something that would never happen. Despite what had happened before. Despite the very bad thing that they were never supposed to talk about. The very bad thing that Alice pretended she couldn't remember. But sometimes she did. Bits of it. She remembered the man. And the blood. And her mum – her real mum.

She had felt safe with Fran. She loved her, in a way. She had no one else. But now, Fran was gone and Alice was the most frightened she had ever been.

She stared down at the phone. Just a little longer, she told herself. Just a little longer.

34

Katie hated being late for her children. She had always promised she would never let them down. She would always be there for them.

Even before Mum's drinking had spiralled into dependency there had been too many occasions when she had arrived blurry-eyed at the school gates, blaming bad traffic or an appointment. Katie had never forgotten that nervous feeling in the pit of her stomach, the embarrassment of her and Lou being the last ones standing there, watching enviously as their classmates skipped off home with their mummies, mummies whose cars probably didn't clink with the sound of bottles in the boot when they drove around a corner.

Katie might not have achieved much in her life. But one thing she *was* proud of was being a good mum. Yes, she had made mistakes. All parents did. But she had always put her children first. Always tried her hardest to give them a happy, *secure* childhood. To not let history repeat itself.

And now, her mum was doing it again, disrupting Katie's life, upsetting her children's lives. She rang Lou's doorbell. Waited. She could hear the usual commotion inside: Mia crying, Sam shouting, 'Mum's here!', Gracie singing some song from CBeebies.

The door swung open. 'Didn't think you'd be this long,' Lou said, letting Katie step through.

'Sorry,' Katie said. 'Something came up and I had to deal with it.'

'Mum?'

Katie hesitated and then said: 'Actually, Fran.'

Lou stared at her. 'Fran?'

Katie recounted as quickly as possible what had happened at their mum's.

Lou's eyebrows rose higher. 'Fran has a *daughter*?'

'Well, that's what Mum said.'

'I can't believe she never told us. I never even understood why she took off to start with. I mean, we all loved Dad. It wasn't as if she loved him more.'

'Maybe she had her reasons.'

'Maybe.'

Katie rubbed at her temples. She could feel a headache edging in. 'Hopefully, she'll turn up and the police will find the little girl.'

If there is a little girl, she thought.

'Anyway, I'd better get Sam and Gracie back home.'

They walked into the open-plan living room and kitchen. Sam was engrossed in his iPad, Grace and Mia were watching *Gigglebiz*.

'Hi, everyone,' Katie chirped as cheerily as she could manage. 'Time to say goodbye to Auntie Lou.'

'I'll just grab their stuff.' Lou darted back out into the hall.

Her sister was being unusually organized, Katie thought. She had also brushed her hair and applied a little make-up, she noticed. She wondered why. And then she spotted the jacket slung over the back of one of the kitchen chairs.

Lou reappeared, clutching Sam and Gracie's bags and coats.

'Where is he?' Katie asked.

'Sorry, who?'

Lou was a terrible liar. She followed Katie's gaze and her shoulders slumped, her face adopting its usual sulky look.

'I wasn't supposed to pick your kids up today. I'd already made plans. I couldn't just cancel. I was doing you a favour.'

Katie opened her mouth to argue but knew that, this time, she was on the back foot.

'You should have told me,' she said. 'I just like to know.'

'Know what?'

They turned. Steve stood in the doorway, shirtless, skin glistening with water from the shower. He was muscular and stocky, with a shaven head and tattoos down one arm. As always, his manner was superficially pleasant, but there was something about him that Katie didn't like. Or maybe it was because she knew the losers Lou normally picked and was always expecting the worst from him.

'Hi, Steve,' she said neutrally.

'All right, Katie.' He smiled, and Katie felt sure that he was enjoying her unease at his semi-naked appearance. He held out a shirt to Lou. 'Could you be a darling and stick that in the wash with my jacket?'

'No problem.'

Lou took the shirt and then picked up the jacket from the chair. A high-visibility police officer's jacket.

'Just off shift?' Katie asked.

'Yeah. Doing a bit of overtime. Got a couple of days off now, though.' Without taking his eyes from hers, he reached over and rubbed Lou's backside. 'Plan to spend it wisely.'

Katie smiled tightly. 'Nice. Well, I should get going. Come on, Sam, Gracie. We need to go home. It's getting late.'

She bundled them into the car, distracting them with questions about their day, their friends, their lessons, what they had for lunch. All of which were generally greeted with the same responses: 'Good.' 'Okay.' 'Can't remember.' 'I've forgotten.' 'Can we watch TV when we get home?' 'I'm hungry. Have you got any sweets?'

It wasn't until they were halfway along the high street that Gracie asked, 'Why were you late, Mummy?'

Katie smiled at her in the rear-view mirror.

'Just bad traffic, sweetheart.'

Once home, she settled the pair of them in the living room and went to make them some bedtime snacks. As she poured milk and arranged biscuits on a plate, she thought about her mother again.

'She was here. Today.'

Okay, her mother had invented dramas before. Worked herself into histrionics, fuelled by drink and paranoia. But something about this afternoon's episode was troubling Katie. She had seemed so certain. And yet it was so implausible. Why would Fran come back after all this time? Did she really have a daughter? It was obvious what the young police officer who responded to her call had thought.

'I'll put out a call,' he had said as she walked him to the door. 'See if we've had any reports of a little girl found wandering on her own. Better safe than sorry, eh?'

Better safe than sorry. Katie got the implication. I think your mother's probably a nutjob, but I'll ask a few questions to ease my conscience.

She had nodded. 'I understand. Thank you.'

'And if you hear from your sister, could you let us know?'

'Of course.'

She had watched him climb into his car and drive away. From the kitchen she heard the clink of the wine bottle.

She couldn't blame him, really. Part of her would like to dismiss the whole thing as a figment of her mother's drunken imagination. But somehow, she couldn't. And that raised questions:

If Fran had come back, why go to their mother? They had never been close. And if she did have a daughter, why on earth would she leave her and disappear? And where *was* the little girl?

She put the snacks on the tray and walked back to the living room. Gracie was intent upon *Peppa Pig* and Sam was spread out across the sofa, watching *Spider-Man* on his iPad. She hovered for a moment in the doorway, soothed by the sight of them, happy and safe in their cocoon.

Her mobile rang. She reversed, put the tray back down on the kitchen table and picked it up.

'Hello.'

No reply, but Katie could hear breathing.

'Hello?'

'Is that Katie?'

A young girl's voice, hesitant, nervous.

'Yes. Who is this?'

Another pause. 'My name is Alice. Fran told me to call you if I was ever in trouble.'

Alice.

'Where's Fran?' Katie asked.

'I don't know. Please, can you help me?'

Katie debated. She peered in at Sam and Gracie. Warm and secure in their cosy home. She couldn't just leave them here, on their own. Then she thought: what if *they* were lost, alone and scared, in the dark? She would want someone to help them.

'We have to find her. Before something terrible happens.'

'Okay. Tell me where you are.'

35

A hotel corridor. Gabe stumbled along it, staring at doors with numbers. It felt as strange and unfamiliar to him as an alien spacecraft. He glanced at the card in his hand: 421. He squinted at the directions on the walls. Right, then left, left again, and he found himself in front of a door bearing the matching number.

For a moment, he couldn't think what to do with the piece of plastic in his hand. Then it came back to him. He swiped it in the slot by the door handle. There was a buzz. He pushed the door and walked inside.

Gabe fumbled for a switch. Nothing happened. He tried again, felt bemused. Then he remembered. The card. He had to put the card in another slot by the door. He stuck it in and the room flooded with light.

He stared around. To most people, this room would probably seem small, basic. To Gabe, it seemed immense. It had been a long time since he'd slept in a proper bed-room. A bedroom with a double bed, a desk, a bathroom. The contrast hit him like a sledgehammer. He had spent so long existing in his small van he'd forgotten what it was like to live like a normal person. The space felt extravagant. As did the cost. Gabe had a reserve of savings from the sale of the house, and his outgoings were minimal. But he couldn't afford to do this for more than a couple of nights.

He chucked his bag on the bed and took out his painkillers. He walked into the bathroom and filled a plastic glass with water to swill them down. He avoided glancing in the mirror. He'd never liked mirrors and he knew what it would show him. A pale, thin man with greying hair and too many lines for his age. A face carved with lost hopes and regret.

We talk about life like it's some magical elixir, he thought. Yet life is your own slow crawl along the dead man's mile. Doesn't matter how many diversions you take, eventually we're all heading one way. The only difference is how long the journey takes. He placed his hand on the wound on his side. Tonight, he almost took the fast lane.

He closed the bathroom door and walked back into the bedroom. He sat on the bed, suddenly at a loss. What to do? He flicked idly through the folder telling him about the hotel's services. TV, free wi-fi, bar/restaurant and something sticky between the final pages. He hastily put it down again.

It took several attempts before he managed to summon a few blurry channels on the TV. He gave up and walked around the room. He looked in the wardrobe – a few hangers fastened to the rail and some extra pillows. He opened the drawers beside the bed. Empty except for a small Bible. He stared at it, thinking about the other Bible. The underlined passages. *An eye for an eye. The Other People.* He slammed the drawer shut again.

He should be exhausted. And a full-sized bed was a rare luxury. But he had gone past exhaustion. He felt alert, wired.

He thought about the hotel services. *Bar/restaurant.* He probably wasn't supposed to drink, after the blood loss and on top of all the painkillers. But he was marooned in a strange hotel, with no purpose, no food and nothing better to do.

He picked up his card key, grabbed his phone and wandered downstairs to the bar.

He ordered a glass of red wine and took it to a quiet table in a corner. From speakers somewhere above him, Neil Diamond crooned about 'Sweet Caroline'. This was after Phil Collins had opined that she was 'an easy lover', following on from Lionel Richie saying 'Hello'. He was pretty sure that somewhere along the line Robbie Williams would be declaring his love for 'Angels'. Which was somewhat ironic on a playlist obviously forged in hell. Bar music, Gabe thought – music for people too drunk to get away from it.

He sipped at the wine. It tasted a bit sour. He wasn't sure if that was a reflection on the quality of the bottle or just the fact that he hadn't drunk wine in a long while. He and Jenny always used to crack open a bottle – or sometimes two – in the evening. They would sit around the breakfast bar and talk to each about their days over the rims of their glasses. At least, they used to. Later, he would end up drinking alone with his reheated dinner after Izzy had gone to bed and Jenny had retreated to the snug with a book.

And yet, he really wished Jenny was here. The thought slunk in out of nowhere like a stray cat. And once settled in his mind, it refused to move. He remembered her arms around him, the citrussy smell of her hair. Her warm breath on his face as she told him that it would be okay.

It had been a long time since Gabe had been comforted by anyone. Touched by anyone. Gabe tried not to think about it too much. But, sometimes, it got to him. He yearned to be part of a couple again. To have a female body next to his at night. To share secret smiles, kisses, jokes. Even if, for a long while, the communication between himself and Jenny had been more in the way of stone-cold silences. He even missed that.

You don't *need* another person to make your life complete. But life, like a jigsaw with missing pieces, is hard to complete on your own. And there endeth the drunken philosophy for the evening. His phone started to ring.

'Hello?'

'Gabriel?'

A woman's voice. No one else called him Gabriel.

'DI Maddock?'

'Can you talk? Is this a bad time?'

'Yes. I mean no, I can talk.'

'Where are you?'

'A hotel.'

'No van?'

'Not tonight.'

'Okay. Which hotel?'

'Erm, Holiday Inn, off Junction 18. In the bar.'

'Okay. I'll be there in about half an hour.'

'Why? I mean, I didn't expect to hear from you again so soon.'

'There's been a development.'

'What sort of development?'

'I'll tell you when I get there.'

'Can't you just tell me on the phone?'

'No.' A pause. 'You need to see this.'

36

Katie pulled up near the park. She felt nervous and guilty. She had never left Sam and Gracie on their own at home before. Christ. She could be reported to the police. She had locked the door but left Sam a key. In her sternest voice she had told him not to open the door to anyone but her. She would be half an hour, tops.

He had rolled his eyes. 'I'm not an idiot.'

'I know. You're very grown-up, which is why I'm trusting you like this.'

'Where are you going, Mummy?' Gracie had asked, hovering at the living-room door.

'I just have to help a little girl who is in trouble.'

'Why?'

'She's your cousin, and she's lost, and I have to bring her back here.'

'We have another cousin? What's her name?'

'Alice. Now, I'll make hot chocolate for everyone when I get back. Okay?'

'Yay! Hot chocolate!'

The park was only a ten-minute drive away. Katie knew it well. She had played there herself as a child and even taken Sam and Gracie once or twice. But this evening it looked smaller and more run-down than she remembered. The street felt narrow and gloomy; several of the street-lights were broken.

Still, the girl had been clever. The school was just up the road and parents would often bring their children here to let off steam on the way home. Of course, at seven thirty, all the other children had gone – back to nice, warm houses with families that loved them. Or so Katie liked to think. Perhaps that wasn't true. Perhaps some went back to homes where their parents argued and threw things, or to homes where Dad was busy, and Mum didn't care, and they were left to fend for themselves. It was easy to imagine that other people had the fairy tale, but the truth was the shiny front doors, hanging baskets and neatly mown lawns didn't tell the whole story.

She locked the car and looked around. No sign of anyone; even the small bungalows that lined the road looked quiet and empty, only the faintest slivers of light through pulled curtains. She shivered.

What are you doing here, Katie? You should be home, with your own children. Let the police deal with this.

She zipped up her jacket and shoved the thoughts away. Whatever was going on, a little girl was in trouble, and if either of her children were ever alone and scared, then she hoped someone would help them. It was something their dad had always said to them: *If not you, then who?*

She entered the park and walked along a pathway that ran past a small pond. The playground was on her left. It looked deserted. She took out her phone and pulled up the most recent number. She pressed call. Distantly, she heard the sound of another phone ringing. She waited and then a small figure emerged from the shadows beneath the climbing frame.

'Alice?'

The girl hovered uncertainly. She was very slight, dressed in jeans, Uggs and a dark hoodie. In one hand, she clutched a small pink rucksack decorated with purple flowers. Katie's heart constricted. She looked so young, so vulnerable.

'Are you Katie?'

Katie nodded. 'Yes, I'm your –' She hesitated. 'Aunt' sounded odd when they had only just met. 'I'm your mum's sister.'

The girl looked down, her face cast into more shadows. 'Fra— . . . Mum told me, if something ever happened, that I should call you. That you would do the right thing.'

'Where is your mum, Alice?'

'I – I don't know.'

'Is she in some kind of trouble?'

Alice nodded then jumped at a rustle of bushes from the right. Katie jumped, too, squinting into the semi-darkness. The girl's twitchiness was contagious. Probably just a bird or the wind. Still, Katie realized that she didn't really want to hang around here in the deserted park any longer.

'C'mon,' she said. 'It's getting late.'

Alice walked slowly out of the playground, clutching her bag like a shield, small shoulders hunched. She stopped a short distance from Katie. When children are scared, Katie thought, they bundle up like hedgehogs, all tightly bound, spikes out. But at some point, especially when they are tired and hungry, they have to let it go.

'Have you eaten?' she asked.

Alice shook her head.

'D'you like cheese on toast?'

A tentative nod.

'So do my children.'

'You have children?'

'Yep. Sam's ten, Gracie is five. They like cheese on toast with brown sauce. What about you?'

'I like cheese . . . but not brown sauce.'

'Okay, just cheese then.'

Katie saw the spikes gradually retracting, Alice's shoulders relaxing. She held out her hand. After a momentary hesitation, Alice took it.

'Let's go home.'

Alice remained silent on the journey back, the bag resting on her lap. It had made a strange rattling sound when she sat down, like she had stones or something inside. Katie was curious, but she didn't push it. Questions could wait. The police could wait. For now, the girl needed food, rest and a warm bed.

Katie glanced at Alice again as they pulled onto her street. She had taken her hood down, revealing more of her face, which was pale and fine-boned. Long dark hair hung lankly either side, except Katie couldn't help noticing that the roots were lighter. Almost blonde. Dyed? *Why would you dye a child's hair?*

As if feeling her eyes on her, Alice looked over.

'What?'

'Nothing,' Katie said brightly. 'We're here.'

'This is your house?'

'Yes,' Katie said, suddenly conscious of how small and twee her tiny terraced house looked, with its hanging basket and cheap potted plants.

'It's nice,' Alice said. 'Like a proper home.'

The longing in her voice squeezed Katie's heart again. What the hell was her sister thinking? What had she got herself into? Katie couldn't claim to have been close to Fran, even before she left. They were very different. Fran had always been highly strung, impulsive, argumentative. More like Mum, in fact. But Katie couldn't believe that she would just desert her daughter, not unless she had a very good reason, or unless . . . something terrible had happened.

'Okay.' She pulled on the handbrake. 'Let's go and get you fed.'

They walked up the short path to the front door. Katie inserted her key and pushed it open.

'We're back!' she called out, leading Alice into the kitchen.

Sam and Gracie bounded out from the living room, curiosity winning out over the television and the iPad.

'This is Sam and Gracie,' Katie introduced. 'And this is Alice, your cousin.'

'We didn't know we had another cousin,' Sam said.

'Alice's mum lives a long way away,' Katie said.

'In Australia?' Gracie asked. 'Jonas and his family moved to Australia, and that's a long way away.'

Katie smiled at Alice. 'Jonas was in Gracie's class last year,' she explained.

'In Australia they have spiders the size of dinner plates,' Sam said. 'But they don't hurt you. It's the little ones that can kill you.'

'Sa–am,' Katie warned, but Alice smiled.

'Redbacks,' she said. 'They live under the rims of toilets.'

'Yuck,' Gracie said.

Sam grinned, regarding Alice with new-found respect: 'Do you like Spider-Man?'

Alice shrugged. 'I prefer Wonder Woman.'

'I like Peppa Pig,' Gracie informed them.

'Peppa Pig is for girls,' Sam announced loftily. 'Spider-Man is for boys.'

'Boys and girls can like both,' Alice said.

Sam thought about this. 'S'pose. D'you want to see my Spider-Man game?'

'Okay.'

'That's a good idea,' Katie said. 'Why don't you all go in the other room while I make Alice something to eat? It's past bedtime and she hasn't had any tea. Alice, you can put your hoodie and bag in the hall –'

'No . . . thank you.'

'Sorry?'

'I – I'd like to keep the bag with me.'

Alice clutched it protectively to her chest.

'What's in it?' Gracie asked.

'Just . . . pebbles. I collect them.'

'I collect Lego cards,' Sam said.

'O-kay,' Katie said slowly. The flowered rucksack was obviously some kind of security blanket. 'That's fine. Just the hoodie, then. Sam, can you show Alice?'

Sam led Alice into the hall, Gracie skipping behind. Katie took out some sliced bread and cheese and tried to ignore the uneasy feeling in her stomach. The feeling that was telling her that something about this was all wrong. Alice was scared and nervous. But not scared or nervous *enough*. She didn't seem surprised by her mother's sudden disappearance. Hadn't even asked when she would be back.

She told me if anything happened to call you.

Why? What had Fran been expecting to happen? Why dye the girl's hair? And there was another thing: Alice had said 'Fran' instead of 'Mum' on the phone, *and* in the park, before she caught herself.

Katie glanced towards the living room, where she could hear Gracie babbling excitedly. Children were much more accepting, Katie thought. Of change, of new people. Which was what made them so vulnerable. Of course, Alice was only a child herself, but there was something about her that unnerved Katie. A sense that her presence here was a risk, to all of them.

She hoped she had made the right decision tonight.

She hoped she hadn't just invited a cuckoo into their nest.

37

Maddock walked into the bar, a bag slung over one shoulder, intent on her phone. She didn't glance up as she sat down at Gabe's table. Gabe waited. He remembered these power plays from the police interviews. The intention: to make him sweat, wondering what they might have on him, wondering if, even though he knew he was innocent, they might somehow find *something* to implicate him.

After a few seconds, Maddock hooked the bag over the back of the chair, put down the phone and met his gaze across the table. She didn't smile. But then, she never did.

'Thanks for meeting me.'

Like he had a choice.

'That's okay.'

'You look like shit.'

'Getting stabbed will do that to you.'

'Right.'

'Why are you here, apart from the sympathy, obviously?'

'This isn't strictly an official visit.'

'Oh.'

'So first, I'm going to ask you again – unofficially – where did you get those photographs?'

Gabe stared at her. 'Why? Have you found something out?'

'Where did you get the photos, Gabriel?'

He sat back and folded his arms. His side throbbed.

She squared him with a look. 'Okay. You know what my average day consists of? Kids stabbing other kids because they wore the wrong trainers on the wrong street. Domestics, some of which we have visited several times, who don't press charges until it's too late because we're dealing with a homicide. Druggies, alcoholics, people with mental health issues who should be in a facility where they can be treated appropriately instead of left to wander the streets until they forget to take their medication, scalp someone with a machete and get put in a police cell.'

'Sounds fun.'

'It's a ball. But then, sometimes, a case comes along that makes you remember why you wanted to join the force. One that really gets to you. One that worries away at the back of your mind, keeps you awake at night.'

'Like mine.'

'I really wanted to find the person responsible. All along, something about it felt off. I never thought it was a robbery.'

'Which was why you thought I had something to do with it.'

'Nine times out of ten it's someone the victim knows. But I never liked that anonymous call. Always wondered if there was an accomplice. Maybe one that got cold feet.'

He tried to stop the familiar feeling of anger, grinding his teeth to stop him saying something he might regret.

'Is this going somewhere?'

'Yes. I have a friend who works at the coroner's office.

I was passing, on my way home, so I asked if I could see the files they held on your wife and daughter, including post-mortem photographs.'

She reached into her bag and took out a thick plastic evidence folder. She placed it on the table and then laid her hand over it. 'Before we go on, in this *unofficial* capacity, I want to ask you a few more questions.'

'Okay.'

'How many photographs of your daughter would you say you had at home?'

'Maybe half a dozen, but the ones on the walls were older. We meant to put up some new ones – they change so quickly, but . . .' He trailed off. But they hadn't got around to it because it hadn't seemed urgent, important.

'Do you have any more recent photographs of Izzy?'

'Yes. On my phone.'

'Can I see the most recent?'

Gabe took out his phone and flagged up the photo. His heart tore a little every time he did. It was Izzy at the local park. She was eating an ice lolly and smiling into the camera, squinting slightly.

They didn't go out very often, just him and Izzy. But Jenny had had a bad cold so he'd offered to take Izzy out for a while so she could rest. It had been unseasonably warm, blue skies, golden sun. Izzy had been excited and chatty.

'Daddy, push me on the swings. Daddy, watch me on the slide. Daddy, look how high I can jump on the trampoline.'

Afterwards, they had fed the ducks and then sat outside the small café, Izzy eating the sticky orange lolly that had left splodgy stains on her pink dress. It had been one of those small pockets of perfect. A few precious hours where everything in his world had aligned. He'd realized that he was happy.

And then it was over. He had promised Izzy they would do it again. And of course, they never did. Because stuff – unimportant, inconsequential things – got in the way.

'When was this taken?' Maddock asked.

'Err, there's a date.' He showed her on the phone.

She squinted at it. 'So, still several months before the murders.'

'Yes. Jenny had been busy. We both were.' He frowned. When had they stopped documenting every moment of Izzy's life? When had they become so fragmented as a family?

'The photo used in the newspapers was a school photo?'

'Yes, from the previous year.'

Maddock drummed her fingers on the table. 'Your father-in-law did the formal identification. Whose decision was that?'

'No one's, really. I was supposed to do it but then I was ill, passed out . . .'

'So, you never saw your daughter after she died?'

'No.'

She chewed her lip. Obviously came to a decision.

'Okay. These are the photographs you gave me.'

She opened the plastic folder and laid the photos of Jenny and Izzy on the table a short distance apart.

She gave him a moment to look at them.

'This' – Maddock took another photo out of the folder and laid it next to the photo of Jenny – 'is the photo of your wife I obtained from the coroner.'

Gabe stared at the photograph. It was identical to the one Harry had given him. His heart didn't fall. He had expected it. Sometimes, you just knew. Jenny was dead. He could feel the vacuum she had left.

He nodded. 'Okay. They're the same.'

Maddock reached into the folder again. 'This is the second photo I obtained from the coroner.'

He felt himself tense. It all came down to this.

'This is the little girl who was found dead at your home. The little girl your father-in-law identified as your daughter.'

She placed the photograph on the table next to the photo of Izzy.

His world seem to expand, contract and shatter all at once. The girl's face was pale and fine-boned, blonde hair swept back from a high forehead. She looked so similar, familiar even, but . . .

'It's not Izzy.'

'No. I also did a little more checking on the coroner's report.' She sighed and showed him a scan of a document on her phone. One sentence had been ringed in red:

'*Front milk tooth missing. Suggests trauma.*'

He stared at her. 'Trauma?'

'The tooth was knocked out. It was recovered at the scene.'

The significance dawned. 'Izzy had already lost her front milk tooth. I told you, in my statement.'

She nodded. 'I can see how the confusion arose but, still, someone should have picked up on it.' She paused. '*I* should have fucking well picked up on it.'

A smile spread across his face. He couldn't help it. He wanted to laugh. To cry. To jump up and down. All this time, he had known, but he hadn't *known*. It hadn't been proven. Now, here it was. Evidence.

'I'm sorry,' he started to say. 'I know it's wrong. Another little girl is dead, but —'

'I understand. It isn't *your* little girl. Don't be sorry. I should be the one saying sorry to you. You were right. Your daughter did not die that night. She may even still be alive.' She leaned forward. 'That's why, if you have any information that could help us find her, I need you to share it with me.'

He debated. He didn't owe Harry anything, but fuck it, Harry still owed *him* an explanation. He wanted to look him in the eye and call him a liar.

'No. Not really.'

'Okay.' Said in a tone that implied she didn't believe him. 'There's something else you should know. We found the car.'

He waited, trying to look less guilty than he felt.

'Right.'

'There was a body – in the boot. Been there a while.'

He tried his best to look shocked.

'Oh God.'

'Yeah. That's not all.'

'It's not?'

'We found another victim nearby. A woman.'

This time, his look of shock was genuine.

'*A woman?*'

'We don't know who she is yet. We're not even sure if she'll regain consciousness.'

'She's alive?'

She gave him an odd look. 'If you can call it that.'

His mind tried to process this new information. A woman. But who was she?

'Gabriel, did anyone else know about the car?'

The Samaritan. Night work.

He shook his head. 'I don't think so.'

'But you can't be sure.'

'No.'

'And you never looked inside the boot when you found the car.'

'No.'

'Good. Stick to that story.'

'*Story?* You think I had something to do with it?'

'No, I don't. But be prepared to answer a lot of questions. You are going to be in the spotlight all over again, okay?'

'Okay.'

'And get a good solicitor.'

38

Remarkably, the children went up to bed with minimal fuss, even Sam, who liked to stretch out his bedtime routine well past breaking point. Staying up for a whole extra hour, and the evening's unexpected excitement, must have tired them out. To be fair, Alice had looked as if she could have dropped off face down in her cheese on toast. She yawned with every mouthful and dark half-moons circled her blue eyes. Katie wondered when she had last slept or eaten properly.

Katie had found her some of Sam's old pyjamas to wear and eventually located the blow-up bed in the cupboard under the stairs, buried beneath several boxes of random junk. She had put it up in Gracie's room, her daughter being delighted to have her first sleepover.

Forty minutes later, when Katie checked in on them, they were all asleep: Gracie half curled on her side, one arm cuddling Peppa Pig, one flung out over the covers; Sam in his usual starfish shape, limbs strewn haphazardly around his bed, enveloped safely in oblivion.

Only Alice didn't look relaxed, even in sleep. Her knees were drawn tightly to her chest and, instead of a soft toy, she still clutched the odd, rattling rucksack, like a shield against invisible monsters.

Katie watched her for a moment then pulled the bedroom door closed and padded downstairs, into the kitchen. She thought about making a cup of tea then changed her mind and headed to the fridge. She pulled out a three-quarters-full bottle of white wine.

Katie wasn't a big drinker. Her hours made it fairly impossible, for a start, unless she got into the habit of drinking in the morning. But also, when you have an alcoholic in the family, the appeal of a cool glass of wine diminishes, mixed up as it is with memories of raised voices, broken crockery, tears and screaming.

Still, right now, she felt like she needed something to numb that nervous, churning feeling in her stomach. She poured a large glass and took a sip, wincing slightly at the sharp taste. Then she sat down at the breakfast bar and picked up her phone.

She hadn't wanted to press Alice too much tonight on what had happened or where Fran was. The poor child was obviously exhausted and traumatized. But she *had* asked if she could have her mum's number. Alice had reluctantly acquiesced. It was a different number to the one Katie had in her phone, but the result was the same. Her calls had gone straight to an automated message: 'The number you are calling is unavailable.'

What's going on, Fran? Why did you come back and where are you now?

Whatever the reason, it must have been desperate for her to leave Alice with their mother. Why hadn't she come to Katie? But then, Katie knew the answer to that one. It was because Katie would have tried to talk her out of whatever it was she was doing. Told her to go to the police.

That was her role. The good one, the reliable one. The

one who everyone took for granted. Fran wouldn't come to her for help. But she would use her in an emergency. A last resort. Good old dependable Katie. The one who would always pick up the pieces, never mind that they might cut her own fingers to ribbons.

She sank her head into her hands. She was tired. The weight of the responsibility, of the day's events, was bearing down on her. Tomorrow she would persuade Alice that they needed to go to the police. But then, what would that mean for Alice? Social workers. Care. Did she really want to abandon her to the state system? She was just a child. A confused, lost child. Katie was her aunt. She was family, and she had a duty to look after her. It was what mothers did. *Christ, what a mess.*

She rose and tipped the rest of the wine down the sink. It wasn't helping. It never did. *Problems float,* she thought. She walked wearily out into the hall and almost went flying as she caught her foot on something by the stairs.

'*Shit.*'

It was one of the boxes from the cupboard. She must have left it lying there after she got out the blow-up bed. She rubbed at her toe. She really should sort some of these boxes. The house was too small, and they were full of junk. Old pictures, cards, leaflets. But Katie found it hard to throw things away. She knew how easily things could be lost. Life, family, love. It was all so fragile. Perhaps that was why she hung onto those faded photos and scribbled pictures on crumpled bits of paper.

She bent down to shove the box to one side and something fluttered from the top. A drawing of Gracie's. A strange stick family with odd-coloured hair, distorted limbs and a huge Gothic house looming behind them, complete with thunderclouds, rainbows and spiders. Part charming, part Tim Burtonesque nightmare.

She smiled and was about to stuff it back in the box when she realized the picture was drawn on the back of something else. She turned it over. A young girl's face smiled back at her.

HAVE YOU SEEN ME?

The flyer. She had meant to look for it but, with everything else that had happened, she'd completely forgotten. She felt a little guilty that she had let Gracie doodle on the back. But at least she had the number. She would call tomorrow and find out how the thin man – Gabe – was doing. After all, he didn't have anyone else to look out for him.

She might curse her family at times, but at least she had family: her precious children. She couldn't imagine the pain of losing everything – your partner, your only daughter – in such a terrible way.

She stared at the picture. Izzy. A pretty little girl. Blonde hair. Blue eyes. Wide, gappy smile. Pretty, and somehow *familiar.* Something about the eyes, the smile. Katie suddenly had the strongest feeling that she had seen her before. Of course, she had seen the *flyer* before. That was probably it. But still, there was something else, something . . .

A stair creaked behind her. She spun around. Alice stood on the bottom step, long dark hair framing her face, eyes wide and haunted, a Japanese horror movie in Marvel pyjamas.

'Alice – you made me jump!'

'Sorry.'

'No, it's okay.' Katie stuffed the piece of paper into the pocket of her hoodie and tried to force a smile. 'What's the matter? Can't you sleep?'

'I need to talk to you.'

'Okay. C'mon. Let's go in the kitchen. D'you want some milk?'

'No, thank you.'

Alice sat down at the table. She still clutched the rucksack. It rattled restlessly. For some reason – stupid, Katie knew – something about the sound set her teeth on edge. *Clickety-click. Clickety-click.*

'Are you worried about your mum?' she asked now.

A small nod.

'Well, look, tomorrow, we'll call the police . . .'

'*No!*' Alice's cry was anguished.

'But they can help.'

'No.' Alice shook her head. 'You can't call them.'

Katie looked at her helplessly. 'Why not?'

'Fran said they would take her away. I'd be left in danger.'

'Alice, why do you say "Fran" sometimes, not "Mum"?'

'I . . .' She looked guilty, caught in a lie. Then she sighed. 'Because she isn't my real mum.'

And there it was. Somehow, Katie had sensed something was wrong – very wrong – about all of this.

'Where's your real mum?'

'She's dead.'

'I'm sorry. Are you adopted?'

'No.'

'Then why is Fran looking after you?'

Alice chewed her lip. Katie got the feeling it was a long time since someone had extricated the truth from Alice; it felt like pulling a sliver of glass from a wound.

'Something bad happened. Mum died. So did Emily. Fran saved me.'

Katie felt more confused than ever. 'Who's Emily?'

'She was Fran's little girl.'

'Wait. Fran had a daughter who *died*?'

A nod. 'That's why Fran has to keep me safe. She can't lose me, too.'

Christ. Katie tried to process this. Fran's daughter was *dead*? So, who was this girl? Where were her family? Did she have a father? Did he know where she was, or was he out there somewhere, looking for her?

And that's when it hit her, the realization sideswiping her like a juggernaut.

That feeling of familiarity. The eyes, the smile.

Something bad happened. Mum died.

Her breath seemed to lodge in her chest. Jesus Christ. Could it be possible?

She took the flyer back out of her pocket.

HAVE YOU SEEN ME?

She looked at the photo, then back at Alice. Of course, she was older, her hair had been dyed and her adult teeth had grown through.

But there was no mistake.

'What's that?' Alice asked.

Katie reached for her hand. 'Sweetheart, I think . . . it's you.'

39

Izzy had loved the *Toy Story* movies. Gabe found them incredibly sad. The end of childhood. The fear of becoming old and unwanted. The realization that life moves on without you.

Gabe had found himself reflecting on this a few months before Izzy's fourth birthday. Jenny had set him the task of clearing out some of Izzy's old toys before the house filled with new ones.

'It's either that or buy a bigger house.'

They both knew that that was not on the cards, not with the unspoken fragility of their relationship. And Jenny was right. The house was overflowing with pink plastic.

He had found Buzz beneath a mountain of more recent acquisitions in Izzy's toy box. He stared at his wide plastic smile: to infinity and beyond, or the charity shop? He put him to one side – *he couldn't, just couldn't* – and set about collecting some of her older toys: cheap Barbie knock-offs, a pushchair, dog-eared cuddly toys and other plastic novelties acquired for Christmas or birthdays and never played with. He had divided them into two bin bags. One for the charity shop. One for the tip. By the time he had finished, it had been too late to take them to either, so he had deposited the bags in the garage – and promptly forgotten about them.

Izzy didn't miss the toys. She had plenty of new bits of plastic for Gabe to spend hours putting together and days tripping over. Then, a few weeks later, the weather turned surprisingly warm. Gabe had opened the garage to get out the mower, to cut the grass. Izzy ran in with him and her face fell.

'Why are all my toys in here, Daddy? Are you throwing them away?'

'Well, you haven't played with them for ages.'

'But I want to play with them *now*.'

She began to root determinedly through the bags. Gabe had checked his irritation.

'Izzy – you have lots of lovely new toys. We haven't got room for all of them. I'm going to take some of your old toys to the charity shop. You know, like in *Toy Story*, when Andy gives his old toys to the little girl.'

'What about the others?'

He hesitated. 'Well, they have to go to the tip.'

Her eyes had widened in horror.

'But then they'll be burned.'

Crap. Why had he mentioned *Toy Story*?

'Izzy, they're broken, missing bits –'

'But we can't let them be burned just because they're broken. Woody was broken and he got fixed.'

Gabe had sighed. 'Izzy, some things can't be fixed.'

'Why? Why can't we save them all?'

And then she had burst into tears. One of those sudden, violent storms of emotion that gather and break out of nowhere. He had knelt down and held her as she sobbed, her tears soaking hotly through his T-shirt.

He had felt her pain. *Why can't we save them all?* Because we can't. Because life isn't fair. Because we have to pick and choose and, sometimes, those choices will be tough. Sometimes, we don't even get the choice. Not everything or everyone can be fixed with some thread and a dab of glue and we won't all end our days on the front porch in the sunshine.

He didn't say any of this. He wiped her eyes and said, 'Shall we go and get an ice cream?'

After it happened, somewhere within that huge chasm of darkness and pain, Gabe had found himself tasked with clearing out Izzy's room. He couldn't do it. He had shuffled around like a bewildered child himself, unable to give her things away, unable to let a single hair clip go. Eventually, he had called a removals company and everything – all of her toys, clothes and furniture – was put into storage.

Here. He stood staring at the anonymous row of shuttered garage doors, illuminated by the security lighting. Number 327. He hadn't been back to this place, an industrial estate just outside Nottingham, for almost two years. Several times, he had thought about emptying the lock-up, giving away the contents, cancelling the direct debit. But the image of Izzy's face that afternoon in the garage always stopped him.

'Are you throwing them away?'

If he let this go, then it would be the beginning of the end. He would be letting her go, casting aside that lifebuoy of hope that had kept him afloat these last three years. He would be admitting that she wasn't coming back. The end.

He walked over to the keypad beside the door and tapped in the code. Izzy's birthday. He stepped back as the door rolled open and the automatic lighting stuttered into life.

He steeled himself, but the pain still hit him, hard enough

to cause him to wince. All in here. Izzy's life. Her bedroom furniture, her toys, her pictures, playhouse, bike. All neatly stacked in this dark, cold storage space, the incongruity of the bright colours against the dismal cinderblock never starker. Toys need to be played with, he thought. Woody was right about that.

He walked forward, touched the headboard of her bed, her pink Barbie scooter, as if they could impart their memories to him. He realized he found it harder and harder to summon up the image of Izzy playing, or sleeping. She was fading, retreating into the past. And he couldn't call her name or run after her because he was rooted in the present and you can't go back, only forward.

'Gabe?'

He turned. Harry stood in the doorway, white hair haloed in the light. He leaned on his walking stick and looked thinner and more stooped than ever.

Gabe smiled thinly. 'Come in – make yourself at home.'

He watched as Harry took an unsure step forward. Then Gabe pressed a switch on the wall. The automatic door slowly lowered, shutting them both inside.

'What the –?' Harry squinted at him across the lock-up. 'What the hell is going on, Gabe? What is this place?'

'It's all I have left of her.'

He saw Harry blink and look around, taking it all in. He watched every small movement: the bobbing of his Adam's apple, the slight twitch above his left eye, a trembling in his hand.

'You said this was urgent. That there was something I needed to see.'

Gabe nodded. 'That's right. I wanted you to see this. I wanted you to understand how I never gave up hope. How

I kept all of this because I wanted to be ready, for my little girl, when she came home.'

'And that's why you've dragged me out here so late at night? For God's sake!' Harry sighed, but it sounded forced. 'I don't know what more I can do to help you, Gabe.'

'You can tell me the truth.'

'I have.'

'No. You have lied. Right from the start. Right from the day when you misidentified my daughter's body. Those pills Evelyn gave me certainly did the trick, didn't they? Or was it something she slipped into my coffee before we left the hotel? Eye-drops, perhaps? I mean, it was a risk, but you pulled it off. I just need to know why.'

Harry's face regained some of the calm superiority that was the norm.

'I feel sorry for you. I really do. But this time, you've lost it.' He shook his head. 'Open that door or I'm calling the police.'

'You do that. I think they'd like to talk to you – about why you faked a morgue photo, wrongly identified a dead girl. They *know*, Harry. But I wanted to talk to you first.'

Harry hesitated, mobile hovering in his liver-spotted hand. Gabe waited, wondered if he was still going to try and brazen it out. And then he saw Harry's shoulders slump, the sag of defeat. He lowered himself onto the edge of Izzy's bed.

He didn't just look old, he looked ill, Gabe thought, and he could suddenly picture Harry in a few years' time, lowering himself onto a hospital bed in much the same way, tubes hanging from his arms, skinny white legs poking out from his thin gown. Once the master of this domain, now at the mercy of doctors who were wielding dummies when he was wielding scalpels. Death might be indiscriminate, but time is merciless.

'I always thought faking the photo was a step too far,' Harry said. 'But I kept it, just in case. When you told me about finding the car, I had no choice. I had to use it, to convince you to let it go.'

'It almost worked,' Gabe said.

'But not quite.'

'It was the cat.'

'Sorry?'

'That morning, the cat scratched Izzy on her chin. I put a plaster on it. In the photo, there was no scratch. It had to have been taken later.'

Harry shook his head. 'Perhaps it's for the best. You don't know how hard it's been for me, keeping this secret, all this time.'

'*Hard for you?*' Gabe stared at him in disbelief. 'You tried to convince me my daughter was dead. You let me torture myself, searching for her. You let another child be buried in her grave. How . . . how could you do that?'

'"Conscience doth make cowards of us all."' Harry's expression was sharper. 'When you have a child, you would do anything for them. *Anything.* Jenny was our only child – our world. Izzy was our universe.'

'That's why you came to visit them so often.'

'Evelyn never liked you.'

'I'm shocked.'

'It caused friction between her and Jenny. When the truth came out – all those secrets *you'd* been keeping, Gabe – I realized Evelyn was right. You didn't deserve Jenny or Izzy.'

Gabe clenched his fists. 'That has nothing to do with this.'

'Are you *sure*?'

'I —' he faltered.

Harry smiled unpleasantly. 'Didn't you ever wonder? Why me? Why my family? Why did this happen?'

Of course he had. He had wondered if this was what he deserved. Karma, kismet, fate.

Or something else.

We share the pain . . . with those that deserve it.

Gabe's mouth felt dry. 'It wasn't a random attack, was it?'

Harry regarded Gabe as though he were a slow child finally adding up two plus two. He shook his head. 'No. It was because of *what you did*. To *her*. The other girl. The girl whose name you gave to your own daughter, like some kind of sick joke.'

Gabe stared at him. Dread crawled up into his throat. 'Isabella.'

She sleeps. A pale girl in a white room. She doesn't hear the machines that beep and whirr around her. She doesn't feel the touch of Miriam's hand or notice as the nurse leaves the room. The pale girl doesn't hear or see or feel a thing.

But she does dream.

She walks along the beach. Her alabaster skin is kissed golden by the sun and her flaxen hair streaked almost white. Now the butter-yellow orb is setting, melting slowly into the sea. There's a faint breeze, and it casts shimmering ripples across the water, crusting the tops with foam.

Isabella loves the beach. But she isn't supposed to be here. She is supposed to be at her violin lesson. Every Wednesday after dinner. On Monday it's vocal coaching, and Friday it's piano. Her mother tells her she has a special talent for music; she is helping her achieve her potential. But sometimes it feels to Isabella as though her mother is squeezing the joy out of the very thing she loves, like a lemon in a juicer.

At least the violin lessons are out of the house. In her teacher's small seaside terrace. She plays better there. The only reason her mother agreed to it. Miriam, their housekeeper, drops her off and picks her up afterwards. Yes, they have a housekeeper. And a cleaner and a gardener. Isabella knows that she is privileged.

Her father made a lot of money and, when he died when she was *just a baby, he left it to her mother. They live in a big house with acres of gardens and her mother likes to believe that she gives her only daughter everything she could ever want, except, of course, the one thing that any fourteen-year-old really desires: freedom.*

Isabella understands why her mother worries about her. Her father died unexpectedly. Her mother is afraid that she might be taken from her, too. So she tries to build walls around her daughter. To keep her safe. Beautiful walls, but that doesn't stop them being a prison.

So, sometimes, Isabella seeks small moments of escape, like this one.

Mr Webster, her violin teacher, is away for three weeks' holiday. She hasn't told her mother. After school she let Miriam drop her at the small terrace as normal. And then she came to the beach.

Isabella never feels lonely on the beach. Even as summer ebbs away there is always life here. Dog walkers, families packing up their picnics for the day, couples sauntering hand in hand. And the beach itself. Alive with the lapping waves, the restless pebbles and the impatient cawing of the seagulls.

Although the beach is mostly shingle, there's sand right at the water's edge. Isabella likes to take off her shoes and socks and walk along the shoreline, letting the waves lap over her feet, feeling the sand suck at her toes.

She can't bring a towel, so she'll sit on the wall at the edge of the promenade to let her feet dry. Sometimes she'll make musical notes in the small pad she keeps in her violin case, melodies inspired by nature. Finally, she will walk along the beach and collect pebbles and pretty shells. She has to be careful to hide these when she gets home, in case her mother realizes she has been here.

At seven o'clock, Isabella knows her time is coming to an end. She glances up. She can just about see her house from here, perched high on the cliffs, in the distance. She knows her mother will be sitting, on her own, in the huge living room, waiting for her. She sighs and traipses slowly back up the beach, treasuring her last few moments of freedom. The seagulls caw goodbye. The waves whisper farewell. Sssssh. Sssssh. She spots something glinting white amidst the brown pebbles. A shell. She crouches down and picks it up.

It's a beautiful pink-and-white conch shell. You hardly ever saw ones this big and unbroken. Isabella checks that it's empty inside. Satisfied, she tucks it into the pocket of her hoodie. She glances at her watch. Ten to seven. She needs to hurry.

She trots up the steps to the promenade. Cars line each side. The last of the day-trippers, perhaps enjoying a coffee or fish and chips in one of the cafés that line the other side of the road.

She takes the shell out of her pocket, unable to stop herself admiring it one final time. She remembers something Miriam said: 'Hold a shell to your ear and you can always hear the sea.'

Miriam is full of funny sayings like that. Sometimes Miriam can be a bit strict, but Isabella knows there's a different side to her. When she was little, Miriam would bake with her in the kitchen, creating sweet little fairy cakes and giant, fluffy sponges. Whenever her mother was feeling too tired, it was Miriam who would play hide-and-seek in the gardens or read to her on rainy afternoons. Now she is older, Miriam sometimes lends her the twisty thrillers she keeps in her room (rather than the literary tomes her mother prefers her to read). Their little secret.

Isabella smiles. She raises the shell to her ear and steps into the road. The sea roars inside her head.

Perhaps that's why she doesn't hear the roar of the car's engine.

40

It all happened so quickly. That's what people always say, isn't it? *Oh God, it all happened so quickly.* But it didn't. Not for him. He could remember every agonizing second, every sound, every tiny detail. Her final moments indelibly stamped upon his memory, in glass and bone and blood.

He wasn't even supposed to be driving. It wasn't his car. But he was more sober than the rest of the gang: Mitch, Jase and Kev. To call them 'mates' was stretching it. Really, they were just kids he grew up with. They lived on the same estate, went to the same school. Thrown together by circumstance and postcode.

This particular night, they were sprawled on a bench on a patch of scrubby grass behind the local Spar. Dale, the manager, knew they were weren't eighteen yet but he was happy enough to sell them cheap booze. The road curved up here away from the promenade and the straggly row of fish-and-chip shops, arcades, run-down cafés and tacky souvenir shops. You could just about see the sea and the pier.

They smoked and drank cider, and even though Gabe knew that he should really head home and make a start on his college coursework, he was feeling pleasantly buzzed. And hungry.

Echoing his thought, Jase suddenly said:

'Fuck, I'm starving.'

'Me, too,' Kev slurred.

Mitch jangled his car keys. 'Let's drive down the pier, get some chips, see if there's any fit birds hanging around the arcade.'

It was about a mile from the estate to the promenade, walkable, but Mitch had an old Fiesta that he drove everywhere. He was the only one of them who had a car. His uncle had got it cheap from some bloke he met in the pub and Mitch had done it up with a stereo, neon lights and all sorts of shit that basically screamed 'Pig Me!' to passing police cars.

'C'mon.'

Mitch jumped off the top of the bench and promptly fell flat on his face. Jase and Kev guffawed like wasted hyenas. Mitch rolled over and wiped at his chin. He stared at the blood on his fingers and laughed again.

'Man, I'm soooo fucked.'

'Maybe we should walk,' Gabe said. He could feel his own buzz waning.

'Fuck that,' spat Kev.

Mitch sat up and seemed to consider. For a minute, Gabe thought he might agree, and if Mitch agreed the rest would follow, like stoned sheep.

Instead, he chucked the keys at Gabe. Gabe somehow caught them. 'I don't have a licence.'

'So? You know how to drive, dontcha?'

He did. Mitch had shown him the basics.

'Gabe-o, Gabe-o,' Kev chanted. Jase just grinned like a loon.

He wanted to say no. The weed and the alcohol were wearing off, but he was still over the limit. However, if *he* didn't drive, Mitch would get behind the wheel, and he was in a far worse state than Gabe.

Not your problem. Walk away. Go home.

But he couldn't. Because saying no wasn't just about driving the car. If he walked away now it would be the moment Gabe-o let them down. The moment Gabe-o was a *fucking pussy*. The moment Gabe-o stopped being one of the gang.

He took the keys, sauntered over to the car and climbed in. Jase and Kev piled in the back. Mitch staggered over and collapsed into the passenger seat next to him. As Gabe started the engine, he leaned over and cranked up the stereo that he'd fitted himself, wires snaking everywhere. The Prodigy pounded out of the speakers, shaking the whole car.

'Fucking yes!' Kev shouted.

Gabe eased the Fiesta out of the Spar car park and pulled out on to the road. He ground the gears, forcing it clunkily into third.

'Man, you drive like my nan,' Jase chortled.

Gabe scowled, face flushing. And actually, he thought, kangaroo-hopping down the road at twenty was probably even more conspicuous than just putting his foot down. He accelerated and whacked the car into fourth, hitting forty, forty-five then fifty as they wound down the cliff road. Despite his initial trepidation, it felt good.

He cruised along the promenade, the bright lights of

the pier drawing closer. To his left, the sun was sinking into the sea, drowning the sky in pink and orange. To his right, rows of shabby B&Bs; a blur of fairy lights, neon and plastic chandeliers. The Prodigy screamed about being a firestarter. His foot pressed down a little harder as the chorus came on . . .

And she was there.

One minute the road was clear; the next, the girl stood in the middle of it.

Blonde hair, almost white, pale skin. No more than fourteen. Dressed in a simple yellow sundress and sandals. She turned. Her blue eyes widened, her mouth made a small 'Oh' of surprise, as if shocked by the suddenness and finality of their meeting.

He saw all of this, even though the moment could only have lasted fractions of a second. And then she was gone, flying through the air and up, over the windshield, like a massive gust of wind had lifted her and carried her away. The impact threw him forward, the seatbelt yanked him back, slicing deeply into his chest and shoulder, head slamming against the headrest.

He heard the squeal of the brakes, even though he didn't remember hitting them, felt the steering wheel fight against his grip as the car bucked, skidded and eventually shuddered to a halt.

I've hit her. I've killed her. I've hit her. I've killed her. Oh fuck, fuck, fuck.

He was vaguely aware of screaming and yelling, the car doors opening, Kev and Jase staggering out. He felt someone – Mitch – grab his arm. He remained crouched, frozen over the wheel, heart trying to escape his bruised chest, breath coming in strange, small gasps. Mitch turned and sprinted away, across the road, disappearing into the side streets.

Gabe raised his eyes to the rear-view mirror. The girl lay in the road, several feet behind the car. Motionless, her body oddly contorted.

He could hear shouting. People emerging from the cafés and bars, drawn by the squeal of brakes, the commotion. A portly man, who he recognized as the owner of the sundae shop, had pulled out a chunky mobile phone and was shouting about an ambulance.

For the moment, no one was looking at him. All horrified eyes were on the girl.

C'mon. Run.

He glanced towards the pier. He could do it. He could still get away. He peeled his hands from the wheel and half fell, half staggered out of the car. He took a step forward . . . and then turned and limped over to the girl.

She lay at odd angles in the road. Her eyes were half open, but her face was a mask of blood and a dark shadow had spread beneath her white-blonde hair. In one hand she held a shell, remarkably unbroken.

He sank to his knees beside her. He could smell rubber, salt and something darker and crueller. He reached for the girl's hand. The fingernails were broken and torn, the knuckles flayed free of skin.

Her eyes rolled towards his.

'An ambulance is on its way,' he said, not really knowing whether it was or not. 'It will all be okay.'

Even though he could already see it wouldn't. The unnatural angles of her limbs. The blood bubbling at the corners of her mouth. Tears burned at the back of his eyes.

'I'm so sorry.'

Her lips moved. Gabe bent his face closer. Her breath was hot and metallic.

'Lisssten.'

She exhaled the word with a fine spray of blood. And, even though it was impossible because she must be in terrible pain and possibly dying, it looked like she was trying to smile.

'I can hear the sea.'

41

'It was an accident.'

'You were drunk.'

'I was seventeen. I made a mistake. I paid the price.'

'A suspended sentence, a fine.' Harry snorted.

'It was an accident. She stepped out right in front of me. Besides, you know that's not what I meant.'

'Maybe it wasn't enough.'

Gabe shook his head. 'It was over twenty years ago. Why? After all this time?'

'I don't know.'

'What *do* you know?'

'Only what the woman told me.'

'What woman?'

'The woman who has Izzy.'

He couldn't stop himself. Despite the sharp tug of the stitches in his side, Gabe launched out of his chair and hauled Harry up by his lapels, slamming him against the lock-up's cinderblock wall. 'What's her name? Where is she? Where's my daughter?'

Harry was almost Gabe's height and Gabe was no Adonis, but he could feel the frailty of the man as he lifted him. The wasted muscle beneath the smart clothes. The faint sour smell of fear beneath the expensive aftershave. He felt a tiny spark of guilt. But only a tiny one.

'I don't know her name. I don't know where Izzy is.'

'Liar.'

'It's the truth.'

'Is Izzy in danger?'

'No. It's not like that.

'Then what *is* it like? Tell me!'

Harry's face paled. He started to wheeze. Gabe released his grip. Harry sank back down on the bed. With a sigh like a death rattle, he said:

'After your call that night . . . Evelyn was hysterical. I persuaded her to take some tablets, to help her sleep. I didn't sleep much myself. I woke early and went downstairs. There was a brown envelope on the doormat. No postmark, but something bulky inside. I opened it and found a mobile handset and a note: "Your granddaughter is alive. Take this phone and go to the park. Wait on the bench by the playground. Do not contact the police."'

'And you just did what the note said?'

'I thought I had just lost my daughter *and* my granddaughter. Now someone was offering me hope, however insane it sounded.' He looked up at Gabe through red-rimmed eyes. 'What else could I do?'

Gabe swallowed. 'Go on.'

'So, yes, I went to the park. You know the one?'

Gabe knew. They had taken Izzy to that park on their sporadic visits to 'Nan and Grandad'.

'I sat down on the bench and waited. I hadn't been there long when the mobile started to ring. I answered it. A woman's voice said: "Look towards the swings."'

'I turned. And she was there – *Izzy* – standing with a

woman in the playground. The woman told me if I wanted to see Izzy again, I needed to do exactly what she said. She would call again in one hour with instructions.'

'And you let them walk away?'

'I was hardly going to give chase. At almost eighty? And I was in shock. Izzy was alive. It was impossible, a miracle.'

'So, what *did* you do?'

'I walked home and told Evelyn. I thought she'd say that I was going mad or demand that I called the police, but she didn't. She took my hand and said: "We must do whatever she says. Anything to get our granddaughter back."'

'Like drugging me, stopping me seeing the body, lying at the identification?'

'The woman told us the only way to protect Izzy was to make sure everyone believed she was dead.'

Gabe stared at him. Something else fell into place with a sickening thud.

'It was *her* daughter, wasn't it? The little girl who died? The little girl you identified?'

Harry nodded, face slack.

'Why the hell didn't she go to the police?!'

'She couldn't. She said she had made a mistake. Become involved in something beyond her control. She had tried to save Jenny and Izzy, and it had cost her daughter's life.'

Gabe tried to imagine how terrified someone would have to be to abandon their own daughter's body, to let her be buried in another little girl's grave. Terrified, or some kind of psychopath.

'How did she even find you?'

'I presume Izzy must have told her where we lived.'

Perhaps because the woman told Izzy she was taking

her back to her family, Gabe thought. He tried to force the anger down.

'What else did this woman say?'

'That what happened was retribution for something terrible you had done. She said that the people responsible would never stop if they knew Izzy was still alive. Because they always settled their debts.'

'Did she say who "they" were?'

'She called them "the Other People."'

Gabe felt his spine bristle with ice.

'You believed her?'

'I'm not sure what we believed. We just wanted our granddaughter back. The woman promised that if we did this, when it was safe, she would bring Izzy to us, we could take her away somewhere. Just the three of us.'

'Just the *three* of you?'

'It was what Jenny would have wanted.'

'How the hell do you know what Jenny would have wanted?'

'I know she wanted a divorce. She told Evelyn.'

Gabe stared at him, stunned. Divorce. The word had hovered in the air between them sometimes, almost spoken but never quite given form, for fear that if it were to materialize, it might turn into reality.

He knew they had come close. It was getting harder and harder to hide his missing Mondays from Jenny. His agency was flexible about hours. It was a creative industry and they were happy for Gabe to work remotely a couple of days a week. But there were still times when Jenny had caught him out, calling his office, only to be told he was working from home.

'Are you having an affair?' she had asked him bluntly one

evening. He had denied it, furiously, fervently and – *thank God* – she had seen the truth in his eyes. But she knew he was lying about *something*. Ultimately, it didn't matter that it wasn't an affair. It was his lack of honesty, the lack of trust that was driving an insurmountable wedge between them.

But he'd had no idea that Jenny had told Evelyn. The woman she once described as '*about as maternal as Maleficent*'.

He shook his head. 'She never said anything to me.'

'She wanted to get away from you.' Harry snarled. 'If only she had done it sooner, then maybe she would still be alive.'

Gabe wanted to argue, to deny it. But he couldn't. It was true. If only she had left. If only she had hated him more.

'So, why isn't Izzy with you right now?'

Harry's lips thinned.

'Let me guess,' Gabe said bitterly. 'It was never safe enough. It was always next week or month or year.'

'It was *your fault*. You couldn't let it go. You couldn't stop searching, stirring things up, looking for the damn car. You ruined it all.'

'Why the hell didn't you go to the police?'

'We were scared. We thought, if we did, we might never see Izzy again.'

'How do you even know that Izzy is still alive? This woman – this *nameless* woman – could have been lying to you all along.'

Harry hesitated. His eyes staggered around as if looking for somewhere safe to settle. 'Every three months we would receive a photo or a video. So we knew that Izzy was safe, looked after.'

'You have the phone? The one she gave you?'

'Yes.'

'Then show me.'

'They were encrypted. Only available to view for twenty-four hours before they deleted.'

'Then call this woman,' Gabe said. 'Tell her you need to meet.'

'It won't work.'

'Make up some story. Convince her. You're good at lying.'

'I tried to call her after I received your message. There's no answer.'

'Try again.'

'You don't understand. The number is unavailable. Even if I wanted to help you, I can't. She's gone.'

Gone. With Izzy. Gabe wanted to punch the wall in frustration. And then he remembered DI Maddock's words:

We found the car. We found another victim nearby. A woman.'

'Harry, when I told you I'd found the car, did you tell the woman?'

He had the grace to look sheepish. 'Yes.'

'Christ!'

'What?' Harry looked at him strangely.

'There was a body in the boot, badly decomposed. It had been there a while. When the police pulled the car out of the lake today, they found a woman nearby, barely alive.'

Gabe saw the realization dawn in Harry's watery eyes. 'You think it's the woman who took Izzy?'

'I think, after you told her I'd found the car, she went back, maybe to destroy the evidence.'

'But, if it's her, then –'

'Where the hell is my daughter?'

42

When the *Titanic* was sinking, the band continued to play. Everyone had heard that story. But often, Katie wondered why. Denial, duty or simply the need to focus on something familiar and comforting when all else was lost? When the worst had happened.

She felt a bit like she was playing on the *Titanic* this morning. Or fiddling while Rome burned. Doing all the normal things, when nothing about this was normal at all.

She poured out cornflakes, splashed milk into bowls, buttered toast and poured glasses of orange juice. She made a cup of tea then settled Sam and Gracie in front of the TV in the living room while she searched in the tumble dryer for missing school cardigans and socks. All the while trying to ignore the voice inside her head that kept screaming: *Iceberg! Iceberg!*

HAVE YOU SEEN ME? *I think it's you.*

Alice (she wasn't ready to answer to Izzy) was still in bed. It had been gone 11 p.m. by the time Katie had wearily tucked her in. She had absorbed the revelation calmly. Worryingly so. Despite Katie's best efforts to coax more out of her, Alice claimed not to remember anything about the night her mum died. Just that it was something bad.

Fran had saved her. She repeated it like a mantra, like she had learned it off by heart. But Katie wasn't so sure.

It was true that most children, once they reached eight or nine, would forget events from their earliest years. *Childhood amnesia*. Something to do with how fast the brain is growing and laying down new neural pathways.

But, if Katie was right and Alice was who she thought she was, she would have just turned five when her mother was murdered. Old enough to summon up *some* memories, even if her brain had done its own whitewash job to protect her from the trauma.

Memories didn't just evaporate like steam. They were more like lost keys. You might have put them somewhere for safekeeping or thrown them into a deep well because you didn't ever want to unlock that particular door again, but they were still there, somewhere. You just had to find a way to retrieve them.

Her first instinct had been to call Gabe. He deserved to know that his daughter was alive. That he had been right, all along. And if Alice saw her daddy, maybe some of those memories of her former life would come back to her.

But then, Katie had caught herself. Gabe might still be in hospital. And Alice needed rest; she needed time to let this settle. If Gabe insisted on seeing her straight away (which he would), it could all be too much. For both of them. Besides, Katie wanted to be *sure*. She didn't want to get the poor man's hopes up just to dash them again.

After she had put Alice to bed, she spent several hours scouring the internet for information about the murders. Three years ago (so, the girl's age was right). It had been all over the television and newspapers at the time. No one had ever been caught and there seemed to be no motive, certainly not after Gabe was absolved. No robbery. No sign of forced entry. Like the killer had just been invited in.

And maybe she had, Katie thought. *After all, who would feel threatened by a woman with a child?*

She felt a coldness steal in and wrap itself around her heart. What was she suggesting? That Fran was somehow involved. But what about *her* daughter? If Alice was telling the truth, she'd been killed, too. Katie refused to believe that Fran would let her own child come to harm. So, what was the alternative? Was Fran just in the wrong place at the wrong time? Or was the answer somewhere in between? Was she an accomplice? Drawn into a situation that spiralled out of control? Where the only option left was to save one child and run? But from who?

She thought about the postcard again.

I did it for Dad.

Katie picked up her mug of tea and took a sip. Predictably, it had gone cold. Sometimes, it seemed like her entire life was measured out in undrunk mugs of tea. She was just about to pour it away and make another when the front doorbell rang. She jumped. Christ, her nerves were shot this morning.

She walked into the hall. Through the glass at the top of the door she could see what looked like the fluorescent jacket of a police officer.

Fran. Had they found her?

She pulled the door open.

'All right, Katie?'

It took her a moment. She had only met her sister's boyfriend a handful of times and, while she was aware of his job, she had never seen him in uniform.

'Steve? What are you doing here?'

'Didn't get you out of bed, did I?'

He smiled. Katie had the urge to pull her dressing gown a little bit tighter around her body.

'Actually, I was just getting breakfast.'

'Right. Can I come in?'

She hesitated. Gracie and Sam were still ensconced in front of the TV. Alice was upstairs asleep. But if she came down . . .

'It's important.'

Reluctantly, she nodded. 'Okay.'

She led him into the kitchen, even as something worried at the back of her mind. How did he know her address? She supposed he *was* a police officer. But there was something else, something niggling.

She closed the kitchen door and turned to face him, forcing a smile. 'So, can you tell me what this is about?'

He looked around. 'Aren't you going to offer me a cuppa?'

She fought down her natural instinct to be polite. 'I have to get the kids to school. You said it was important.'

His face immediately darkened. She thought about Lou. Her poor choices. How a uniform was no indicator of character.

'It's about your sister Fran.'

She stiffened. 'What do you know about my sister?'

'I know she's got herself into trouble and she's going to get you into trouble, too.'

'I haven't seen my sister in nine years.'

'Where's the girl, Katie?'

A jolt of fear shot through her. How the hell did he know about Alice? What was this?

'Sorry?'

'If you're hiding her, you're obstructing justice.'

She tried to keep her voice steady. 'I thought you worked in Traffic, not Missing Persons?'

'I know she's here. Just fetch the girl and we'll all be sweet.'

And suddenly she remembered what else was bothering her. Yesterday, Steve had said he had two days off. But here he was, in uniform.

Iceberg. Iceberg.

'Are you even on duty?'

He sighed, held out his hands. 'You're right. This isn't police business. Call it debt collection. Your sister owes and it's time to pay.'

'I'd like you to leave, please.'

'Fine.' He smiled. And punched her in the face.

Her nose exploded with an agonizing crack. She tried to scream, but her throat was full of blood. She gurgled and staggered backwards. He caught her before she could hit the floor, pushing her against the sink.

'Nothing personal. Just earning a little overtime.'

She forced out the words: 'Furr . . . who?'

'Oh, I think you know.' He whispered the name in her ear, his lips brushing her skin. Terror squeezed her insides.

'Whut . . . 'bout . . . Lou?'

A sneer. 'That fat-slag sister of yours? She was business, not pleasure. Keeping tabs.'

He wrapped his hands around her throat and squeezed. She tried to scream, to draw in breath, but her nose was a mushy mess and her throat was half choked. Faintly, from the living room, she could hear the *Scooby Doo* theme. *Oh God, what if the children came in here?* What if he hurt them?

She grabbed for his face, scratching at his skin with

her nails. He squeezed her throat harder. She kicked and writhed, trying to throw him off, but he was too strong.

He pressed his face into hers. 'I'd rather it had been you. If I had more time, we could make this a lot of fun.'

Out of the corner of her eye, she saw a flicker of movement. The door opened. Alice stepped into the kitchen. *No*, Katie thought. *No. Don't come in here. Get away. Run. Get Sam and Gracie and run.*

But Alice didn't run. She moved forward and swung something over her head. There was a rattling sound, a heavy thud, and the pressure on Katie's throat was released. She gasped for air. Steve staggered to one side, toppling into the table and chairs.

Before he could recover, Alice raised the rucksack and swung it again. It connected with his skull with a satisfying crunch. This time, he slumped heavily to the floor, out cold.

Christ. Alice had just assaulted a police officer.

A police officer who was trying to kill you.

If she hadn't have been scared, and in so much pain, Katie would have laughed at the sheer insanity of it. She dragged in a couple more rasping breaths. Alice stood, still clutching the rucksack, as though debating whether to use it again. Katie forced her trembling legs to walk over to her and wrapped an arm around her thin shoulders.

'What have you got in there?' she croaked. 'Rocks?'

Alice shook her head. 'Pebbles.'

Of course.

'Mum? What's happened?'

She turned. Sam stood in the kitchen doorway with Gracie. They stared at her in horror. Gracie started to sob.

'Mummy! Your face.'

Katie hurried over and hugged them. 'It's okay, it's okay.'

'Why is Uncle Steve on the floor?

She glanced back at Steve. The blow had knocked him out, but she couldn't see any blood. On one hand, that was probably good. Murdering a police officer was something else. On the other hand, he was going to wake up.

'We could make this a lot of fun.'

'I'll explain later. Right now, I want you to get your shoes and coats on. We need to leave. *Now.'*

43

'I want you to visit Isabella.'

And so began his real sentence.

When it came to the trial, Gabe's age and former good record had counted for him. Witnesses confirmed that the girl had just walked out, right in front of the car. He couldn't have stopped in time. While the others had fled the scene, Gabe had stayed, holding the girl's hand and talking to her until the ambulance arrived. In the shock and confusion, the crowd hadn't realized that he was the driver. However, he had probably been speeding, he was over the limit and, even though the girl was alive, barely, his solicitor had told him that there was very little chance he could avoid a custodial sentence . . .

If it hadn't been for the letter.

Charlotte Harris, the mother of the girl – whose name he now knew was Isabella – had written to the judge. He never saw the contents of the letter, but he would learn later that Charlotte was someone of influence. She had asked for leniency.

And she had asked to meet him.

They sat in an enormous living room. Balconied windows and wide French doors looked out over the chalk cliffs. Lush lawns unfurled, like a thick green carpet, down to a shimmering swimming pool. Around them porcelain, marble and glass sparkled and shone.

Beautiful. And yet . . . Gabe found it hard to imagine a teenage girl, with all her clumsiness, colour and mess, ever living here. The huge space felt empty. He wondered if it had ever felt alive.

Charlotte Harris poured water into crystal glasses. Like the house, she was polished and poised; pale blonde hair, immaculate cream dress, shiny pearls.

'The visits will take place every Monday at precisely 2 p.m. For exactly one hour. Wherever you are, whatever you are doing.'

'Wh–why Monday?'

Charlotte regarded Gabe coolly. 'Isabella was born at 2 p.m. on a Monday.' She let this thought weigh upon him before continuing. 'You will not deviate from the day or time. You will continue to visit Isabella without fail until the day she recovers.'

Gabe stared at her. Isabella remained in a persistent vegetative state. No one knew when, or if, she would ever regain consciousness, let alone recover.

'But what if' – he swallowed – 'she doesn't?'

Charlotte smiled and Gabe felt her hatred emanate from every pore.

'Then you will visit her without fail until the day one of you dies. Do you understand?'

He understood.

Every Monday Gabe sat at Isabella's bedside while machines whirred and beeped around her. He talked to her, read to her; sometimes he held her soft, cool hand.

Isabella slept. A pale girl in a white room.

He visited her while he studied at the local polytechnic, chosen because it was within walking distance of the hospital.

He visited after he had finished his degree at the poly, working evenings in a pub and doing freelance work for a local advertising agency to free up his days. When the agency offered him a permanent copywriting position, he negotiated a cut from the already meagre salary in exchange for every Monday afternoon off, lying about visiting his dying mother in hospital, even though his mother was already dead by then.

He visited when Isabella's mother moved her from the hospital to a specially constructed annexe in the remote cliff house, catching two buses and walking a mile from the bus stop to get there.

He visited after he was headhunted for a job at a top agency, miles away in Nottingham, insisting on working remotely for two days a week so he could drive the four hours to Sussex and back.

He visited after he met Jenny. The urge to tell her, to share everything with the woman he loved, was overwhelming, but he couldn't. He couldn't bear to see the disappointment in her eyes.

He visited when he should have been spending holidays with his wife and daughter, inventing ever more elaborate excuses to avoid a whole week away. He had booked earlier flights home, deliberately missed trains, faked food poisoning and even invented an old friend whose funeral he needed to attend. All to keep his promise.

He visited when Jenny was in labour.

He visited when Izzy performed in her first nativity and on her third birthday.

He visited when his wife was being slaughtered and his daughter kidnapped – the hideous irony of this only sinking in later.

He visited afterwards, fighting through throngs of reporters and photographers outside his home, chasing him with accusations and stories about his former crime.

Man questioned over murders of mother and daughter left girl in coma.

Father whose family were slain visits teenage girl he left for dead.

The first victim.

Oh yes. Gabe understood.

He understood that Charlotte had made him more of a prisoner than if he had been behind bars. Chained to Isabella for life.

'That's why none of this makes any sense. Charlotte wanted me to pay. But not like this.'

He turned to the Samaritan. They stood on the motorway bridge, vehicles parked a short distance away. The policeman had not returned to Gabe's van last night. Gabe thought that the Samaritan had sounded a little disappointed when he told Gabe this.

'You destroyed her daughter's life,' he said now. 'Sounds like she had a pretty good reason to want to destroy yours.'

The wind gusted cold drizzle into their faces. Gabe pulled his collar up to his chin. The Samaritan leaned on the railing, in his usual black jacket and T-shirt, seemingly oblivious to the weather. Below, the motorway flowed with fast-moving early-morning traffic. Like a river, it never stopped, not entirely. Always more cars. Always more journeys.

'Charlotte isn't behind this,' Gabe said firmly. 'She didn't contact the Other People.'

'Why are you so sure?'

'For a start, Charlotte hated technology. Miriam once told me that she didn't even own a mobile phone. She had no idea what Google was, let alone the Dark Web.'

'Maybe she got someone to help her?'

Gabe shook his head. 'No. She was a virtual recluse. No family. No friends.'

'People will surprise you,' the Samaritan said. 'Not usually in a good way. And Charlotte Harris sounds like a piece of work.'

'Oh, she was.'

Charlotte Harris was a polished shell full of poison. And Gabe was sure she would have taken great delight in his torment over losing his wife and daughter.

But she never had the chance.

The Samaritan shot him a look. '*Was?*'

Gabe smiled thinly. 'Charlotte Harris is dead. She died a year before Izzy was born.'

44

They sat at a sticky table in a corner of the motorway café. The place smelt of stale food, and the fluorescent lighting lent everyone the pallor of zombies. A young girl served customers behind the counter. Katie half expected to see a parallel version of herself walk out and start collecting cups.

They were a few junctions south of Newton Green. Katie didn't dare risk returning to her own place of work. For a start, Steve knew where that was. He could come after her. Once, that might have sounded paranoid. Not any more.

This café was about a third full, the other tables occupied by a mixture of travellers: a couple of young labourers tucking into bacon butties and studying their mobiles; a group of pensioners chatting over tea; a young mum with a toddler in a high chair.

Customers came and went here with more regularity than in a high-street café. A constant stream of strangers. That was what Katie was counting on. Somewhere safe, anonymous, well populated. So she could have some time to think. To recalibrate.

She had bought activity books and colouring pens from

the shop, plus some ibuprofen and plasters for her swollen nose. Then she had fetched milkshakes and chocolate cake and settled the children at a quiet table in a corner.

For now, they seemed to accept the situation. Children did. They were able to adapt, to just get on with the moment in hand. Of course, they still had questions, which Katie had attempted to field as best she could.

Why did we run away? What happened to Uncle Steve? Wasn't he a policeman? Are we going to jail?

She had told them that Steve was a bad man, even though he was dressed as a policeman. They had to run away until the good police could sort things out.

'Like the Terminator?' Sam had asked. 'He pretended to be a policeman, but he wasn't. He pretended to be John Connor's mum, too, and put a spike through his dad's eye.'

'Something like that,' Katie had said, and then told him not to talk about spikes through eyes in front of his sister (and wondered at which friend's house he had seen *Terminator 2*).

While they ate their cake and slurped milkshakes, she texted the school to say that Sam and Gracie were sick and wouldn't be in today. And then she texted Louise.

'Are you okay?'

'No, Steve broke up with me last night.'

'Good.'

'Thanks.'

'Steve is dangerous. He came to my house and attacked me this morning.'

'Is this a joke?'

'No joke.'

'WTF?'

'Are you at home?'

'Lucy's.'

Lucy was Lou's oldest friend. Sensible, mumsy, the complete opposite of Lou. Katie felt relief wash through her.

'Can you stay there tonight?'

'Suppose.'

'Steve doesn't know where Lucy lives?'

'No.'

'If he calls, don't answer. Don't tell him where you are.'

'Scaring me.'

'Good. Promise you won't speak to him?'

'Promise.'

Katie just hoped she would keep her promise. She took a sip of coffee. Alice was helping Gracie colour a trio of Disney princesses. Sam doodled superheroes while picking at a piece of chocolate cake with his fingers, hardly any of the crumbs making it to his mouth.

Despite what she had told them, she didn't know if she could call the 'good' police. What if they didn't believe her? Whatever else he was involved in, Steve was still one of their own. They would take his word over hers.

She couldn't go home. Couldn't call her mother. It struck her that she didn't really have any other people she could turn to. No friends, not even any casual acquaintances. She was always so busy working, looking after the children, getting by, she had no time left to form relationships.

Plus, she wasn't built for emergencies. She was a creature of routine. She didn't have a panic protocol. Fran did. Fran had always been the rebel. The one who skirted trouble. Headstrong, impulsive. She had had the hardest time from their mum, perhaps because they were so alike. Both always sure they were right; quick to anger, slow to forgive. Katie could still remember the blazing rows, the slammed doors and screaming, Dad trying to play peace-maker between his favourite daughter and his wife.

Yet she also remembered Fran defending her when their mother had had too much to drink. And when some older boys once gathered around to torment her on her way home from school, Fran had waded in with a hockey stick, laying into the boys with such ferocity that Katie had to beg her to stop.

Where are you, Fran? What the hell would you do to get out of this mess?

'Mu—um?'

She looked up. Sam wriggled on his seat. 'I need the toilet.'

'Okay.' Katie glanced at Alice and Gracie. 'Can you go on your own?'

He rolled his eyes. 'Of course. I'm ten.'

'Well, be quick, don't talk to any stran—'

'Strange men. I know.' He slipped from the table.

Katie immediately felt anxiety kick in. The toilets were only just along the corridor. But what if someone snatched him? Suddenly, everything and everyone around her seemed suspicious, full of threat. Other people, she thought. They were everywhere. And you never knew which ones were dangerous.

She realized that Alice was watching her warily.

'Are we running away again?' she asked.

'What? No. We're just working out what to do next.'

'That's what Fran used to say.'

'Right. What else did Fran say?'

'That we just had to get far enough away, and we would be safe.'

'And were you?'

'For a while.' Alice looked over at Gracie, who was still intent on Rapunzel, Jasmine and Belle. She lowered her voice. 'Then a bad man came.'

Katie felt herself tense. 'When was this?'

'A long time ago. Fran thinks I was asleep, but I woke up. He came to the house at night. They had a fight and Fran got rid of him.'

'How d'you mean?'

Her voice dropped to a whisper. 'I crept downstairs and saw her put him in the boot of the car. The old one she kept locked in the garage.'

Katie swallowed. 'Then what happened?'

'I went back to bed and pretended to be asleep. Fran came up and said we had to leave. We drove the car to a hotel, a long way away. Fran went out for a bit. The next day, the car was gone.'

Katie thought about the boys and the hockey stick. How far Fran would go to protect those she loved.

But she wasn't Fran. *So, what should Katie do?*

And then she knew. There was really no choice.

'No more running.' She reached out and took Alice's hand. 'We're going to sort this mess out.'

She picked up her phone.

45

He hadn't driven this way for a long time. All the miles he had covered, all the treks up and down the motorway, this was one road he had not been able to bring himself to travel.

The road back home.

Woodbridge, Nottinghamshire.

He and Jenny had bought the rambling Victorian vicarage at an auction, sight unseen. When they got the keys, he realized that they had not only paid over the odds for what was essentially a derelict wreck held together by woodworm and rat droppings, but that the meagre budget they had set aside for renovation wouldn't even cover the cost of replacing the roof.

Jenny had wanted to ask her parents for help. Gabe had said no. Harry and Evelyn's wealth had always been a bone of contention between them. Harry had paid for their wedding, a lavish affair which had made Gabe feel a little uncomfortable at the time. But he reasoned that Jenny was Harry's only daughter and it was tradition. However, he didn't want accepting their money to become a habit. For Jenny, it was too easy. She was used to being given everything she asked for. Gabe didn't want to be a charity case. He had worked hard not to owe anybody anything.

It became their first real argument, and it had festered for weeks. Eventually, just to cease the hostilities, he had acquiesced, on the condition that they pay back every penny.

It had taken them several years to turn the house into something not just habitable but beautiful. A labour of love, and Gabe had been so proud of their achievement. The hours they spent together covered in plaster and paint. Cuddling around the real fire while it snowed outside and plastic sheets formed makeshift windows. The house that Gabe and Jenny built.

It was a dream home, at least for him. Red brick, draped in a glossy shroud of ivy, sash windows, a long gravel drive-way and gardens that surrounded it on three sides. When Jenny fell pregnant, life seemed complete.

They had put a trampoline and a swing out the back for Izzy. In summer, they filled a huge paddling pool and the slide became a water flume.

A home for their family. A home Gabe had hoped they would grow old in, watch Izzy grow up in, maybe even welcome grandchildren into.

And they *had* been happy there. Mostly. He had tried so hard to believe that. To put aside the dark feeling that the house had come to represent everything that was so very different about Jenny and him: their backgrounds, their wants, their hopes for the future.

For Gabe, it was the pinnacle of his achievements. For Jenny, it was the sort of home she had grown up in, the sort of home he felt, sometimes – uncharitably – that she *expected*.

Jenny was a kind person, a brilliant mum, a saint for putting up with him, but he could never quite shake the feeling that he would never be good enough for her. He would always be the boy from the estates who got lucky. One day, his luck would run out.

And he was right.

The home he built for his family might as well have been made of straw. All the time, there was a big, bad wolf lurking in the shadows, just waiting to blow it all down.

The house hadn't changed that much. The driveway had been paved, two Range Rovers parked outside. The garden, where Izzy used to love to run and play, had been landscaped, with new decking and a hot tub.

It had been sold to a professional couple in their forties with no children. Gabe didn't understand why two people needed a five-bedroomed house with grounds. But then, all the people with families had pulled out of buying it once they found out what had happened there. As if the house's grim history could somehow rub off on them. As if tragedy were contagious.

He stared up at his former home. When the police had arrived that evening, the electric front gates and the rear patio doors were both open. Jenny *always* shut the front gates. They were both security conscious, Jenny because of growing up with parents who wanted to safeguard their wealth, Gabe because he grew up in a place where people would steal the glue from your gran's false teeth, so you protected what little you had.

Now he wondered if someone had ensured those gates were open. Had that been the woman's role? To get Jenny to let her guard down, leave the gates open and let the real killer in? But something had gone wrong. Jenny had died, the woman's daughter had died, and she had run, with Izzy.

The police had spoken to everyone at Izzy's school, other mums, colleagues at work. Everyone she knew. Or, at least, everyone they thought she knew.

Could your wife have let the killer into the house?

Had she arranged to meet someone?

Do you know the names of her friends?

And of course, he didn't. He had never realized what a stranger his wife had become until she was gone. He didn't know her friends, her routine. They shared a house, a bed, but at some point, they had stopped sharing their lives. When did that happen? he wondered. Maybe that was why the word 'divorce' was never spoken. They didn't need to. They were already retreating, ending their marriage stealthily, slipping away from each other so slowly that neither even noticed the other one was disappearing.

His phone rang in his pocket. He pulled it out.

'Hello.'

'Gabriel, it's DI Maddock.'

'Yes?' He waited.

'Just to inform you – your father-in-law presented at the police station, he's being interviewed now.' A pause. 'I also wanted to let you know that we have revisited blood and forensic samples taken from the body of the girl we found at your home.'

Blood and forensic samples. Such cold, clinical words. He swallowed. *Not Izzy,* he reminded himself. But she had been somebody's daughter. Somebody's little girl. And, just like Izzy, she had probably giggled at *Peppa Pig*, written letters to Father Christmas and cuddled a favourite toy to ward off bad dreams. He hoped she was sleeping soundly now. He hoped, despite him never having been big on God or religion, that she was somewhere safe and warm.

'Gabriel?'

'I'm here,' he croaked through a hot, hard lump in his throat.

'It confirms that she is not your daughter, Gabriel.'

'Okay.'

It should have felt good. He should have felt vindicated. But he didn't. Izzy was still lost and, even in death, this other little girl was being discarded and abandoned all over again.

'There's something else,' Maddock said. 'The woman we found –'

'Do you know who she is yet?'

A longer pause. 'That's why I'm calling.' The silence echoed down the line. 'I just spoke to the hospital. She never regained consciousness. I'm afraid she died fifteen minutes ago.'

He let this sink in.

'What about the man in the boot?'

'Forensics are still working on it, but no luck yet.'

'So, there's no way of knowing what's happened to Izzy?'

'There may be one thing. Does the name Michael Wilson mean anything to you?'

'No. Why?'

'He was killed in a burglary gone wrong nine years ago. When we searched the database for familial matches to the samples taken from the girl's body, his name came up.'

'He's her father?'

'More likely, grandfather. And our records show that Michael Wilson has three daughters.'

He tried to process the significance of this.

'We are now comparing his DNA with the unidentified woman,' Maddock continued. 'I'm pretty certain we'll get a match.'

The girl's mother, her grandfather. Both dead. But . . .

'You said *three* daughters. What about the others?'

'Trust me, Gabriel. We are pursuing every lead.'

'Not quickly enough.'

'If Izzy is out there –'

'*If?* Izzy is out there, and you have to find her!'

'We are doing all we can.'

'Right – along with pursuing every lead. Are lessons being learned along the way, too?'

'Gabriel –'

'I don't need platitudes and clichés. I need you out there, searching for her.'

'We don't have unlimited resources.'

'You think she's dead, don't you?'

'No. I didn't say that.'

'You didn't have to.'

'We are doing our best. *I* am doing my best. Is there anything else you can tell us that would help?'

He hesitated.

'*Until the day one of you dies. Do you understand?*'

'I've told you all I can'

'Right. Then let us do our job.'

He ended the call, just about resisting the urge to hurl the phone out of the window. So near, he thought. So near to finding all the answers. And yet, so far. He had pieces of the story. Fragments. But only one person knew the truth, and she wasn't talking to anyone. And if the woman had, as Harry said, been caring for Izzy, looking after her all this time, who was doing that now? *Who had his daughter?*

Could he face more years of not knowing? Worse, could he face knowing? Could he face the crushing inevitability of that call when the police told him that they had found her, they had found Izzy's body?

He brought up the photo of Izzy on his phone. HAVE YOU SEEN ME? Yes, sweetheart, he thought. I see you all the time. In every dream. In every nightmare. But there's so much I didn't see. I never saw those first adult teeth come through. I never saw your hair darken and thicken. I never saw you learn to swim or stop saying 'lellow' instead of 'yellow'. You're fading, slipping from my memories. Because memories are only as strong as the people who hold onto them. And I'm tired. I don't know if I can hold on for much longer.

He let the tears slip from his eyes. They hit the screen, blurring the picture, until he could barely see Izzy at all. *Going, going, gone.*

And then his phone buzzed with a text.

She sleeps. A pale girl in a white room. Around her, machines whirr and buzz and an alarm flashes red. The window bangs open and the conch shell lies on the floor, shattered into sharp shards. The air resonates with the discordant chime of the piano keys.

This is what alerted Miriam first, even before the alarm on her pager. She runs into the room and takes in the scene. Her heart is pounding, legs trembling from where she has scrambled up the stairs from the kitchen. She stares around at the mess, the shell, the open window. What on earth is going on?

Then, as always, practicality takes over. She goes to the girl's side, checks her pulse, heart rate, fluids. She resets the machines, presses buttons, makes adjustments. The machines resume their steady whirring.

She breathes a small sigh of relief. She's getting too old for this, she thinks. It's time she retired. But she can't. She has a responsibility here. But sometimes she feels so weary. The burden of it all too much to bear.

She touches the soft piece of paper in her pocket again. He gave it to her when he first started searching for his little girl. She kept it to remind herself how much he has lost, too. Sometimes, she finds herself looking at it and wondering if it's true – if his daughter really is out there, somewhere, just as she stares at Isabella and wonders if she is inside there, somewhere. Two young girls. Both lost. Except, as long *as someone is still searching for you, you are never really lost. Just not yet found.*

She brushes a tendril of hair from the girl's face. It feels damp. Sweat? But Isabella doesn't sweat. And, there's a smell. Seawater, she thinks. Isabella's hair smells of seawater. It must be from the open window.

She goes to close it. Outside, the sky looks sullen and thunderous. A storm brewing on the horizon. Miriam shivers. She is not given to flights of fancy, but she knows when something is wrong. She can feel it in the air.

She turns. A movement in the shadows behind the door catches her eye. A figure emerges. Miriam jumps. Her heart flutters against the brittle bones of her chest.

'Who are you?' she stammers. 'What do you want?'

He smiles. White teeth glint.

'I got a lot of names.'

He raises a gun. Miriam clutches at the crucifix around her neck.

'But some people call me the Sandman.'

46

A traffic jam. Of all the times. Gabe would have laughed at the irony, if he didn't feel like crying and screaming and punching a fist through the windscreen.

The line of cars in front stuttered and stopped. He watched the speedo creep up to thirty, pushed the car momentarily into fourth gear and then immediately had to hit the brakes again.

He thumped the steering wheel. Once again, fate seemed to be conspiring against him. Stopping him from reaching her. Déjà vu. Always too late. Always just out of reach.

I've found your daughter. Meet me at the coffee shop. Junction 12.

Of course, the text could be a cruel joke. A prank. But why?

A dream is never more fragile than when it's about to come true. The slightest wrong move and it could disintegrate into dust. He felt like a man teetering on a tightrope across a river of hungry crocodiles, heading towards a mirage. Risking everything for something that could vanish into a haze.

He heard sirens, and an ambulance flashed past on the hard shoulder. There must be an accident ahead. Someone's routine journey suddenly cut short by a momentary lapse of attention, a missed lane change, a fractional delay on the brakes.

The traffic crawled forward another few feet. He felt his frustration inch up another notch. He saw a sign coming up. The next junction. Half a mile. It wasn't a quick diversion, but was it better than sitting in traffic? He drummed his fingers. Could he cut across the lanes in time? Or should he just wait out it on the motorway?

The same dilemma he had faced three years ago. He couldn't afford to make the wrong decision again. The traffic edged forward. The slip road was fast approaching. A few cars had already turned off. He was leaving it too late.

He debated with himself, then quickly slammed on the indicator and darted into the inside lane, in front of a lorry, which hit the horn and flashed him angrily. He ignored it. The slip road was running out. He yanked the steering wheel to the left, felt the wheels of the camper van bump over the white hazard lines, and he was off.

He hoped that, this time, he wasn't too late.

47

Where was he? The activity books had been discarded; crumbs and empty cups littered the table. Katie had given Sam and Gracie her phone to play with, to ward off the boredom whinges, but she could sense that they were getting restless. Alice sat, ostensibly engrossed in a word puzzle, but Katie noticed that she hadn't filled in a single letter in the last ten minutes.

She checked her watch again. Over an hour since she sent the text. The phone told her that it had been delivered. He hadn't replied or tried to call, not that she would have answered. Some conversations needed to take place in person. Maybe he hadn't read it. Maybe he thought it was some sort of cruel prank. Maybe he wasn't coming.

What to do? How long should she wait?

Her eyes scanned the coffee shop again. She tensed. Two men in fluorescent jackets and police uniforms walked up to the counter. Her heart beat faster. Were they just stopping for a coffee or here on more official business?

She jumped as Alice gripped her arm. 'I know,' Katie whispered.

The police officers appeared to be talking to the girl behind the counter. As Katie watched, one of them turned

291

and surveyed the café. Was he looking for someone – *for them?* Katie had chosen a table behind another couple and partially shielded by a pillar, but if the police officers started to walk around, if they were looking for a woman on the run with three children, then their little group – in hoodies, pyjama bottoms and boots – stood out like a sore thumb.

She nodded at Alice and then whispered: 'Sam, Gracie, get your coats on.'

'Why? Where are we going?'

'We're just *going*.'

They grabbed their coats. The police officers were still at the counter. Katie motioned with a finger to her lips and they pushed their chairs back and rose from their seats.

The police officers turned. Katie froze . . . and then spotted the two large takeaway cups of coffee. She felt her heart sag in relief. The officers smiled, waved to the girl behind the counter and sauntered out of the coffee shop.

'It's okay,' she said. 'False alarm.'

She turned to Alice. But Alice wasn't looking at her.

She was staring at another figure walking slowly towards them. A tall, thin figure with straggly dark hair and a tired face. His gait was slightly lopsided, and he clutched his side as if he had a stitch. His eyes searched the café and then, as if drawn by some magnetic force, they fell on Alice.

Shock. Disbelief. The man stopped, raised a hand to his face, dropped it again and took a faltering step closer.

His mouth opened, but nothing came out. It looked like he was searching for a word, a name he hadn't used in a very long time. Katie willed him to find it.

But Alice got there first.

'Daddy?'

48

All this time. All these years. All the moments he dared to let himself imagine this.

And for a fraction of an instant, he thought it was all a big mistake.

Her hair was dark and longer than he remembered. She was so much taller. And thinner. Those once-stocky limbs had lengthened and become lanky. Her cheeks had lost their plumpness and her eyes had changed. He could see in them a wariness, a hurt. He couldn't equate this skinny young girl, dressed in an oversized hoodie, pyjamas and Ugg boots, with his chubby-cheeked, blonde-haired daughter.

And then she spoke:

'Daddy?'

The years fell away. Like a dam breaking. He surged forward and wrapped his arms around his daughter, ignoring the painful twinge from his stitches. She stiffened briefly and then collapsed against him, her frail body surprisingly heavy.

He held her as tightly as he dared, scared he might crush her with the strength of his emotions. Three years. Three years of searching for a ghost, and she had been brought back to him. His daughter. In his arms. Real, substantial. Alive.

'Izzy.' He buried his face in her hair, breathing it in. 'I've been looking for you for so long. I've missed you so much.'

HAVE YOU SEEN ME? Yes. And now he was, never letting her go, lest she might disappear again, evaporate into thin air.

'Gabe?' Another voice spoke, softly.

Reluctantly, he looked up, over Izzy's head. And he realized it was the waitress. *Katie.* He barely recognized her. Her eyes were blackened and her nose was sore and swollen. She looked like she had been in an accident. There were two other children with her, dressed in hoodies over pyjamas. As if they had left their home in a rush. What was she doing here? How had she found Izzy?

'I know you have a lot of questions –' she started to say, her voice thickened by her injured nose.

'What happened to your face?'

'Uncle Steve did it,' the little girl piped up. 'He was Auntie Lou's boyfriend, but he was a bad man. He hurt Mummy.'

'That's why we can't go home,' the boy added. 'Because he might come back. We're on the run.'

Gabe stared at the boy. His felt like his brain had gone into freefall. Thoughts tumbling helplessly around his head. 'I don't understand any of this.'

'I know,' Katie said. 'And I promise I will tell you everything. *Later.* Right now, we need to get the children somewhere safe, where no one will look for us.'

He shook his head. 'Right now, we need to go to the police.'

'No!' Izzy pulled away from him.

'Izzy –'

'The bad man will come back. He'll find us.' Her voice rose in panic. 'No!'

'Okay, okay,' Gabe soothed his daughter. 'We won't do anything you don't want to.' He eased her back to him. 'I'm your daddy. I'll look after you now. I'll protect you from the bad man.'

He glanced back at Katie.

Somewhere safe.

He considered. And then he found himself saying: 'I know a place.'

49

Gabe drove south. Izzy sat beside him, a small rucksack clutched on her lap. She held it tightly, possessively, and he wondered what was inside that was so precious. Katie dozed with her children in the back, exhaustion and the motion of the van lulling them.

What was Katie's connection to all of this? A waitress in a service station? She can't have just stumbled over his daughter. So how did she find her? Was she somehow involved? It seemed so unlikely. On the other hand, could it be a coincidence that she just happened to work in the café where he always stopped for coffee? Always smiling, always nearby. Could he even trust her? But then, she had saved his life. And wasn't she the one making the leap of faith here, letting a complete stranger drive her and her children who knows where?

Secrets, he thought. It's not the big lies but the small ones, the half-truths — those are the ones that mount up, one on top of another, like a giant, stinking fatberg of deception. And when that blew, you really were in the shit.

He forced his attention onto the road. They had left the motorway a few miles back. It was a dank, dark day, mist starting to lumber in from the hills. As they broke out of suburbia and onto the country roads, it felt more like night, just the flare of cat's eyes and the occasional glow from a farmhouse guiding the way.

Gabe didn't need them. He knew this way well. In a few more miles they would be heading towards the coast.

'Where are we going?' Izzy asked.

'Somewhere the bad man won't find us,' he told her.

She bit her lip, hugged the bag tighter. Something inside rattled and clicked. 'Fran used to say that. She promised . . . but she was wrong.'

'Who's Fran?'

'She was . . . she looked after me.'

The woman, he thought. *The woman who took her.*

'Was she kind to you?'

'Yes. Mostly.'

'Mostly? Did she ever hurt you?'

'No . . . but she got cross sometimes, and she was sad.'

'Did you love her?'

'I suppose.'

He swallowed down a bitter wedge of anger.

'Well, I never want to break a promise to you. But I will do everything in my power to look after you and make you happy. Okay?'

He felt her eyes on him, searching for the truth.

'Okay.'

'However, I will still make you do your homework – and no boyfriends until you are at least thirty.'

Her lips moved a fraction. Nearly, so nearly a smile.

'Okay.'

And then she yawned and closed her eyes.

He watched her for a moment, drinking in the sight, then he reached for his phone, in the holder on the dashboard.

He tapped the screen and brought up a contact, one he hadn't been forced to speak to in a long time. And then he pressed call.

Another hour, and he saw the familiar dark swell of the Downs start to rise ahead of them. Soon the winding country roads that snaked through the Sussex countryside would start to rise, the forests and funnels of trees falling away as they started to climb, up to the cliffs.

A beautiful part of the country. A rich part of the country. A lot of 'refugees' from London moved here when they decided they had had enough of – and earned enough from – their city lifestyles, investing in renovated farmhouses with acres of land that they tried to prevent walkers from crossing, kidding themselves that they were living the rural life because they owned a Range Rover and wore their Hunter wellies to Waitrose (because, obviously, they paid someone else to walk the Labradoodle through the muddy fields).

However, it was also an area with several impoverished seaside towns where unemployment and crime ran high. Where there was always the undercurrent of violence and a persistent resentment – at the rich Londoners, at the tree-hugging lefties in Brighton and, in particular, at the immigrants who had settled in many of the poor council estates, like the one he grew up in.

But they weren't heading there.

They turned off the main coast road, on to a small private lane, and the house drew into view. Just the upper storeys visible above the high walls that surrounded it. From a distance, in the fog, it looked grey, like some kind of stone castle perched upon the clifftop. Up close, it was whitewashed bright white, like a lighthouse. Beyond the wrought-iron gates stretched a long gravel driveway and acres of green lawn, and almost every room had a view of the sea.

That was the property's name. Seashells.

Gabe pulled up outside the imposing iron gates. Katie had woken up and she peered out of the window.

'What is this? A hotel?'

'No.'

'Who lives here?'

'A woman named Charlotte Harris used to live here with her daughter.'

'Not any more?'

'Her daughter was hit by a drunk driver when she was fourteen. She was left in a persistent vegetative state. She's cared for by private nurses in a special wing of the house.'

'Oh God.'

He waited a second and then said: 'I was the drunk driver. I visit her every week. I have done for over twenty years.'

He climbed out of the car and walked up to the gates, leaving this information to sink in. For Katie to put the pieces together. After a moment, he heard her climb out of the car after him.

'And her mother is going to let us stay here?'

'No.' He tapped numbers into the security pad set into the wall. 'Charlotte Harris is dead.'

'Then who actually owns this place?'

Gabe pressed a button and the gates started to swing open.

'I do.'

50

A gift is never just a gift. Sometimes, it's an apology, sometimes an expression of love. Sometimes, it is leverage or a subtle display of emotional blackmail. Sometimes, it's a way to assuage guilt. Sometimes, it's a way to make yourself seem benevolent. Sometimes, it is a show of power or money.

And sometimes, it's a trap.

When Charlotte Harris's solicitor had requested a meeting 'at his most urgent convenience' that grey Monday in November, Gabe hadn't known quite what to expect; he hadn't even known that Charlotte was ill.

He never saw her on his visits to Isabella. Hadn't done for years. Always a private woman, she had become a total recluse. Miriam, the housekeeper and head nurse, had confided that she only left her room to sit with Isabella. Never even ventured out into the grounds. Both captives, Gabe had thought, in their own way.

But with Charlotte dead, what would happen to Isabella? he had wondered. Who would look after her, pay the staff, ensure that her care continued?

And then the solicitor had told him.

Gabe had stared at the dapper little man, with his shiny bald head and small round glasses, and felt his jaw slacken.

'The whole estate?'

'That is correct.'

'I don't understand.'

Mr Barrage had smiled curtly. He looked like a caricature of a solicitor, Gabe thought. He just needed a bowler hat and an umbrella.

'Mrs Harris had no other family apart from her daughter, Isabella, who is obviously in no position to administer her own affairs. Charlotte wanted the house and her estate to be looked after by someone who understands Isabella's condition and will ensure that she continues to receive the highest levels of care. That is one of the conditions of the will. The property cannot be sold, but you and your family are welcome to live there. It is yours to do with as you wish, up to a point.'

Gabe had tried to process this. Charlotte Harris was wealthy. But Isabella's care must cost hundreds of thousands a year. All the money would have to be kept safe to ensure that her care continued. He supposed he had always thought that, when Charlotte died, then his visits would stop, or at least reduce. His sentence would be lifted. But he should have known she would make provision. He just hadn't expected *this*.

'And if I don't accept?'

'The money will continue to be held in trust for Isabella and the estate will be administered by the executor of the will.'

Mr Barrage had smiled thinly at Gabe. The executor. The executor was *him*. He had agreed to it a few years

302

ago. Saying no to Charlotte wasn't really an option. But it was just a formality, she had told him. Just paperwork. He hadn't really thought much of it. Now, he understood. *Snap*. The doors of the cage slammed shut.

He considered. 'What if I felt that it was in Isabella's best interests for her care not to continue?'

'Then you would have to go to court to justify that course of action. Which could be costly. And I would draw your attention to clause 11.5 in the will, which prohibits the use of any of your inheritance for "any action which would cause the cessation of Isabella's care or shorten her life". You'd be on your own.'

Of course. Charlotte really did think of everything.

'And then there are all the people who depend upon you, Mr Forman. The staff at Seashells. They are your responsibility. You can ensure they keep their jobs and are well looked after.'

The solicitor took his small, round glasses off and offered what Gabe presumed was supposed to be a warm smile. It barely scraped past frosty.

Still, he was right about the staff. They were good people. Especially Miriam. She had cared for Isabella for most of her life, firstly as a housekeeper and then, using her nursing experience, to oversee her care after the accident. She deserved this far more than him.

'What about Miriam? She's worked for Charlotte for years. This should really be her inheritance.'

'Miss Warton has been provided for in the will.'

'She should have the house. I want to give her the house.'

'I'm afraid you can't do that.'

'But the house is mine to do with as I wish.'

'To a point.' The solicitor picked up the will and slipped

his glasses back on. Gabe got the impression he got a real kick out of doing that.

'"Seashells shall not be sold or given as a gift by the beneficiary to any other person/s. Doing so will render the will null and void and the estate will revert to the executor.

'"Exceptions are permissible only in the following circumstances: i/ The death of the beneficiary. In this event, Seashells shall pass to his next of kin. ii/ Incapacitation by serious illness or any other circumstances that mean the beneficiary is unable to adequately fulfil the duties of the will. In this event Seashells shall pass to his next of kin. iii/ If the beneficiary has no next of kin/his next of kin are dead or incapacitated by serious illness or any other circumstances that mean they are unable to adequately fulfil the duties of the will, then the house and estate will pass into a trust fund administered by a legally appointed trustee."'

She had him. Even in death, Charlotte Harris was not about to let him off the hook. The house was beautiful, worth millions, and yet Gabe would have happily seen the whole damn pile go crashing off the cliffs on to the rocks below.

She knew that. She knew the greatest gift she could have given him would be to never see the place again. Its echoing rooms, its sterile smell. It wasn't a home. It wasn't even a hospital. It was a morgue. Just no one was willing to admit that their patient was dead. It was only the physical shell that was left. Isabella existed. She didn't live.

And he had caused it. He had put her here. That was why he couldn't say no to the will; why he wouldn't refuse or contest it. He could never leave Isabella. Never desert her. She was his responsibility. Charlotte knew that, too.

But there was something else. Something that Charlotte didn't know. Jenny was pregnant. Three months. One day, Isabella would die. It was a miracle an infection hadn't taken her by this point. One day, he and Jenny would no longer be around. Whatever his feelings about the house, it would be a wonderful inheritance for their child. Could he really refuse that?

He had bowed his head.

'All right. But I have one condition. All day-to-day care is looked after by Miriam. She immediately gets a 50 per cent pay rise and the house is hers to live in as long as she wants, completely free. I will pay all the maintenance and bills, but I won't live there.'

Mr Barrage had almost shrugged. Not quite. Solicitors didn't shrug. Just like they didn't laugh at jokes, have dress-down days or chew gum.

'As you wish, Mr Forman. I just need you to sign here, and here.'

Mr Barrage held out a pen. Gabe had hesitated. Then he took the pen and scribbled a signature.

Never had a man become a millionaire with such a heavy heart.

'You look terrible,' Jenny had said when he arrived home later. She handed him a large glass of wine. 'What's up?'

He had looked at her. At her clear green eyes, wavy blonde hair, her slightly rounded belly beneath the loose T-shirt. Their baby. The thought still took his breath away.

He should tell her. He *had* to tell her. He couldn't keep something this big from his wife.

But telling her one part meant telling her everything. And he knew his wife. Once she had finished calling him a dickhead and a liar and a fucking idiot, she would want to see the house. She would insist. And once she set eyes upon Seashells, that would be it. She would want to live there. Finally, the house of her dreams.

He could see her eyes lighting up. Could almost hear her enthusing about which room would be the nursery and which the playroom, where they would put the trampoline and play area – and an infinity pool would really take advantage of the sunsets. Oh God, and maybe there was enough land on the other side of the house to turn into a paddock, for a pony?

The rest would follow. It would be better to move Isabella to a separate facility, in the grounds. This was a home, not a hospital. And Miriam could find somewhere else to live, couldn't she? They could help her. After all, Charlotte had left the house to *him*. Didn't he want the best for their family? Jenny wasn't heartless, but she was practical, pragmatic and, ultimately, the burden of guilt was not hers.

He couldn't let that happen. So he kept the document stuffed in his pocket. Another secret. Heavy as a brick. And, like bricks, secrets eventually drag us down and drown us.

He took the wine and smiled at Jenny. 'Nothing. Just work.'

51

Lights glowed dimly from the south wing of Seashells. Gabe eschewed the main entrance and led their small group around to the opposite side of the house. The children stared up with wide eyes.

'This is all yours?' Sam asked.

'Yes.'

'It's like Wayne Manor,' he breathed out in awe.

'Or Ariel's castle,' Gracie added.

'You don't have a front-door key?' Katie asked.

'I don't want to disturb Miriam – she's the head nurse – if she's in the main house, and the south wing is where Charlotte's daughter is . . .' Gabe hesitated. 'He didn't want to say 'kept', but what could he say? 'Maintained'? 'Looked after'? '. . . where she sleeps,' he finished. 'We'll go through the family kitchen.'

'There's more than one?'

'The south wing is pretty much self-contained. Sleeping quarters for the nurses on shift, a kitchen, bathrooms. Charlotte had the extension specially built when she brought her daughter home from hospital, not that you'd know it was a later addition to the house.'

'I can't believe the hospital let her remove her daughter

from their care. I mean, I've read about court cases where parents have been stopped from doing that.'

Gabe inserted his key in the side door and it swung open.

'The hospital couldn't do anything more for her. And money lets you do a lot of things most people can't.'

They stepped inside and Gabe flicked on the lights. He heard Katie let out a small gasp.

The kitchen was huge. Gleaming chrome appliances, smooth granite worktops and a shiny tiled floor that reflected the spotlights set into the ceiling. A large American-style fridge-freezer faced them. An island stood in the middle that was the size of, well, most people's kitchens.

'The original kitchen was getting a bit old,' Gabe explained. 'Miriam asked if she could put a new one in.'

Katie gazed around. 'Miriam has expensive tastes.'

'She works hard. This is her home.'

'Wait? You don't live here?'

'No,' he said shortly, throwing the keys onto the massive island.

'Never?'

'No.'

'How long have you owned it?'

'Nine years.'

He crossed the kitchen to a door which led out to a short corridor and then to a large oval hallway. Off this was the living room, dining room and a winding staircase which led to the second floor, the master bedroom and three guest bedrooms.

Miriam would probably be working on the other side of the house, or asleep if she wasn't on duty tonight, in which case she would be in the nurses' quarters, close to Isabella. He didn't want to wake or alarm her or have her calling the police because she thought there were burglars in the house. He took out his phone and quickly typed a text:

'Miriam, just stopping at the house tonight. Will explain later. Gabe'

She was bound to realize something was wrong, of course. He had missed a visit, and he had only ever stopped at Seashells once before, a couple of weeks after Jenny and Izzy.

He had been aimlessly driving, not wanting to go back to the house which would never again feel like a home, not knowing where to go, and he had ended up here. Miriam found him weeping at Isabella's bedside and she had taken him into the main house, forced him to eat something and made up a bed. She hadn't asked questions, although she must have seen the news. She had simply looked after him. Gabe supposed that was her job. But whether it was duty or compassion, he had gratefully accepted it.

Gabe looked back at the small, bedraggled group: his long-lost daughter, a waitress he barely knew and her two children, thinking that he could do with some of Miriam's no-nonsense care right now. What was he supposed to do with them?

He felt someone touch his arm. Katie. 'It was a long journey. We're all pretty worn out and hungry. Why don't I make something to eat and we can talk after the children are in bed?'

'Right. Okay.'

Of course. He realized it had been a long time since he had had to consider anyone's needs but his own. He was out of practice at being a parent. Or a partner. The warm imprint of Katie's fingers lingered as she walked away towards the fridge.

She pulled open the doors and peered inside, wrinkling her nose. 'A lot of ready meals, but not much else.'

She started opening cupboards. Gabe joined her and found several multipacks of baked beans. Katie smiled and brandished a loaf of bread.

'No finer feast.'

They ate around the breakfast bar. Gabe turned on the flat screen on the wall and CITV played in the background in a way that was both vaguely irritating and immensely comforting. Funny the things you forget you miss, he thought. Like the sound of kids' TV, or tripping over children's shoes, or their lack of tact and subtlety.

'So your real name is Izzy?' Sam asked.

Izzy nodded.

'And you're her real dad?' he said to Gabe.

'Yes.'

'Our dad left to live with stoopid Amanda,' Gracie said.

'Right.'

'She stinks of perfume,' Sam added.

'And she won't push me on the swings in case she breaks a nail,' Gracie said. 'Then she goes like this.'

The pair pulled weirdly contorted faces.

Izzy giggled. Gabe felt something strange happen. A surge of warmth in his stomach. A desire to giggle with her. It felt strange, but nice. *Happiness*, he thought. *This is what happiness feels like.* It had been so long, he had forgotten the sensation.

He found himself staring at Izzy again. She was alive. This was real. On the way here, he had felt as though he was burning up with questions. How? Where? Why? But right now, he didn't care about the answers. He didn't care how this had come to be. He just wanted to enjoy sitting eating beans on toast with his daughter. Something most parents wouldn't think twice about, but a moment of banal ordinary life he had thought he would never experience again.

After the plates had been scraped clean Gabe found a family packet of biscuits in another cupboard. They managed to maintain the sheen of normality as they munched on them, keeping the conversation generic. It helped, Gabe thought, that children have a shorter attention span and a much greater adaptability to new situations than adults. They just accept stuff for what it is. Sam was more fascinated with the house than how they came to be here. He wanted to know how big it was, how many bedrooms it had, did it have a swimming pool, was there a butler?

After exhausting the questions and the Custard Creams and Jammie Dodgers, Gracie started to yawn. It had somehow got to almost seven o'clock.

'I think it's bedtime,' Katie said meaningfully. She glanced at Gabe. 'We'd better sort out where the children are going to sleep. I mean, obviously, you're not short of rooms.'

Gabe thought. 'Well, the master bedroom is probably made up. I'm not sure about the others.'

'I don't want to sleep on my own,' Gracie immediately said.

'Me neither,' Sam added.

Izzy didn't say anything, but she seemed to shrink a little closer to Gabe.

'Okay, well –'

'Why don't Sam, Gracie and Izzy share the master bedroom?' Katie suggested. 'I'm presuming there's a double bed, so they can top and tail?'

'Right. Good idea.'

'And what about us . . . I mean?'

'Erm, well, there are two more doubles. I can probably find some bedding.'

'Great.'

'I'm tired, Mummy.' Gracie yawned again.

'Okay, sweetheart. Let's get you upstairs.' Katie smiled. 'Hey, at least you're already in your pyjamas.'

Gabe led them into the hall, flicking on lights as he went. The vastness still surprised him. He watched Katie and the children staring around in awe. Imagining it through their eyes, it also seemed unnecessary. Who needed this much space, this many rooms? A small home could burst with love, and yet this place, despite the plush carpets and silk wallpaper, seemed threadbare of joy.

They trailed up the winding staircase. It had been a long while since he had been on this side of the house, and it felt more unfamiliar than ever. He paused on the landing. Which was the master? Right, he thought.

'Just down here,' he said.

'You could get lost in this place,' Katie said, but something in her voice made it sound more like a criticism than a compliment. He felt a strange urge to defend Charlotte.

'I think Charlotte's husband bought it as a family home, but then he died, Charlotte never remarried, never had any more children and then . . . there was the accident.'

His fault. All his fault.

He pushed open the bedroom door.

'In here.'

'Whoah,' Sam muttered.

The bedroom, like everywhere else, was huge. The bed was a four-poster, easily enough room for four adults, let alone three children. Sam and Gracie threw themselves on it, the long journey, the exhaustion, the strangeness of this unfamiliar house instantly forgotten.

A massive bay window took up most of one wall. The curtains were open. In the day, you could see views that stretched out over the ocean. Tonight, you could just make out the dark body of water, rising and falling restlessly. Above it, the wind whisked scudding clouds past the semi-circular moon.

Izzy walked towards the window. The windows were double glazed, but you could still hear the buffeting of the wind, the distant roar of the waves.

Against the dark panes, she looked frighteningly small and fragile. Gabe had an urge to grab her, to pull her back from the storm building outside.

Instead, he walked over and stood beside her. Their own shadowy reflections stared back at them, ghosts hovering in thin air.

'You can see miles out to sea on a clear day,' he told her.

Izzy raised a hand and touched the glass. 'The beach is down there.'

'Yes.'

'Have I been here before?'

Gabe frowned. 'I don't . . .' And then he remembered. Jenny had been ill. He had told her he would take Izzy to work for the day, but it had been a Monday so they had come here. Izzy could only have been eight or nine months old.

'Once,' he said. 'But you were just a baby.'

She withdrew her hand and clutched the rucksack to her chest. It rattled and clicked, and Gabe realized what the sound made him think of. *Pebbles*. But why would Izzy carry around a bag of pebbles? And then he remembered some-thing else, something he hadn't thought about in years.

When Izzy was a toddler, she used to have these odd sleep episodes. Obviously, toddlers napped quite a lot, but she would just suddenly fall asleep, anywhere, one minute awake and gabbing, the next gone. Gabe had felt sure she would grow out of it (like her weird fear of mirrors), but Jenny had insisted it wasn't normal. Then, one day, when Izzy was about three, he'd arrived home from work to find Jenny hysterical.

'She did it again. Just fell asleep and, when she woke up, I found this in her hand.'

'What is it?'

'A pebble?'

'Oh. Where did she get it?'

'That's it. I don't know. What if she'd put it in her mouth, what if she'd choked?'

He had tried to be sympathetic, but he had been tired and distracted and probably made Jenny feel that she was overreacting. Kids picked up stuff, right? And it hadn't happened again, at least not that Jenny had mentioned.

But now, he wondered. *Pebbles.* The beach. And then another thought thrust itself into his head – the strange shiny stone in the Samaritan's tooth. An icy draught seemed to seep through the windows and wash over him.

'She wanted us to come.'

He glanced back down at Izzy. 'What? Who?'

But Izzy was already backing away from the window, shaking her head, whether at him or something she could see in the glass, he wasn't sure.

'No. Not now.'

Who was she talking to?

314

Then he jumped as Katie clapped her hands briskly together.

'Okay. Let's get you all into bed.'

The children climbed into bed with surprisingly few complaints. The room smelt a little fusty but the bed was large and comfortable and the somnolent effect of soft pillows and clean sheets soothed them almost instantly.

Katie kissed Sam and Gracie on their heads. 'Night, night. Sleep tight.'

Gabe hesitated for a moment and then sat down beside Izzy at the other end of the bed. He bent and pressed his lips to her forehead. Her skin felt ridiculously soft. Her hair smelt faintly of shampoo. He breathed her in. Her scent was so familiar and yet so strange. Once, her small, supple body had felt almost like a part of his own. Now, it was all new to him. All of this, having a daughter, being a father, he had to relearn it. Relearn it and do it *better* this time.

'Night, night.'

'Daddy?'

'Yes?'

She stared up at him with sleepy eyes. 'You won't go away, will you?'

'No. I'm not going anywhere.'

'Never ever?'

Never ever. If only there was such a thing, such a place, he thought.

He brushed a wisp of hair from her forehead. 'Never ever.'

He rose and walked to the door.

'I'll leave a light on outside,' Katie whispered, but the only reply was a trio of heavy breaths.

She pulled the door to. Gabe stared at the sleeping form of his daughter through the gap. He didn't want to leave her. Didn't want to ever let her out of his sight again. *Never ever.*

But right now, there were things he needed to know. He turned to Katie.

'Shall we?'

52

The ornate hands on the gilt clock above the fireplace read twenty minutes past seven. With the heavy emerald curtains pulled, Katie could no longer have told you whether that was morning or evening. The last twenty-four hours felt like some terrible, surreal dream.

She sat in the living room while Gabe poured drinks in the kitchen. She hugged herself to contain a shiver. The room was beautiful. But cold. And she wasn't sure that had anything to do with its size or the heating. The whole house lacked warmth. But that wasn't all. There was something else. Something just slightly 'off' about this place. Like a sealed exhibit. A place not even blessed with ghosts because it had never been full of life.

Despite the elegance of this room, there were incongruous touches. The flat-screen television on the wall beside the fireplace, two large tan leather recliners and a gas fire glowing in the hearth, where she presumed there had once been a real fire. Although, tonight, she was grateful for convenience over aesthetics.

Gabe had mentioned that Miriam, the head nurse, lived here. She supposed she had to make it more liveable in but, still, it seemed that the house was crying out for someone to love it properly, to appreciate it, to reanimate it.

And then she thought about the girl lying in the south wing. This house wasn't really a home. It was a living mausoleum. And Gabe was its keeper. She wondered why he didn't just sell it, but then perhaps he couldn't. Perhaps he felt duty-bound to look after the girl he had almost killed.

Rereading the news stories online had refreshed her memory. The night his wife and daughter were murdered, Gabe had been visiting the girl he had put into a coma years ago in a car accident.

The very thing that had given him an alibi, proven him innocent of their murders, had been the thing the papers had used to crucify him with. Nail after rusty nail. A hit-and-run, they called it, except Gabe had not run. He had stayed with the girl, handed himself in to the police and visited her ever since. But that part was missed out. He was already as good as a killer. He was a drunk driver. He had left a girl brain dead. The none-too-subtle implication was that, somehow, he had brought all of this on himself. It was justice. Karma.

She remembered feeling sorry for him at the time. A mistake from his youth dredged up and used against him. And then she thought about her dad. About the young man who had killed him. About how it had destroyed her family.

An eye for an eye.

'Brandy?'

Gabe walked back into the room holding two large glasses of amber liquid. Hefty measures. She never drank brandy, but she had heard it was good for numbing shock.

She took a gulp. *Jesus Christ*. Talk about numbing. She felt like it had seared the nerve endings from her throat. From the way Gabe gagged when he sipped his, it seemed like he wasn't much of a drinker either. But then he took a second, larger gulp and she guessed that, like her, he needed it.

He sat down on the opposite sofa and they perched awkwardly, clutching their glasses, a large oak coffee table between them, unsure if they were allies or opponents.

And then he said, 'Thank you.'

It wasn't what she was expecting.

'However this happened, you brought my daughter back to me. There were times when even *I* doubted that she was still alive. When I thought that, maybe, everyone was right and I *had* lost my mind. It's impossible to tell you how much this day means to me.' He paused, took another swig of drink. 'But if you had anything to do with what happened to Izzy, I will hand you over to the police without a second thought.'

She said steadily, 'I didn't. The first I knew about any of this was last night. I didn't even know for sure that Izzy was your daughter. She was calling herself Alice.'

'*Alice?*' His face darkened. 'I suppose that was the name this woman – *Fran* – gave her.'

She looked down into her glass. 'I want you to keep in mind that, whatever you think about the woman who took Izzy, she has looked after her and kept her safe all this time.'

He barked out a hard laugh. 'She *kidnapped* my daughter. She made me believe she was dead. Why the hell are you defending her?'

She took another sip of brandy and grimaced.

'She's my sister.'

'*Your sister?*' Something changed in his face. 'Of course.' He shook his head. 'I'm such a fucking idiot.'

'Look, I hadn't seen or heard from Fran in over nine years. Then, yesterday afternoon, I got a phone call. From a girl I believed was Fran's daughter – asking for my help.'

'Completely out of the blue?'

'Yes.'

'And you just believed her?'

'Whatever was going on, she was a child, scared and alone. I fetched her and brought her home.'

'What did she tell you?'

'Not much at first. She said her name was Alice and that Fran had told her to call my number if she was ever in trouble.' She swallowed. 'But, from the start, there were things that didn't feel right. She forgot to call Fran "Mum" and I noticed that her hair had been dyed. I wasn't sure why you would dye an eight-year-old's hair.'

'Seven,' Gabe said.

'Sorry?'

'Her birthday isn't until April. Two months away. She's seven.'

Katie felt her cheeks flush. 'I'm sorry.'

'Go on,' he said tersely.

She took another gulp of brandy. She was getting more used to the burning sensation now.

'Later that night, she admitted that Fran wasn't her real mum. She said her real mum was dead. Fran had saved her and kept her safe. But now she's disappeared.'

'Why didn't you call the police?'

'I was going to, this morning . . .'

'And?'

'This happened.' She pointed at her face. 'A man came to the house. He was after Izzy. I think he would have killed me, but Izzy knocked him out with her bag of pebbles. She saved my life.'

The smallest of smiles tilted the corners of his lips. 'That's my girl.'

She felt a momentary loosening of the tension, the mistrust, between them. Then he frowned.

'Why didn't you call the police then?'

'Because the man who attacked me was a police officer.'

She saw his eyes widen, realization dawning. 'The man who stabbed me was dressed in a police uniform. Young, stocky —'

'Shaven head?'

He nodded, and she felt a chill. All this time. Steve *had* been using her sister. Just not in the way she thought.

'That sounds like him.

'Why would a police officer be involved in this?'

She shrugged. 'Everyone has a price.' She thought about the look in Steve's eyes. *The enjoyment.* 'Some are just cheaper than others.'

It seemed as if he were about to say something to this, then he shook his head.

'That's why you ran?'

'And then I called you.'

He nodded, considering. 'I still don't understand, though. How did you realize that "Alice" was Izzy? How did you even get my number?'

Katie reached into her pocket and pulled out the crumpled flyer. She held it out to him.

'I kept hold of it.'

'And you recognized Izzy from this picture? Isn't that a bit of a leap?'

She hesitated. How much to say? How much to admit? She placed the brandy glass carefully on the large coffee table. 'My sister is not a bad person. I really believe that what she did, she did for Izzy, to protect her –'

'How do you know? You haven't seen her in nine years. Or is that a lie?'

'No!'

'I mean, when you think about it, it's all a bit convenient. You just happen to work at the service station where I stop for coffee. And your *sister* turns out to be the person who kidnapped my daughter. What are the odds?'

She glared at him. 'You think I'd waste my life working for years in a shitty café just on the off chance that you might call in once a week and ignore me? Yeah, great plan. In the last twenty-four hours I've been attacked in my own home, forced to take my children and run. I don't know if we'll ever feel safe going back. I have no idea if my sister is alive or dead. How do you think that makes me feel? I never asked for any of this.'

She felt tears burning and tried furiously to blink them back. She would not cry in front of him. *Keep it together.* Like you always do.

He stared at her, a strange look in his eyes. Then he sighed and sagged back on to the sofa, the anger subsiding.

'If your sister isn't a bad person, why was she in my house that night? Why did she take Izzy and run? Why did she abandon her own daughter's body? What sort of mother does that?'

'I don't know. I can only think she was terrified. She

must have seen the killer. Maybe she abandoned her daughter to save yours.'

'Why didn't she just call the police?'

'Maybe she couldn't. Maybe she had got herself involved in something she couldn't get out of.'

'*What?* What could she have been involved in that could lead to this?'

Katie wavered. Now or never. She took out her purse. Her hand shook. She slipped out the dog-eared business card and laid it on the coffee table.

THE OTHER PEOPLE.

Gabe stared at the card and then looked up at her. 'What do you know about the Other People?'

'What do *you* know?'

'Vigilante justice. Quid pro quo. An eye for an eye –'

'Requests and Favours,' she finished bitterly. 'My sister owed the Other People a Favour.'

'What for? What did she ask them to do?'

'Kill the person who murdered our dad.'

53

Nine years ago

Gone, Katie thought, staring at the card, '. . . but not for-gotten.' Still gone, though. For ever. *Gone.*

The word seemed to have lodged in her brain.

She couldn't get past it.

'You don't have to decide on the words right now,' the elderly lady behind the counter told her kindly. 'You can always call back.'

But she couldn't. There had been enough disagreement about the flowers/plants. She needed to get this done. And it was stupid, really. Because it wasn't as if Dad was going to read the card. It wasn't like she was writing it for him. But she still felt a burden, a responsibility to get the words right, if nothing else. To avoid the clichés, the bland platitudes.

But what could she say? This wasn't the funeral of a father who had died peacefully in his sleep. He hadn't suf-fered a long illness from which death was a merciful release. What were the right words when your beloved father had been brutally and sadistically murdered?

The florist was still staring at her.

She was short, with straggly white hair in a bun and thick glasses which she peered through like a myopic mole. A myopic mole dressed in a blue dress, shabby cardigan and sensible black shoes.

'It's always more difficult in these circumstances.'

Katie looked at her more sharply. 'What do you know about my circumstances?'

'I'm sorry. I didn't mean to intrude but, well, I read the news and . . . I'm so sorry.'

Katie cleared her throat. 'Thank you. It's just –'

'You're still angry.'

She looked up sharply, about to retort that it was none of this woman's business. But then she realized the florist was right. That was exactly it. It was hard to write words of remembrance when you were still so angry that you were doing this at all. When this was not right. When what you really wanted to do was shout and scream and rail against the God who had let it happen.

And this was the first person who had recognized that. She nodded. 'Yes. I am.'

The florist smiled. It wasn't exactly sympathetic. Katie wasn't sure what it was. It only occurred to her later that it was satisfaction – as if she had answered correctly.

'Would you like a coffee?'

'Erm, thank you.'

The woman gestured for her to come around the counter. In the back of the shop there was a small kitchenette and a couple of comfy chairs. Katie sat down while the woman boiled the kettle.

'You know, a lot of people think that grief is all about acceptance. But that's not always the way.'

'Then what am I supposed to do?'

'How do you really feel about the man who murdered your father?'

Katie took a breath, so sharp it physically hurt, like a cracked rib.

'I hate him. I know I'm not supposed to say that. I know I'm supposed to try and forgive. He was just a kid, only eighteen. Deprived background, in and out of care. I get it. But he murdered my dad. He crushed him against a wall and then left him there to die. He could have still saved him. One call. One sign of remorse. Instead, he went to a party. While my dad was bleeding to death, he was snorting coke and getting wasted.'

She stopped for breath. It was the first time she had said it; had really let it out. To a complete stranger.

The florist brought two mugs of coffee over. 'At least they caught the person responsible.'

'For what it's worth. Our solicitor is telling us to prepare for a plea of manslaughter and a light sentence because of his age. Maybe only two or three years. My dad is dead for ever and he gets a few years. It doesn't feel like justice.'

'What would?

The question caught her by surprise. Her answer even more so:

'For him to die, in pain and alone, just like my dad.' She shook her head. 'God. That sounds awful, doesn't it?'

'No, it sounds honest. Here.'

The woman handed her a card.

Katie stared at it. The card was black with three words written in white.

THE OTHER PEOPLE.

Beneath the words two white stick people held hands.

'What's this?'

'A website where you can connect with people who've been through the same thing as you; who might be able to help.'

'Right – thank you. I'll take a look.'

She had no intention of taking a look. It was probably some happy-clappy Christian site. This was obviously a ploy to spread the good word.

'You won't find it on the normal Web.'

Katie frowned. 'Then?'

'You've heard of the Dark Web?'

Katie stared at the frumpy, bespectacled florist. The Dark Web. Was this a joke? Some hidden-camera show?

She frowned. 'I thought that was illegal.'

'Not always. Sometimes it's just for individuals who want to be more private.'

Katie flipped the card over. A sequence of letters and numbers was written on the back.

'That's the Web address and password. If you want to visit,' the woman said.

'So, it's just a chatroom?'

'Not just. If you're serious about finding justice for your father, they offer other services.'

Other services.

The conversation had taken a surreal turn. The small room suddenly felt claustrophobic; the smell of the flowers sickly, the taste of the coffee bitter. Why had she confessed all of that to a stranger? *Grief*, she thought. It was playing with her mind. She needed to get out of here.

'Well, thank you – for the chat and the coffee, but I should really go now.'

'What about the words on your card?'

'Just . . . "We'll miss you, Dad."'

She hurried from the shop, out into the flow of midday foot traffic, gulping in the cool air. She walked briskly along the pavement, towards the car park. She meant to throw the card into a litter bin, but she didn't see any, or maybe there were people in the way.

Somehow, when she got back home, it was still in her purse. She took it out; her intention, she was sure, to chuck it into the recycling bin. But she must have been distracted because, instead, it ended up sitting on the small table in the hall.

She was busy with Sam and work and it continued to sit there with unopened junk mail for several days. She had almost forgotten about it when Fran came round to finalize the funeral arrangements.

Her sister didn't come round very often. She had always maintained a distance from the rest of the family. To be fair, Katie didn't mind all that much. She found her elder sister hard work, in the same way that Mum could be hard work. Spiky, often confrontational. Difficult to love. Which made it sound as though you were the one with the problem when, in fact, it was more that Fran put obstacles in the way of affection. Katie wasn't sure why and, after all this time, she wasn't sure if she had the energy to climb over them.

This particular afternoon Fran hurried in, saying she couldn't stop long. And then her eyes fell to the card on the table.

'What's this?'

Nothing. Just junk. I was about to throw it away.

That's what she should have said.

But she didn't. She felt a compulsion to share it. Perhaps

because it was something she and her sister could actually have a conversation about.

She said: 'It's a weird story, actually . . .'

The funeral was a week later. It passed. That was probably the best thing she could say about it. Their mum managed to stay sober enough not to embarrass herself during the service, although a couple of times Katie had to grab her arm to hold her steady.

There was no one to do the same for her because Craig was at home looking after Sam. Again. Although they had agreed that they couldn't bring a screaming baby to a funeral, Craig hadn't made much of an effort to persuade his parents to step in and babysit so he could support his wife. Katie tried to convince herself he was just being a good father, and almost succeeded.

The vicar delivered a speech which talked a lot about their dad in life, as Katie and her sisters had requested, but omitted the brutal and senseless nature of his death. He also talked about acceptance and forgiveness, but every time she glanced at the plants arranged around the coffin, which she would take away and put in his beloved garden, she thought about the myopic mole – *other services* – and fought to contain a shiver.

Standing at the graveside felt surreal, like she was in a movie, playing the role of the grieving daughter. Despite the very real sound of Lou wailing and sniffing beside her, red-faced and snot-full of grief, it didn't seem possible that this was actually happening. It couldn't be *her* dad, in that hard, wooden coffin being slowly lowered into the earth. This wasn't his ending. This wasn't the way things were supposed to be. It was inconceivable that she would never see his smile or feel his warm touch again. *Gone*, she thought. For ever. The tears rolled down her cheeks and she felt a hand take hers. Fran.

Katie had booked a small village pub for the wake. It was crowded. Dad had been popular, and she knew he would have been happy to see so many people there. The room buzzed with conversation and, away from the bleak solemnity of the church, she felt some of the heavy grief not exactly lifting, but dissipating. This was Dad, she thought. Not that cold grey church and hard wooden coffin. This. Here. People. Friends. Laughter.

She had put Lou in charge of monitoring Mum, but it was a pointless task. People kept buying the grieving widow drinks and she was already pretty drunk. In a way, Katie envied her. She wished she could just throw back the gin and surrender to oblivion. But she couldn't. Someone had to circulate, to accept condolences, thank people for coming, chat to the vicar, make sure that there were enough sandwiches. A funeral certainly seemed to make people hungry.

Finally, face hurting from the forced smiling, she managed to get away and find a quiet corner, where she stood, sipping a warm white wine, nibbling a breadstick. Fran emerged from the crowd and came to stand by her side.

'I visited that website,' she said, with her usual lack of preamble.

'What? Why?'

Fran held out the business card. 'I borrowed this. I was curious.'

Katie took the card back with a shaking hand. She hadn't even noticed it was missing. 'And?'

'I did it.'

'Did what?' Katie stared at her, a tight knot forming in her stomach. 'Fran, what did you do?'

Her sister glanced out of the window. Katie realized a taxi had pulled up. She frowned. 'You've booked a cab? I thought I was giving you a lift.'

'I have to go home and pack.'

The knot grew tighter.

'Pack? Where are you going?'

'I'm sorry. I can't stay here any more. Not now Dad's gone. I need a fresh start. It's best for everyone.'

'What are you talking about?'

Her sister turned and suddenly grabbed her in a fierce tight hug. 'For Dad. Just remember that.'

'Fran?'

Releasing her, leaving Katie feeling a little dazed and breathless, Fran turned and walked briskly from the pub. Katie wanted to run after her, to scream at her to come back, to explain. Then she heard a smash of glass from the other side of the room. *Mum.* She couldn't make a fuss at her father's funeral. Her mum had that covered. She would not let anything else ruin this. She watched her sister climb into the waiting taxi and then she turned. Smiling and nodding, she crossed the room to deal with her mother, even as Fran's words reverberated around her brain.

'For Dad.'

The phone call came a week later. Katie was in the kitchen trying to soothe a grizzly Sam when her mobile rang. She snatched it up, wedging it between her shoulder and her ear.

'Hello?'

'Katie?'

'Yes?'

Sam wailed. She tried to ease a dummy into his mouth.

'It's Alan Frant here.'

Their family liaison officer.

'Oh, hello, Alan.'

Sam spat the dummy out onto the floor.

'There's been a development in your father's case.'

'What sort of development?'

She bent awkwardly, clutching Sam, and rescued the dummy from the floor.

'Jayden Carter has been found dead.'

She froze. *Jayden Carter.* The teenager who had murdered their dad.

'What happened?'

'I'm not sure that –'

Sam wriggled in her grip. She stuck the dummy briefly into her own mouth then wedged it back in his. This time, he accepted it.

'Tell me.'

'His wrists and throat were slashed with a razor.'

'Oh God!'

The room spun. Every bit of saliva seemed to have been sucked from her mouth.

'Yes. Very unpleasant.'

'But . . . it was suicide?'

She wanted him to say yes. *Please say yes.*

'There will be a full investigation. Obviously, Jayden was on remand and there are some, well, inconsistencies. But, as far as your father's case is concerned, the CPS can't prosecute a dead man.'

Inconsistencies. Other services.

'No,' she whispered. 'I see.'

'I'm very sorry.'

'Yes. Thank you. Bye.'

She put the phone down. Her stomach rolled. She walked into the living room and placed Sam in his playpen.

I'd like him to die, in pain and alone, just like my dad.

Oh, Jesus Christ. She ran to the kitchen sink, but could only heave. She splashed her face and tried to catch her breath.

I did it.

Coincidence. It had to be a coincidence. Surely. She was reading too much into it. And yet . . .

She grabbed her mobile, pulled up Fran's number. She had tried calling her several times after the funeral, but each time it had gone to voicemail. Now, an automated voice told her: 'The number you have called is no longer in service.'

She tried again, just to be sure, but got the same message. Shit. Okay. What to do? And then she knew. She grabbed Sam, bundled him into his buggy and left the house.

A young woman with short blonde hair was serving behind the counter at the florist's. She smiled pleasantly as Katie came in.

'Can I help you?'

'Erm, yes. I was in here the other day and there was an older lady serving?'

The pleasant smile vanished. 'Martha?'

'I didn't catch her name. Is she going to be in again?'

The girl shook her head. 'No. That's why I'm covering. She called in yesterday and said she wasn't coming back. She's supposed to give a week's notice and she's really dropped us in it.'

Katie just stared at her, feeling her world start to disintegrate beneath her feet.

'I don't suppose you have her contact details?'

'Even if I could give them to you, it wouldn't help.' She lowered her voice. 'They're all fake. My boss is pretty pissed off, to be honest.'

Katie stared at her. *Fake*. She left the shop in a daze. Breathe, she told herself. Keep calm. Think rationally. Chances are, all of this is just a weird, horrible coincidence. Not a conspiracy. Real life. She needed to sit down, have a coffee, put all of this in perspective.

She found herself a seat in the local coffee shop, ordered a cappuccino and gave Sam some juice and a banana. Then she took the business card out of her purse.

THE OTHER PEOPLE.

Fran, what did you do?

What does it matter? Dad's killer is dead. Justice. Rip the card up. Forget it. Get on with your life.

'Cappuccino?'

She glanced up at the waitress.

'Oh, yes, thank you.'

The waitress put the overflowing cup down on the table. Katie smiled politely, waited until she had walked away and picked her phone up.

Forget it. Get on with your life.

She opened Safari and googled: how to access the Dark Web.

Whatever Fran had done, she had to see for herself.

54

There was only one problem with hatred, Gabe thought. And it wasn't that it would eat you up or destroy you. That was bullshit. Hatred could fuel you through the worst of times. Grief, despair, terror. Love and forgiveness might keep you warm, but hatred would power your rocket all the way to the moon.

No, the problem was that, eventually, hatred burned itself out. And now, when he really wanted it, when he needed to summon it for the woman who had taken his daughter, he found that his tank was dry. Running on empty.

He looked at Katie wearily.

'That's why your sister was there. Repaying her Favour.'

Katie nodded. 'I think so.'

'Why didn't she just refuse?'

'You've seen the website. Do you really think refusing is an option?'

He would have like to have said yes. It was just a website. Probably run by a couple of geeky kids with acne, an inferiority complex and a grudge against the world. And then a twinge in his side reminded him of the eight stitches pulling his serrated flesh together. The hot burn of the knife. The look in the man's eyes.

Failure to complete a Favour threatens the very integrity of the site.

She was right, he thought. And her sister had had a daughter. A daughter she would probably have done anything to protect. Except it didn't work out like that.

'I suppose she thought, better my family than hers?' he said bitterly.

Katie's lips thinned. 'I don't believe Fran would have been involved if she had known what was going to happen.'

'But she *was* involved, even if it was just in getting Jen to let down her defences so the killer could get in. She was still complicit in my wife's death.'

'I know.'

She sipped her drink and winced as the glass touched her injured nose. Gabe felt the anger subside. This wasn't her fault.

'What a fucking mess.'

'Yeah.'

'Who are these people?'

'Anybody, everybody. Obviously, there's someone pulling the strings, but mostly it's ordinary people looking for a way to ease their grief and pain. That's what the website takes advantage of. And once you're pulled in, that's it.'

'What is it they say about six degrees of separation? We're all connected in some way?'

'Exactly. Everybody has a use. However small. Perhaps the florist who gave me that card was just repaying a Favour.'

'Pyramid selling for the homicidal,' he muttered. 'You sound like you've done your research.'

'After I found out about Jayden, I spent a lot of time lurking on the website. Trying to make sense of it all. I thought about passing on the details to the police but –'

'What?'

'I was scared. If they could get to a prisoner on remand –'
She didn't need to finish.

'So, I just put it to the back of my mind, resolved not to think about it any more, to concentrate on my family, the living. That's what Dad would have wanted.'

'Shame your sister didn't feel the same.'

'Don't blame her. I was angry about Dad, too. If I hadn't spoken to that woman, none of this would have happened.'

'Those were just words.'

'But I meant them.'

'Most of us, in our darkest moments, have wished some-one dead.'

'The difference is, the Other People grant those wishes.'
Like a fucking psychotic fairy godmother. Gabe looked at Katie.

'In the morning, we need to go to the police. You need to tell them everything you know.'

She nodded. She looked pale and drawn, the bruising around her eyes darker, although the swelling on her nose had gone down a little. And he was about to make her night even worse.

'There's something else. The police found the car Izzy was taken in.'

She seemed to sit up straighter. 'And?'

He thought about the decomposed body. He was pretty sure that Fran was responsible. But mentioning it would only complicate things, and now was not the time to tell Katie that her sister was a murderer.

'They also found a woman. Badly injured. I'm afraid she died in hospital this morning.'

She drew in a breath. 'Have they identified her?'

'Not yet.'

'Right. I see.'

'I mean, it might not be Fran but . . .'

'What are the odds?'

'I'm sorry.'

'No.' She cleared her throat and shook her head. 'I think, in my heart, I knew she was dead.'

'Right. Well.' He tipped up his glass but, to his surprise, it was empty. 'I guess that's all the cards on the table.'

'Not quite. There's one thing you haven't explained.'

'What?'

'Who hated you so much that they wanted to kill your family?'

55

Izzy lay motionless in bed, her breathing slow and steady, eyes closed. But she wasn't asleep.

She hovered over sleep in the same way an owl might hover over the dark fields below, occasionally letting herself drift down, close to the whispering grass, but soaring up again before she could let herself settle.

At the other end of the bed, Gracie snuffled into a pillow and Sam lay, sprawled, half in, half out of the covers. Downstairs, she could hear Katie and her dad (it still felt so strange to use that word) moving around, talking.

Her dad seemed nice. She could only remember bits of him, from before. Fran had told her it was too dangerous for her to see her dad, that he couldn't keep her safe. But she wasn't so sure that was true. She had recognized him straight away, and the feeling he gave her, when they hugged, had been of comfort, warmth, protection. There were a lot of things Fran had told her that Izzy was beginning to doubt.

Even about that day. The day it happened. The day the horror came.

Izzy had loved Fran, in her way. She tried to be kind, and Izzy knew Fran cared for her, would have done anything to protect her. But there was always something hard about her. Even when she hugged Izzy, her body felt sharp and bony, like she had managed to armour herself against the world, inside and out.

And now Fran was gone. Izzy knew, in a way she couldn't explain, that she was dead. Not having someone around, knowing they were somewhere else, was one type of being away. But this felt different. Like there was some sort of space, a gap in the world where Fran had been. *Dead.* Izzy let the word settle. Like her mum. Like Emily. Some people thought that 'dead' meant going to heaven. Fran had told her that that was lies. 'Dead' meant never coming back.

The wind whistled outside and Izzy reached for her rucksack of pebbles on the bedside table. She hugged the bag to her chest. Inside, the pebbles shifted and rattled. They were restless. *They know this place*, she thought. And, weirdly, she felt like she knew it, too. The feeling had grown stronger and stronger. And then, when she had looked out of the window and seen the beach, she had realized.

The girl in the mirror. She was here.

That was why Izzy couldn't sleep. She could feel her presence, hear her voice, whispering to her from just the other side of the door.

I need you.

Of course, she didn't have to go. She could just stay in bed and pretend to sleep. But the compulsion was so strong. Almost like a physical tug.

Pleeeaaase.

The girl needed her.

And she needed the girl.

She sat up and swung her legs out of bed. Gracie stirred and rolled over, murmuring something, but her eyes remained closed. Izzy pushed aside the covers and tiptoed across the carpet.

She reached the bedroom door and eased it open. The bathroom was to the left along the long landing. She padded out into the darkness, the light from the hall throwing up a faint illumination. She supposed it didn't matter too much if anyone heard her. They would probably just think she was going to the toilet.

She walked along the plush carpet, reached the door and slid inside, pulling the door closed behind her. She didn't lock it. Fran had always told her not to, in case she fell and Fran couldn't reach her.

Like everything else in this strange but familiar house, the bathroom was huge. But cold. Painted white and dark green. A large claw-footed bath stood in the centre, across a checked tiled floor. There was a sink and a separate shower which looked newer. On the windowsill were bowls of pebbles and shells.

Izzy took a breath and walked towards the sink. She looked down into the basin, counted: '*One, two, three.*'

And then she looked up. Into the mirror.

The pale girl looked back at her. Behind her, the sea churned. The wind tugged her white hair this way and that. The girl smiled. Then she raised a hand to her lips.

Shhhhhhhh.

56

Gabe padded softly along the silent corridors. Too quiet. Too still. Like Isabella, the house existed in a state of suspended animation. Neither living nor dead. In perpetual limbo.

He reached the door to the south wing. A double fire door with a keypad for entry. He typed in the code and the door buzzed open.

Whenever he entered this wing of the house a heavy melancholy settled on him. He sometimes wondered if this was what men walking the green mile felt like. A long, slow trudge to a certain fate. Despite attempts at homeliness, with pictures of brightly painted beach houses on the walls, low lighting and carpet, there was no escaping the institutional feel, the chemical smell and the staleness of the air.

He found himself wishing, again, that he had the strength to let Isabella go, to release her once and for all. But he didn't. He was too afraid of the consequences and unwilling to bear the responsibility for her life. What right did he have to determine how and when it should be ended? Him, of all people?

He passed the kitchen, the store cupboard, a small

bathroom. There were two bedrooms down here, where the nurses slept, but the doors were ajar and they were empty. Upstairs, there was another spare bedroom, bathroom and the master, where Isabella was sleeping. He took the stairs, slowly, pausing on each step, conscious that he was only delaying the inevitable.

Finally, he reached her room. He hesitated. Waiting for something – anything – to prevent him entering – his phone to ring, the ceiling to cave in, the earth to open up. But there was nothing, except the stern stillness of the house.

He pushed the door open and walked inside.

The pale girl sat near the shoreline. Izzy hesitated for a moment and then sat down beside her.

The sea was hard and choppy today. Angry brown waves drew themselves up into small mountains before throwing themselves recklessly at the shore. The blustery wind tugged at the girls' hair. One light. One dark. But Izzy didn't feel the cold. She didn't feel anything when she was here.

They sat for a while in silence. Then the pale girl said, 'He's near.'

'The Sandman?'

The girl nodded.

'Who is he?'

'Death. Salvation. A man. The coming of the end. He came here once. A long time ago. He took a piece of the beach back with him. And now I sense him all the time, like a discordant note, getting louder and louder.'

'Is he a bad person?'

The girl turned. Izzy realized it was the first time they had sat so close. The girl was far older than she had thought. Not really a girl at all but, somehow, still childlike.

'You know what a mirror does?'

'Reflects?'

'It reverses everything. There is no good or bad. It just depends which side of the glass you're standing on.'

Izzy thought about Fran. How she loved her but was also sometimes scared of her.

'I suppose.'

'Miriam used to tell me two stories about the Sandman. In one, the Sandman sprinkles sand into the eyes of children to send them to sleep and give them wonderful dreams. In another, he steals their eyes. Two sides of the mirror. The giver of dreams. The stealer of eyes.'

'That's horrible.'

'It's like this place,' the girl continued. 'I'm safe from the darkness here, but the longer I stay, the more in danger I am of losing myself.'

Izzy looked out to the sea, rippled with black and silver. The sky loomed overhead, full of pent-up fury.

'I don't understand.'

'Do you remember when we first met?'

Izzy tried. She searched her mind, scrunched her eyes.

'Not really. It feels like I've always been coming here.'

'You were just a baby. But we made a connection. You kept me tethered here. To life. It made my existence bearable. But it's not enough. Not any more.'

'Why? What will happen if you stay?'

'What do you think the beach is made of?'

Izzy glanced around. The beach was mostly shingle that petered out to sand at the water's edge.

'Pebbles, sand?'

The pale girl held up a hand. The wind blew through her fingers and the tips slowly crumbled, flesh dissolving into fine grains which sprinkled back down to the beach.

'That's what this place does eventually.'

Izzy stared at her in horror. 'What can I do?'

'Help me leave. With a friend, I don't think I'd feel so scared. Are you my friend?'

Izzy stared into the pale girl's eyes. For a moment, they didn't seem friendly. They seemed . . . something else.

She hesitated and then said: 'Yes. Of course.'

The girl held out her mutilated hand.

'Then come with me.'

57

She slept. A pale girl in a white room. Machines surrounded her. Mechanical guardians, they tethered the sleeping girl to the land of the living, stopping her from drifting away on an eternal, dark tide.

Their steady beeps and the laboured sound of her breathing were Isabella's only lullabies. Before the accident, Gabe knew that she had loved music. Loved to sing. Loved to play.

She still looked like that young girl. Perhaps that was why he continued to think of her that way, despite her now being a woman of thirty-seven. The intervening years had not carved their mark upon her face. No grief or joy. No excitement or pain. It remained smooth and unblemished by the passage of time. By the experience of living.

A small piano had been placed in one corner of the room. The cover was up, but the keys were coated in a fine layer of dust. On top of the piano there was usually an ivory shell, its silky pink insides like the delicate curves of an ear.

But not today. Today, there was no shell.

And Isabella was not alone.

A figure sat beside her bed.

Her grey hair was cropped short. She wore a plain blue

nurse's uniform and a single crucifix around her neck. Her head was bowed, as if in prayer. The machines beeped and whirred.

'Hello, Miriam,' Gabe said.

She raised her head slowly. 'Gabe. This is a surprise.'

But she didn't look surprised. She looked resigned and a little weary.

Gabe hovered at the end of the bed.

'I needed somewhere to stay, for a little while.'

'Well, of course, this is your house.'

'And yours.'

'Thank you.'

He moved around the bed and sat down in the other chair. 'How's Isabella?'

A pointless question, as the answer was always the same.

'She's as well as she can be. We keep her clean and comfortable – and sometimes I pray.'

He nodded as she fingered the crucifix around her neck.

'Is that why you're here? I noticed there were no other nurses on.'

'Often, it's just me. I'm perfectly capable.'

'Of course. Look, Miriam, I thought you should know that there's been a change in circumstances. It's why I missed my visit yesterday.'

'Oh?'

'I found Izzy.'

'Your daughter?'

Her eyes widened. She clutched the crucifix tighter.

'Yes.'

'She's alive?'

'Yes.'

'Oh, my goodness. Well, that's wonderful. But how?'

'It's a long story.' He paused. 'It involves a group called the Other People.'

She frowned and half shook her head. 'I don't think I've heard the name.'

'They claim to offer justice to those who have lost loved ones, who have been let down by the courts. An eye-for-an-eye, tooth-for-a-tooth kind of justice.' He paused. 'Someone asked them to murder my wife and child as pay-back for what I did to Isabella.'

She stared at him. 'Forgive me, but this all seems a little far-fetched. Who would do such a thing?'

'Someone who was angry, bitter, grief-stricken?'

'You mean Charlotte?'

'I thought so, to start with . . . but no, I don't think it's her style. She already had me where she wanted me. Besides, Charlotte died before Izzy was even born.'

'Then who?'

'How long have you worked here?'

'Over thirty years.'

'You've looked after Isabella all that time. Without question, with total devotion. You must care for her a great deal.'

'Yes, I do.'

Gabe nodded, his heart feeling like it might just burst with sorrow.

'Then please tell me that's why you did it. For Isabella. Not just for the money.'

58

Katie woke with a start, catapulted from her dreams by . . . what? She blinked, her eyes adjusting to the dimly lit room. It took her a moment to remember where she was. Then it all came flooding back. The living room, in the big house. She must have fallen asleep on the sofa. What time was it? She checked her watch: 10.15 p.m. Hardly late, but it had been a long day.

Gabe had told her he was going to the other wing, to see Isabella. She had decided to stay here and finish her brandy before going to bed. The glass still sat, half drunk, on the coffee table.

She sat up and listened to the house settle. Something had woken her. A faint noise, a thud? She strained her ears. Any mother becomes attuned to the nocturnal noises of their children. She knows when they are sleeping peacefully and she knows, instinctively, when something is wrong.

Something was wrong.

She heard it again. A creak of a floorboard. Faint, stealthy. Someone was moving around. Not Gabe. His steps were heavier. This was a child.

She stood up, padded out of the room and up the huge staircase. The master was to her left, the bathroom at the end of the landing. She could see a thin yellow strip of light beneath the door. So maybe that was it. Maybe one of the children had just needed to use the toilet. Still, something – instinct – told her she should check. She walked along the landing, fingers tracing the wall in the darkness until they found a light switch. She flicked it on and the landing flooded with pale yellow light.

She reached the bathroom door and knocked gently.

'Hello?'

Silence. No reply. Not even the sound of water running.

She knocked again. And then she pushed at the door. It was unlocked and swung open. She stepped inside. The bathroom was empty. But the mirror above the sink was split with a huge, jagged crack and the sink was smeared with bright red blood.

Shit.

She hurried back across the landing to the master bedroom, fear squeezing her heart. She could make out Sam straight away at the bottom of the bed, one leg poking out of the covers. Another curly blonde head poked out of the top. Katie padded across the room, up to the grand double, and gently pulled back the covers. Next to Gracie, just a faint dent in the pillow.

Izzy was gone.

59

'You're wrong.'

'I really hoped I was. And I admit, it took me a while to see it. Perhaps I didn't want to. The will was watertight. Even if something happened to me and my family, the estate went into trust.' He paused. 'I called the solicitor on the way here and asked who the trustees were. That's when it all fell into place. There's only one. You, Miriam.'

She stared at him, appraising. Her fingers fell away from the crucifix. 'I've devoted my life to caring for Isabella. Sacrificed so much. When Charlotte died, I thought I might see some reward for my dedication, for all those years.'

'Instead Charlotte gave her whole estate to the man responsible for almost killing her daughter.'

'She left me her crystal,' she sneered. 'Her *crystal*. How is that *fair*?'

'I would have given you everything if I could. That's why I let you live here, in the house.'

'And what good is this place to me, a sixty-five-year-old woman with osteoporosis? I want to retire. I don't want to rattle around this death house. But I'm stuck here. As long as you're alive. As long as she's alive. And if I leave, what will I get? A state pension and a draughty little flat somewhere?'

'I would have made sure you were looked after.'

'I deserved more. And Isabella deserved justice.'

'So, you contacted the Other People. How did you even find them?'

'A nurse who worked here for a while. We talked sometimes. On the day she left, she gave me a card. "They might be able to help you," she said. "But you won't find them on the normal Web." I admit, I didn't have a clue what she was talking about. But I was curious. I did some research . . .' She touched the crucifix again. 'And I found the answer to my prayers.'

His fists clenched. 'That Monday night I was *supposed* to drive straight home and discover the bodies of my wife and daughter. I'd be the prime suspect in their murders, especially with my past. If I was in jail and my family dead, everything would go to you.'

'It's what I deserve. It's what I'm due.'

'Isabella would have to suffer a tragic relapse but, without me around, that would be easy.' He paused. 'Still, you had no guarantee I would be convicted.'

'Even if you weren't, I know you, Gabe. You're weak. You wouldn't be able to live without your wife and daughter. It would only have been a matter of time before you killed yourself.'

'Except I didn't. Because I saw the car. Because I knew Izzy was still alive.'

Her face darkened.

'Did *you* know?' he asked.

'I was informed that something had gone wrong. That there was a possibility Izzy was still alive. But I was assured that the Other People would find her and fulfil my Request.'

'And you had to be sure she was dead, didn't you? You

couldn't run the risk that she would come back and claim her inheritance. We all had to be dead for you to get what you were due.' He stood, her presence suddenly sickening him. 'I'm calling the police now. I want you out of this room and away from Isabella.'

She nodded. 'I presume you've been recording our conversation on your phone?'

'Of course.'

She drew something from the pocket of her uniform. It took Gabe a moment to realize what it was, the object was so incongruous in her vein-stippled hand.

'Jesus!'

Miriam looked down at the gun, as if its appearance had surprised her, too. 'I had a visitor earlier today. He called himself the Sandman, and he gave me this.'

'Miriam, please, put the gun down.'

'And he gave me a choice. To end things peacefully, to do the right thing, or to suffer greatly by his hand.' She raised the gun. 'There's only one bullet, you see.'

She pressed the barrel against the side of her head.

'Miriam, don't.'

'But he misjudged me.'

She turned the gun around and pointed it at Gabe.

'He didn't understand that I don't fear him. And I *will* get what I deserve.'

'Miriam . . .'

She held her finger against the trigger. And then a voice cried:

'*No!*'

60

Izzy stood in the doorway, wearing just her T-shirt and knickers. Her hair was wild with static, eyes wide and glazed, and her hands were streaked with blood.

'Izzy,' Gabe said desperately. 'You have to go back to bed. Now.'

But she didn't hear him, didn't even seem to see him.

'Your daughter.' Miriam smiled. 'How nice.' She swivelled the gun around.

'*No!* Shoot me. You leave her alone.' Gabe turned and grabbed Izzy by the shoulders. 'Izzy!' he pleaded. 'Wake up! Get out of here.'

LET GO.

He felt the shock shoot up his arms. His hands were hurled back, repelled by an invisible current. And now, he could feel it all around him. Energy. Pulsing and crackling in the air. The hairs on his body stood on end; pressure bulged behind his temples.

'Stop this!' Miriam cried. 'Whatever you're doing. Stop it!'

Izzy gazed at the nurse, unblinking. The gun wavered in Miriam's hand then spun from her fingers and flew across the room. Miriam screamed and clutched at her fingers as though scalded.

Izzy walked past her, towards the bed. Her eyes were fixed upon the sleeping girl now. They seemed a more intense blue than Gabe had ever seen. And he suddenly felt more afraid than he had ever felt in his life. Izzy reached the bed.

'It's you,' she whispered.

No, Gabe thought.

She took the sleeping girl's hand.

'Don't!'

Isabella opened her eyes.

The windows blew out with a crash. Gabe was thrown backwards, against the far wall, the force snatching his breath away. A furious wind clawed at the curtains, tossing lamps across the room, snatching at the bedding. Seawater stung his eyes. The piano lid crashed up and down, keys shrieking in a furious discord.

Miriam struggled to get up from her chair. The wind obliged her wishes. It picked her up and held her there, scuffed black shoes dangling in mid-air, before slamming her back down again, so hard the chair skidded halfway across the floor. Miriam landed with a scream, cut abruptly short.

The two girls silently held hands as the storm raged around them.

Gabe fought to force his words out:

'*Izzy!*'

But she couldn't hear him. She was somewhere else, staring at some point beyond him, beyond this room, beyond anywhere.

'*Izzy!!*'

And then, in desperation:

'*Isabella!*'

The wind seemed to dip. Isabella turned her head on the

pillow. For the first time since the accident, he stared into her eyes. And he saw it all again. The beginning. The end. The ceaseless existence between. *The beach*.

'I'm sorry!' he cried. 'I'm so, so sorry. But please, let Izzy go. I can't lose her.'

She stared back at him, grey gaze unfathomable.

And then she closed her eyes . . . and let go of Izzy's hand.

The wind immediately dropped. The lid of the piano fell with a heavy crash.

Izzy crumpled to the floor.

Gabe staggered across the room and gathered his daughter into his arms. She was still breathing. *Thank God.*

'Gabe?'

He turned. Katie stood in the doorway. He blinked at her. 'What are you doing here?'

'I woke up. Izzy was gone. I was trying to get in the door when it just opened.'

She looked around, only just taking in the whole scene.

'Oh God.' She raised a hand to her mouth.

He followed her gaze. Miriam was slumped in the chair beside the bed, still holding her crucifix. Her neck was crooked at an odd angle and her eyes were flat and empty.

Gabe turned to Isabella. She looked, once again, as if she were sleeping. But he could see that the faint rise and fall of her chest had ceased and the machine beside the bed now emitted a single jarring beep. A final note.

She was gone. *No*, he corrected himself. *She was released.*

He clutched Izzy tighter.

'Goodbye, Isabella,' he whispered. 'Safe journeys.'

61

He drank black coffee, plenty of sugar. He rarely ate. Occasionally, he would blow out a cloud of steam from a vape, despite a sign on the wall that read: NO SMOKING OR VAPING. But no one was going to call him on it. This was his place.

He wore black: overcoat, T-shirt and jeans. His skin was almost as dark. He was tall, but not overly so. Muscular, but not obtrusively so. His head was shaved clean. Sitting, still, in the corner, he was little more than a shadow. A shadow that most patrons gave a quick glance then chose a seat far away from. Nothing to do with race or prejudice. More a sense of unease. A feeling that if they looked at the man for too long, they might see something they could never erase.

Gabe walked across the dimly lit café and sat down opposite the Samaritan.

'Still can't believe you're running a café.'

The Samaritan grinned. 'I'm a man of many talents.'

'*That* I can believe.'

'You look almost human for a change. Fatherhood suits you.'

Gabe smiled. He couldn't help it. The word 'father' did

that to him. The thought of Izzy. It had been only a few months but already they were feeling more familiar to each other. She was calling out to him when bad dreams woke her in the night. 'Daddy' was sounding more natural on her tongue. She no longer looked at him with a slightly suspicious expression. They still had some way to go to get to know each other again. But he felt eternally grateful that he had the opportunity.

Before, he had taken fatherhood for granted. He had been too busy, too tied up in his own life and his commitment to Isabella to devote enough time to his daughter. Gabe didn't believe that 'things happen for a reason'. People tried to make sense of tragedy, when the point of tragedy was that it was senseless. Bad things didn't happen for a greater purpose. They just happened. However, he did feel that he had been given a second chance. A chance not to make the same mistakes again.

His daughter still held mysteries. They had talked a little about her narcolepsy, or 'falling', as she called it. It seemed to have started again after the day the 'bad man' came – the day her mother was murdered. It worsened during her time with Fran. Probably the trauma. But Gabe couldn't explain what she had told him about the beach, or the pebbles. It seemed insane, impossible. But then, he had seen what had happened in that room, with Isabella. He couldn't explain any of that either. So, for now, he just accepted it. Although, fortunately, since that night, it seemed to be getting better. Slowly.

Izzy saw a counsellor once a week. Gradually, they were easing out some of the story; her time on the run with Fran. But the details of the day Jenny died were harder to retrieve. Izzy had locked them tightly away. The counsellor had warned Gabe and the police that they may never release those memories. But that was okay, Gabe thought. Frustrating as it was, sometimes, some things are best left alone.

DI Maddock already thought they had a reasonably full version of events. It transpired that Fran and her daughter, Emily, had recently moved to the same town as Gabe's family. Emily had gone to Izzy's school. Fran must have known Jenny casually, in the way mums at school gates do. Gabe had probably seen her once or twice. Perhaps he had even mistaken her daughter for Izzy when they ran out of the school gates at pick-up time. Apparently, the two girls were 'almost identical'.

At some point, Maddock believed, Fran had been contacted by the Other People to repay her Favour. It seemed likely that this Favour was to go to Gabe's house, get Jenny to let her in and ensure that the front gates were left open to give access to the killer. That was important, he realized now, because for Gabe to be implicated in the murder of his family, there must be no signs of a break-in.

But Fran had never intended to go through with the plan, not fully. Maddock told him that, in the days prior to Jenny's murder, Fran had given notice on her rental property, booked two train tickets and a holiday cottage in Devon. She had then excused Emily from school for the rest of the week, on the pretext of visiting her sick grandmother. She had also bought two cheap pay-as-you-go mobiles.

On the day of the murder Fran made an anonymous call to the police before reaching Gabe's house, reporting a break-in at his address. She must have hoped that the police would arrive in time to prevent whatever was about to happen. Then, she would disappear with her daughter, somewhere the Other People wouldn't find them.

But the call wasn't given priority; the police arrived too late. Fran went on the run with Izzy in the killer's car.

The police still didn't know who the man in the boot was. But from what Izzy had told them, it seemed as though the Other People must have found them at some point. Fran had killed the man and dumped the body and the car in the lake.

Gabe still didn't understand why Fran took her daughter to his house that day. Perhaps she simply had no one else to look after her. He didn't know how Emily ended up dead or why Fran didn't go to the police straight after the murders. *How could she have just abandoned her daughter's body?* That piece of the puzzle was missing. But he knew, at some point, there had been two little girls in his house. Then a killer came. Only one little girl had survived. Izzy. And he had seen her that night. On the motorway. In the car in front of him.

The police had Miriam's confession, recorded on his phone. Harry had given a statement, too, but would not face prosecution. It was not deemed in the public interest. Gabe had to agree. However, that didn't mean he had to let Harry and Evelyn see their granddaughter. Not yet.

DNA tests had confirmed that Emily was Fran's daughter. Her ashes had been re-buried in a plot beside her mother. Together, at last.

Katie had asked him to come to Fran's funeral. He had refused at first, and then changed his mind. She had tried to save Jenny and Izzy, he reminded himself. And she had kept Izzy safe. He should thank her for that.

Katie's mother wasn't there, but her younger sister was. She sobbed noisily into a stream of tissues. Katie wept, more quietly, beside him. He had stood there awkwardly, unsure what he should do. Then, perhaps a moment before it was too late, he had slipped an arm around her shoulders. He felt her tense and then lean against him. And it was all right.

The police were still trying to trace the Other People, but it was a pretty hopeless task. The website had been removed, although it was undoubtedly still active, under a new URL, somewhere on the Dark Web. Just invisible to them.

Louise's ex-boyfriend, Steve, had been arrested but had so far refused to comment. Two charges of attempted murder were obviously still preferable to whatever else the Other People might have in store for him. Maddock had told Gabe that he was also under investigation for witness intimidation and falsifying evidence in several other cases.

It looked unlikely they would ever find the person responsible for Fran's murder. Whoever it was had been professional. So professional that the police believed he hadn't intended Fran to die right away. He had wanted her to suffer.

'So,' the Samaritan said. 'You've given up the travelling life.'

'I suppose I have.'

'That's good. That shitheap van of yours was an embarrassment. You want to take that straight to the junkyard. Crush it.'

Gabe smiled, but couldn't hold it.

'There's still a few loose ends.'

'That's life. It's not neat, like in the movies.'

'Yeah. But there's one thing I keep coming back to. One thing that keeps niggling.'

'Yeah?'

'Who knew Fran was going to be at the lake that day, at that particular time?'

'Maybe someone was watching her?'

'That's what the police think. They found some remnants of masking tape and broken branches in a tree. They think that someone may have set up some surveillance.'

'So you have your answer.'

'Except *we* were the only ones who knew that the car and the body were there in the first place.'

'I see your point.'

'It got me thinking about something Katie said, about the teenager who killed her father. Jayden. Apparently, he was put into care at an early age. His mum had died, and his dad was a career criminal.'

'Usual cliché,' the Samaritan said. 'Absent father. Kid doesn't have the guidance. Falls in with a bad crowd. History repeats. Sometimes the dad doesn't even know he has a kid till he's grown. When he does, the kid looks up to his dad. Hard to put your kid on the right track when you've spent so long following the wrong one. But maybe you try. Maybe you do your best to steer him in the right direction. Then he makes one mistake . . .'

Gabe stared at him. 'I managed to unearth a mugshot of his dad. It's pretty old. He disappeared off the radar years ago.'

He reached into his pocket. Before he could get his hand halfway out, a fist closed like iron around his wrist.

'Don't do it.'

The Samaritan's eyes bored into his. He felt the bones in his wrist shift and something inside wilt. Gabe suddenly wished he had agreed to meet the Samaritan somewhere other than his own place. Here, if the Samaritan wanted to kill him, he would, and no one would see a thing or say a word.

'Okay,' he muttered.

The Samaritan released his arm. It fell, like a dead weight, to the table.

'I will tell you this once, and once only. You understand?'

Gabe nodded.

'You're right. He was my boy. And he was only eighteen when that bitch had him killed. He wasn't a bad kid. I know what he did was wrong. But he had a lot of good inside him, too.'

'He killed a man and went to a party.'

'And you ran over a girl when you were drunk and left her brain dead. And yet here you are. You, with your white privilege, get a second chance.'

'You don't know me.'

'Oh, I know you were poor. But white poor ain't the same as black poor, and don't try and say it is. The white trash who almost kills a girl drink-driving gets a suspended sentence. A black kid, up for manslaughter – take a card and go straight to jail. Boom.'

Gabe remained silent.

'Jayden felt remorse. He told me. He wanted to make amends, to change his life. Like you did. But he never got the chance. Because some bitch, blinded by revenge, got him killed. You know what they did? They didn't just cut his throat. They beat him first. Pulverized every organ in his body. He died slowly, alone. Just eighteen.'

'How did you find out?' Gabe asked.

'It took some time, but I've got my ways. I started searching for her, following the trail. And I found her. Tracked her down to some little village in the Midlands. I watched her and I planned what I would do to her.'

'She had a daughter.'

'And *I* had a son.' He glared at Gabe. 'But then she disappeared, never came back. I lost her again.'

'But you put two and two together. You knew she was involved in what happened to Jenny and Izzy. That's why you found me, became my friend. You weren't looking out for me, you were looking for Fran and you thought I might help you find her.'

He shrugged. 'You were easy to find, man. Hanging around service stations with your flyers. I did what I had to. And I did you a favour.'

'How?'

'If Fran was alive, you don't think she'd come back for Izzy? You really want that?'

Gabe couldn't reply.

The Samaritan nodded. 'Yeah. Thought so.'

Gabe had known it. Feared it. But knowing you're right doesn't make it any easier to swallow.

'There's something else,' he said.

'What?'

'Miriam. Someone must have worked it out and got to her before me. Gave her a gun. Told her to kill herself.

'Sounds like good advice.'

'She called him the Sandman.'

'Cool name.'

'Yeah. It is. On the bridge you said you had a lot of names. Is that one of them?'

The Samaritan sat back and regarded Gabe silently for a moment. When he spoke again his voice was low and grave: 'Y'know, I've stood on that bridge, too. After Jayden

372

died. Except my bridge was a bottle of whisky and a lot of tablets. I waited for the darkness to take me. But it didn't. Not all the way. I found myself on a beach. But not a beach like anywhere on this Earth. This was some other place. It was cold. And the sea was black and angry, like the waves might reach out, grab me and drag me down . . . I couldn't stay there. I ran and I scrabbled up that shore. I woke up in hospital, vomit down myself, shit in my pants. And *this* in my hand.'

He tapped his tooth and Gabe felt his insides turn to ice. 'A pebble.'

'Yeah. Weird shit. Like I'd walked through a nightmare and brought back a souvenir. I had it broken up and a piece set in my tooth. To remind me.'

'Of what?'

'Of what lies waiting. For people like me.'

'That's how you got the name?'

The Samaritan shook his head. 'That wouldn't make sense, man. Pebbles, sand. No.' His voice hardened. 'I got the name because I put people to sleep.'

Gabe felt goosebumps dust his skin.

'You done with the questions now?'

He nodded. 'Yeah. I should go. I have to fetch Izzy from school.'

The Samaritan held out one large hand. 'Good seeing you again, man. Stay safe and look after that little girl of yours.'

Gabe hesitated and then shook his hand. The Samaritan waited until he had turned from the table before he said:

'You know, if you really want tie up all those loose ends, there's one thing you've forgotten.'

Gabe sighed. He turned back. 'What's that?'

'The car?'

'What about it?'

'You were driving back home that night, right?'

'Yes.'

'And the car with Izzy in was in front of you.'

'Yes.'

'Wrong.'

'Sorry?'

'It should have been driving *away* from your house. It was heading in the wrong direction. You never ask yourself why?'

62

It was a beautiful sunny day. The sort of day children draw in crayon, with a bright round sun, garish blue sea and toxic-yellow sand.

They walked down to the beach from the house. Gabe and Izzy, Katie, Sam and Gracie. He had never thought he would actually move into the big house. But Izzy had wanted to. She said she liked being near the sea, the beach. And he couldn't deny her that.

It hadn't really been part of the plan to invite Katie and her children to move in either. It had just sort of happened. They had visited a lot over the holidays when Gabe was redecorating. Sam and Izzy played well together, and Grace was a sweetheart. Katie had helped him choose colour schemes, furniture, pictures: things to make the big old house feel more like a home. He was grateful for her input – after three years living in a camper van, he had found himself helpless in a new world of flat-pack furniture, fabric samples and tester pots.

When Katie asked what he would do with all the space he had jokingly said that maybe she should move in. Izzy had immediately and enthusiastically seconded this. They had laughed it off, but he had found himself thinking about it more and more. The house was way too big for just him and Izzy. He didn't want to end up with empty, dead rooms, not like before. So he suggested it again to Katie, more seriously. Fresh start. No need to pay rent. Built-in babysitter. No strings.

To his surprise, Katie had accepted. She had found herself a new job at a hotel not far away. It had been six months now, and things felt settled, calm. The huge house, which had always seemed more like a morgue, now echoed with laughter and life. They weren't quite a family, not in the traditional sense. Katie and he were still getting to know each other. He wasn't entirely sure where it would lead, if anywhere. But this was one road he found himself excited to follow. He hadn't quite rejoined life but, somehow, life had found him.

Today, they took a picnic, as they often did. A cliché, but one he had been robbed of for three long years. When you've been denied the pleasure of such small things, they mean the world. They spread the chequered blanket on the shingle and put up deckchairs. They plonked sunhats on the children's heads and Katie rummaged in the beach bag for the sun cream.

She tutted. 'I can't find it.' She looked up at Gabe. 'Did you put it in?'

He frowned. 'I thought I did.'

'Well, it's not here.'

'Are you sure? Let me look.'

'It's not in here. I've looked.'

Izzy, Grace and Sam giggled.

'What?' Katie and Gabe said in unison.

The children exchanged knowing looks.

'What?' Katie said again.

'You two sound like you're married,' Sam said.

Katie and Gabe looked at each other, both flushing red.

'Well, that's –' Katie started to stutter.

'Awful,' Gabe said, pulling a face. 'Yuck!'

'Oy!' Katie play-punched him on the arm. It hurt. Still, he grinned, rubbing his arm.

'Sun cream!' Katie said again, sternly.

'I must have left it in the kitchen,' Gabe said. 'I'll go back.'

'Can we go in the sea, Mum. *Please*?' Sam said.

'Okay. But T-shirts on. I don't want you to burn.'

'Yay!'

The children tore down the beach to the sea. Gabe watched them for a moment, still finding himself reluctant to let Izzy out of his sight for too long.

'D'you want me to go?' Katie asked, reading his mind.

'No, no, it's fine.'

He turned and trudged back up the shingle towards the cliff path. It wasn't that far, but it was steep. By the time he reached the top he was drenched in sweat, his T-shirt sticking to him like a second skin. From here, the path zigzagged along the edge of the cliff towards the rear of Seashells, where Gabe had put a gate in the fence for access. It was usually deserted, except for the occasional hiker or birdwatcher. But not today. Halfway along the path a woman stood, right at the cliff edge, staring out to sea.

Shit. The cliffs a few miles away at Beachy Head were notorious for suicides. Not so many people knew about these ones. But they were just as high and just as lethal, especially around this side, away from the beach. Nothing but a sheer drop to sharp rocks and the clamouring waves below. Your shattered bones would be washed out to sea before you were even missed.

'Hello? Excuse me?'

The woman turned. A black hole opened in his heart. She looked older. Her hair was short and dyed blonde. She was leaning on a stick. But he recognized her right away.

'I thought you were dead.'

63

'I'm not asking for forgiveness.'

'Good.'

'I just wanted to try and explain.'

'You could start by explaining your miraculous recovery?'

Fran regarded him steadily. 'They thought it would be safer.'

'Who's they? Are you in some kind of witness protection?'

'Something like that. There's a lot of interest in the Other People. Not just here. In other countries. They wanted my help. It was easier for me to be dead. For the Other People to stop looking for me.'

'Does Katie know?'

She shook her head. 'And she mustn't. It's too dangerous.'

'Then why are you here?'

'I told you – to explain.'

Gabe stared at her. Part of him wanted to push her off the edge of the cliff. To savour her screams as she fell. Another part needed to know. Questions. There were still questions. What happened in the house? And the car. How did he end up following the car?

'It should have been driving away *from your house. It was heading in the wrong direction.'*

'Then explain. And don't fucking tell me you did it all for Izzy.'

'I saved your daughter's life.'

'She wouldn't have been in danger if it wasn't for you. My wife would still be alive.'

'Do you really believe that? If it wasn't me, it would have been someone else.'

He wanted to argue, but he knew she was right. She was just a pawn. There would always be other people. That was the whole point.

'What happened in the house that day?'

'You know most of it. I was supposed to go around, get Jenny to invite me in and then open the front gates.'

'And let in a killer.'

'I never intended to go through with it. I wanted it to *look* as if I was going to so they'd think I had fulfilled my Favour, but I had a plan.'

'You called the police before you got to the house and reported an intruder.'

'I thought they would get there in time to stop anything bad happening. Then Emily and I would just disappear.'

'Why take her with you that day?'

'I had no one to leave her with and I was scared of leaving her on her own.' She gave a short, bitter laugh. 'Ironic, don't you think?'

He felt a small tug of sympathy. Just a small one.

'The police said there was a struggle, in the house. They thought Jenny had fought back against her attacker?'

'He shot Jenny first. He came in through the patio doors. I threw myself at him, tried to stop him but, somehow, the gun went off.' She paused, swallowed. The horror never far from the surface. 'Emily was shot. She fell. I managed to hit him with a saucepan that was on the hob, to daze him, but there was no time. I . . . I knew Emily was dead. I had to make a choice. Grab Izzy and run, or we'd die too. We made it out to his car. He'd left the keys in the ignition. I bundled Izzy inside and drove away as fast as I could.'

'Why didn't you call the police after you'd got away?'

'I was in shock. I didn't know what I was doing or where I was going. But then reality started to kick in. Izzy was crying for her mummy in the back. I realized I'd driven miles away from the house. I turned around, got on the motorway. I meant to drive straight to the police station. But then we hit the roadworks and there was this car, behind us. A four-by-four. It started beeping, flashing its lights –'

Honk if you're horny. Gabe felt a coldness steal into his veins.

'I tried to pull away, but it accelerated after us. Chasing us. I thought it was *them*. The Other People. They had found us and they were going to kill us. I panicked. I forgot about the police. I forgot about everything. All I knew was that I had to get away. And once I did –' her eyes met his – 'there was no going back.'

Gabe's legs felt weak. Despite the fresh sea breeze buffeting him, there didn't seem to be any oxygen in the air. He thought he might throw up.

'It was me. You ran because of *me*.'

A small, sour smile. 'Fate's a real fucker, isn't it?'

He didn't know whether to laugh, cry or hurl *himself* off the cliff. If he had never been driving behind her. If he had never given chase. A few seconds either way. A change of lanes. Another car pulling in between them. It could all have been so different. Blame fate, karma, an alignment of the stars. Blame God's sick sense of humour. But really, when it came down to it, *right down* to the marrow of the bone, blame it on simple *fucking* bad luck.

'You could have still gone to the police,' he croaked. 'Afterwards, when you realized your mistake.'

'It was too late. I was scared of what would happen. Scared of the Other People. But mostly, I was scared of losing her. This little girl who looked so much like Emily. Who I could almost imagine *was* Emily if I tried hard enough. You were right. I didn't do it for Izzy. I did it for me. Because I needed her. I was drowning in grief. I couldn't live without my daughter and I needed Izzy to fill that gaping hole in my heart.'

Gabe didn't reply for a moment. Then he said, 'I understand.'

She shook her head. 'No, you don't. Because you're a better person than I am. I'm lying to you even now. I didn't come here to explain, not really. I came here because I wanted to see Izzy one last time. To know she's happy.'

'She's happy,' Gabe said. 'She's with her family.'

'Good.' She looked down at the rocks. Gabe felt a wave of vertigo wash over him.

'You know, when I was unconscious, in the hospital,' she said, 'I dreamed I was on a beach, just like this. Emily was there, too.' She looked back at him. 'Do you think they wait for us?'

He swallowed, thinking about Jenny. 'I don't know. I hope so.'

She nodded. 'You should get back. They'll be missing you.'

'What about you?'

'Don't worry, you won't see me again.'

He hoped that was true. He wanted to believe her. But he had to say it.

'If I do, you know I'll kill you, don't you?'

'I'm already dead, remember?'

He turned away and walked down the cliff path. Half-way, he realized he hadn't fetched the sun cream. He turned back. She was gone.

64

Katie stood at the shoreline, the sea lapping at her toes. As Gabe approached, feet crunching on the pebbles, she turned.

'You took your time,' she said.

Gabe held out the sun cream, shrugged. 'I'm old and slow.'

'Nothing else?'

He smiled. 'No. Why?'

She looked at him a little curiously then shook her head. 'Nothing.' She waved the sun cream in the air. 'Kids!'

They obediently splashed out of the water and allowed Katie to slather them with factor 50 before tearing back off into the waves. Gabe stood by Katie's side, watching them play.

After a moment she said, 'We're safe here, aren't we?'

'As safe as we can be.'

'Do you think they're still out there? The Other People?'

Gabe glanced down the beach, to where a young couple lay sunbathing and an older woman sat on a deckchair, mottled legs poking out from beneath a floral sundress, a large sunhat shielding her face.

'I suppose we'll never know,' he said. 'We just have to live with that.'

'I suppose.'

'I can always use my superpowers to protect us.'

'What are those?'

'Old age and slowness.'

'Impressive.'

'Basically, my enemies just get bored of waiting for me.'

She smiled. 'I can see how that would work.'

He reached out and took her hand. She looped her fingers through his and leaned against his shoulder.

Gabe stared over her head, back towards the cliffs. To the point where the waves lashed the sharp rocks and anything that fell would be obliterated and consumed by the sea. Yes, he could live with that.

Epilogue

The old man walked solemnly through the cemetery. He wore a fusty black jacket and held a slightly wilted bunch of flowers. When he reached the right grave he placed the flowers gently beside it and murmured a small prayer.

Nearby, a younger man, little more than a teenager, sat on a bench, staring desolately at a shiny new headstone that signified a recent departure, a raw loss. He wiped at his eyes with the sleeve of his hoodie.

The old man stood. 'Are you all right?'

The young man stared up at him for a moment, bemused, eyes swollen, unsure whether to answer or to tell him to get lost. And then he spotted the white clerical collar and offered a weak smile. 'No, not really.'

The old man glanced at the headstone, even though he already knew the name. Ellen Rose. Nineteen years old, killed by an overdose of drugs supplied by her on-off boyfriend. This young man was her twin, Callum, and he came here every week at this time.

'Ellen Rose,' he said. 'What a beautiful name.'

That was all it took. The grief and recrimination spilt out in a black torrent. People wanted to talk, he found, and usually to a stranger. It was easier than talking to family or relatives. They were too close, too caught up in their own misery and despair.

He let the young man get it all out, the gaping chasm left by his sister's death, the bitter hatred for the boyfriend, the resentment that he was still out there, enjoying his freedom, while his sister was dead.

'He should be in jail. He should pay.'

The old man nodded sympathetically. 'Most people don't understand how it feels, to lose a loved one so senselessly. To know that the person who did it is still out there.'

'But you do?'

'My wife was murdered. Mugged on her way home from church. They never caught the person responsible.'

The young man stared at him, eyes widening.

'I'm sorry. I didn't –'

'It's okay. I've made my peace with it.'

'You've forgiven them?

'In a way. But forgiveness should not preclude justice.' He fumbled in the pocket of his jacket and held out a card. 'Here. You might find this useful.'

The young man glanced at the card briefly. 'Is it some kind of religious thing?'

He shook his head. 'Not at all. But after my wife died, it helped me get some . . . resolution. They could help you, too.'

The young man hesitated and then took the card.

'Thank you.'

The old man smiled. 'Sometimes, it helps to talk . . . to other people.'

Acknowledgements

Writing books doesn't get easier. In fact, if anything, it gets harder.

I was a bit gutted to discover this.

So, firstly, thank you to my husband Neil for keeping me (mostly) sane while writing this, my third book. Without his support I would have even less hair, Doris would have to walk herself and the dishwasher would never get unloaded.

Thanks to Max, my brilliant editorial 'ogre' who manages to make me feel like a fantastic writer while also pointing out all the bits where I'm really not. And to Anne, my equally wonderful US editor, who has been such a cheerleader for this book.

Massive thanks to everyone at MM Agency for everything they've done and continue to do for me. You're the best. Big love.

Thanks to all my publishers and every one of the brilliant people involved in getting a book 'out there'. The publicity teams, proofreaders, cover designers, bloggers, reviewers. And, of course, the booksellers who do such a great job of spreading the book love. Really, my bit in this is quite small.

Thanks to former Met Detective, John O'Leary, who provided invaluable guidance on all the procedural stuff in this book. Top bloke.

Thank you to the LKs for their friendship, laughter and support – and to all the lovely authors I've met on this journey.

Thanks to my mum and dad. It's been a tough year. I love you both.

Thank you to my beautiful daughter Betty for filling my heart with total, unconditional love and for constantly reminding me what's important in life (glitter and unicorns). Being your mum is my greatest joy and privilege. There is no road I would not travel for you, my incredible, gorgeous girl.

Finally, thanks to you, the reader, for coming along with me on this journey. I hope you had fun and I hope you'll stick around for the next one. It's going to be aces!

C. J. Tudor
will be back in 2021

Read on for the gripping
first chapter . . .

Prologue

What kind of man am I?

It was a question he had asked himself a lot lately.

I am a man of God. I am his servant. I do his will.

But was that enough?

He stared at the small, white-washed cottage. Thatched roof, bright purple clematis crawling up its walls, bathed in the fading glow of the late summer sun. Birds chittered in the trees. Bees buzzed lazily amongst the bushes.

Here hides evil. Here in the most innocuous of settings.

He had not wanted to come. He had asked the mother to bring the girl to the church. That was where such things should take place. Within the safety of consecrated walls. Under the watchful eye of the Lord.

But she had been insistent. The girl was beyond help. They could not move her. They could barely restrain her. He must hurry. Please.

He gripped his leather case tighter and walked slowly up the short path. Fear and anticipation mingled in his belly. It felt like a physical pain; a cramping in his gut.

I am a man of God. I am his servant. I do his will.

He raised his hand to knock on the door, but it opened before his knuckles could scrape the blistered wood.

'Oh, thank God.'

The girl's mother sagged at the doorway. Lank brown hair stuck to her scalp. Her eyes were shot through with blood and her skin was grey and lined. She disgusted him. Old. Maggoty. Like she was already half-dead.

This is what it looks like when Satan enters your home. A sickness of body and soul.

He stepped inside. The house stank of faeces and vomit. Sour, unclean. He looked up the stairs. The darkness at the top seemed thick with malevolence. He rested his hand on the banister. His legs refused to move. He squeezed his eyes tightly shut, breathing deeply.

'Father?'

He started. Looked down at himself. The black coat. The robes.

I am a man of God.

'It's . . . nothing . . . I'm fine.'

He started to ascend. At the top, there were just three doors. The girl's lay to his right. A boy, lumpen and slope-shouldered in a stained t-shirt and shorts, stood in front of it. He stared at the priest as he approached.

'Will you help her?'

He looked at the boy and smiled.

'I will do what is necessary.'

He pushed open the door. The heat and smell hit him like a physical entity. He placed a hand over his mouth and tried not to gag. The girl lay upon the bed, caked in her own filth. Her hands and ankles were secured, her face turned away from him. She was naked and very thin, ribs sharp ripples beneath her skin. The bruises from their last encounter lay stark against the white of her flesh. Every fingerprint traced in purple and black. He stared at them.

What kind of man am I?

For a moment, he felt his resolve falter. Was this right? Was *he* right?

And then she turned her head. He recoiled. Her face was contorted, eyes black orbs in her skull. She hissed like a serpent and a flicker of forked tongue slipped between her cracked lips.

He swallowed, his mouth as dry as the summer fields. She was lost. And it was up to him to release her. He had tried with the other girl and failed. Now, he could not afford any doubt. That was just Satan trying to deceive him. He must not weaken in the face of evil.

He turned away and opened his case with shaking hands. Inside, the case was lined with red silk. Sturdy straps held the contents in place: a heavy crucifix, holy water, muslin cloths. On the other side: a scalpel, a sharp serrated knife, and one more item, more unusual perhaps, a small black box. He removed this first, checked the contents and pressed a button along the side.

He turned to the mother and son hovering near the door.

'You must leave.'

'But –?'

'It will not be pleasant.'

The mother nodded and turned to the door.

'I want to stay.' The boy stared at him, chin raised, eyes suddenly bright. 'I want to watch.'

He regarded the boy. There could be promise in him. He nodded. 'Very well.'

He laid the black box on the bedside table beside the girl.

'Dear Lord, give me the strength to expel the demons from this child.'

Next, he took out the rags and the holy water. He poured a little of the water over his hands. Then he took a rag, walked over to the girl and, seizing her by the roots of her greasy hair, stuffed it deep into her mouth.

She choked, bucking and fighting against the restraints. He selected the crucifix and walked back to the bed. He murmured an incantation over her body and held the cross high. Behind him, he heard the boy murmuring prayers of his own, voice tight and urgent.

He laid his hand upon the girl's body. It felt hot and feverish. At the touch of his palm, purified with Holy water, she twisted and spat. The gag flew from her mouth and thick spittle hit his cheeks. He wiped at his face, his resolve strengthening.

'The devil must be purged. Here. Tonight.'

He laid the crucifix down and turned to his case to fetch the serrated knife.

The knife was not there.

He looked up. The boy stood in front of him, the heavy blade clasped in his hands.

'Son –'

The boy plunged the knife into his chest. Pressure. Burning. He struggled for breath, and warm, metallic liquid filled his mouth. He staggered, twisting back towards the bed.

The girl sat up. Her bindings hung loose. She had never been restrained. She and the boy must have . . . but before his mind could fully comprehend the deception, his legs gave way and he crumpled to his knees.

Fire in his lungs. Blood in his throat. He clutched at the handle of the knife, wheezing hotly. Bare feet padded across the floorboards. The girl crouched down beside him. She smiled and he saw now that her eyes were not black, but clear and brown; her skin milky and soft. She was just a young girl. How could that be?

'Please,' he whispered. 'I am a man of God.'

She raised her hand. In it, she held the scalpel. She pressed the sharp tip into the soft flesh beneath his left eye.

'You're a sick bastard.'

She drove the scalpel into his eyeball. Crimson flooded his vision. He screamed. The scalpel rose again, and the sliver of metal pierced his right eye. Agony obliterated thought. His world began to darken.

What kind of man am I? What kind of man? What kind of —?

But the darkness did not reply.